Journey Through an Arid Land

Journey Through an Arid Land

by

G. Davies Jandrey

Journey Through an Arid Land by Gayle Davies Jandrey

ISBN-978-1-61179-337-6   (Paperback)
ISBN 978-1-61179-338-3   (e-book)

BISAC Subject Headings:
FIC044000FICTION / Contemporary Women
FIC033000FICTION / Westerns
FIC051000FICTION / Cultural Heritage

Address all correspondence to:
Fireship Press, LLC
P.O. Box 68412
Tucson, AZ 85737
Or visit our website at:
www.fireshippress.com

Journey Through an Arid Land is a work of fiction. Though based on events that happen all too frequently along the border between the United States and Mexico, any resemblance to actual persons or crimes is coincidental.

Dedicated to those whose lives have been shattered by illegal trafficking along the border between the United States and Mexico.

Acknowledgments

They say it takes a village to raise a child. To my mind the saying also applies to writing a book that might stand a chance of publication. As is always the case, the village chief is my husband, Fritz Jandrey. I am forever grateful to him for his patience and critical ear. I thank the Writers of the Rodeo Circuit for their camaraderie and support. For their encouragement and endurance, I thank my dear friends and early readers, Diane Cheshire, Mary Goethals, Jennifer Vemich and Lee Sims. Many thanks to Lynn and Mike Harris for reading the manuscript and providing technical information about all things equestrian, and to Cameron Hintzen of the U.S. Border Patrol, who was generous with his time, wry insights and plot points. Francis and Peter Grill shared their knowledge of ranching. Randy Armenta of the Luna A Ranch allowed me to perch on the fence by the squeeze shoot so I could witness, up close and personal, what actually happens once the cattle are rounded up. Abrazos y besos to Maria Gabriela Espinoza, who checked my Spanish and made sure I had all the accents and tildes in place. My gratitude and more to my friend and near cousin, Bonnie Lemons, for giving "Journey" its final once-over. Thanks to Albert Downs for providing the beautiful photo of the Chiricahua mountains that is used on the front cover. Lastly, many thanks to Mary Lou Moynahan and Chris Paige at Fireship Press who pushed hard to make this book happen.

G.L.F.M.

Part 1

Crossing Over

Water in the desert is an ocean of tears.
– Tina Moyer

Day 1

Belen Verales motioned to her children to hurry across the wide, pocked street. Nine-year-old Edgar grabbed his sister's hand. They ran ahead of the woman, who was toting a large woven plastic bag. Adriana, a slender 12-year-old, turned to check on her mother's progress. The large hooded sweatshirt Belen wore nearly concealed her pregnancy. Still, her daughter knew exactly how big her mother's belly was, and the girl's face showed concern.

"Andale, mija." Wreathed with exhaust and the smoke from thousands of small cooking fires, Belen waved to hurry her daughter on.

Even at this early hour banda music bled into the street. Here it was different from the muddy lanes of her village in the wet green of Veracruz. There the family had a small farm where they once grew coffee. Now that the beans were worth less than a peso a kilo, they could no longer afford to grow them. She missed the quiet life in her village, but in the weeks since leaving their home, Belen had become almost accustomed to the noise and rush of big cities. She'd negotiated her way through sprawling Mexico City. Agua Prieta did not daunt her.

"Run, run!" she cried to her children and they raced to the curb and into the shadow of the Hotel Las Palomitas, a single-story, concrete block building where they would wait until it was time to leave.

Belen tucked a whip of black hair back under a baseball cap emblazoned with a rattlesnake, the logo of the Arizona Diamondbacks. Her husband, Jacobo, had sent one to each of them months ago. She wore hers for luck now. With luck and the grace of the Virgin of Guadalupe, they would soon be reunited in a city called Phoenix; it was just on the other side, she'd been told. And in a month or so, the new one, si Dios deseo, would be born en los Estados Unidos. At the thought, which was also a prayer, she made the sign of the cross with her right thumb and index finger, touched it to her shoulders and then her lips.

It was cold here in the north. Yesterday she had rummaged through a pile of used clothing spread out on a table in the parish hall of the Catedral de Santa Margarita. Under the stern gaze of the sisters, she chose three hooded sweatshirts, all the same faded, rusty black, and hoped they would not tell her she was being too greedy.

The owner of the hotel stood in the doorway. "Buenos dias, señora." He stepped into the dark hallway and placed one arm against the wall. "And how are the children?"

"Fine. We're all fine," she mumbled, pushing Edgar and Adriana ahead.

"Why are you in such a hurry, little mother? It's early and you have hours to wait." Smiling, he took Adriana's face between his two thick palms. "Qué linda. And you, little man, take good care of your pretty sister and your dear mamá." Laughing like a good uncle, he patted the boy on the shoulder and waved them past. "Andenles, pues."

As she hustled the children past him, she felt his cold, pale eyes on her back and fought an impulse to run. Once in their room, a cubicle without toilet or sink and only a single barred window, Belen spread her rebozo on the narrow bed. The shawl, woven from dark blue cotton, had long, knotted fringes. It was a reminder of her mother, her grandmother and her village. The rebozo, her jet and silver rosary, and a few changes of underwear were the only personal possessions she would carry to the other side. All else, the extra clothing, their old shoes, even her hairbrush would be left in this room.

She arranged packages of crackers, hard white cheese, a sausage on the rebozo, then divided them among the three backpacks already containing the oranges and water.

"Now try them on," she ordered, then watched as the children practiced walking with the fully loaded packs on their backs.

"Mamá, mine's too heavy," Edgar complained.

"Once we get started, your pack will get lighter with each passing hour. When it's finally weightless, we will be with your father."

And she was confident that this was the truth because she was well prepared. On their feet they wore running shoes, newly purchased. They would serve them well, she'd been told, on the long walk north.

She opened her bolsa and spread tortillas, still warm and fragrant from the comal, avocados, bananas and a half-dozen little empanadas de calabazas on a sheet of newspaper. The package of saladitos – the salty, sweet dried plums that every child loved – she would save for later when the children would most need encouragement.

"Eat," she commanded. Belen would make her children stuff themselves. A little later, though the children would resist, she'd give each the herbal suppository. The curandera from their village had promised it would give them stamina and prevent them from falling behind. Then all they'd have to do is wait for their guía, a muscular young man, muy indio, darker even than Jacabo, with a droopy left eye. Known only as El Camaleón, he had been a boxer until a blow to the head had nearly blinded him, or so she'd heard.

At dusk, El Camaleón would come for them and the others resting in the hotel, and they would begin the final, most dangerous part of their journey. Two nights it would take. Two nights until they would all be together again at last. Together, she and Jacabo would begin to build their children's future.

El Corcho, so-called because he was short and stocky as a cork, stood in the hallway for some moments after the woman closed the door. He ran his fingers through his pale brown hair. As the owner of Hotel Las Palomitas, he had an investment in all his pilgrims, but women crossing without their husbands, brothers or boyfriends were always of special interest. He tugged at his belt, which circled below his taut, round belly, then plucked his cell phone from his pants pocket.

Though she was trying to disguise it, the woman was clearly pregnant. At first he had thought it unfortunate, but now he could see how it might work in his favor. Smiling, he made a call.

Wiona rushed down the hallway and into the bedroom again. This time she looked in the closet, pushing aside the old clothes that were crammed in there. Not in the closet. She peered under the bed. Not there, either. "Damn!" she whispered. "Damn, damn, damn!" She didn't have time for this.

She grabbed her father's old cord jacket from the hat tree by the front door. Wrapped in the familiar aroma of wood smoke and hay dust, she scanned the yard, hooded eyes the color of strong tea. People once thought her a fine looking girl, not a beauty, but nice looking enough, with those broad shoulders and long legs – and strong, a good quality in a ranch wife.

She slapped a John Deere cap on her head. A messy braid flapped between her shoulder blades as she strode toward the barn, trying to avoid looking at the sagging corral gate, the busted squeeze chute and the three rotten posts, all of which needed to be shimmed or shored up, jury-rigged, salvaged – anything but replaced – by the time she brought in the calves for branding and castration.

A runty Aussie shepherd, mostly black with a bib of white and russet paws and brows, bounded up, wagging her tailless rump. She whined until Wiona bent to scratch her scruffy ears. No matter how cold it was, the pup refused to come in the house for more than a few minutes at a time, preferring to keep her eye on things from under the front porch.

"Hey, Osa. Where's Emma gone to this time?" The dog's ears perked like two black flags and she raced ahead.

"Mother?" Wiona called. "Emma?" From her pocket she produced the metal whistle that she used to call in the cows. She blew on it twice. Sometimes, that would bring her in.

Even in the desert, April mornings at 4,500 feet were still cold. The canyon itself was a giant bellows, sucking air in during the day, blowing it out at night, and the steady breeze added to the chill. She took a pair of worn leather work gloves from the pocket of her jacket and tugged them on.

Wiona detoured into the corral. With her gloved fist, she punched through the ice that had formed on the horse trough overnight. Link nosed the gate chain, reminding her that it was time to feed him. "In a minute, boy." She smoothed her hand over the sorrel flank. The gelding craned his neck and nibbled at her braid. She pushed his nose away.

Thunder, the farty old jack burro her father had once used to breed mules, stuck his head out of the shed and brayed. He was ancient, placid and a good companion for Link. Wiona peered into the shed. Not here either. She headed for the barn.

At the back of the barn was the ranch office, a cubby with an old metal desk and swivel chair, a narrow mattress on a metal frame and a small wood stove. As a child she had spent many nights napping on the bed under a horse blanket while waiting for something to give birth, a ewe or nanny usually. But her mother was not there either.

The current barn cat, a rather stringy orange, black and white affair, was curled in the office chair. Wiona had broken the long established rule governing barn cats and had given the animal a name, Punkin. Wiona should be sitting in that chair right now finishing up the accounts, not only her own, but those of a half-dozen small businesses in Douglas, Arizona. Her accounting jobs, not the ranch, paid most of the bills these days. But that would have to wait – would wait forever if she had a choice.

Calm, stay calm, she ordered even as her heart raced. What if her mother had fallen and was lying in the cold, unconscious. What if she'd … dropped dead? Where had she not looked? Just as she was about to climb into the hayloft, she heard the truck engine turn over. She loped out to the yard just as the truck was rolling past. Wiona flung open the passenger-side door, climbed in and yanked the key out of the ignition.

"What do you think you're doing?" her mother shouted, snatching at the key. "I'm going to be late as it is."

"Late for what, Mother?"

"Why, my sewing club. What else?"

"Sewing club?" The sewing club hadn't met for years. Wiona couldn't think of a soul still alive who'd been a member other than her mother.

"Oh, you've got plenty of time," Wiona said in an even tone. "It's still early. Look the sun's not near over the rim."

Emma passed a plump hand over her short, steely, gray hair as she looked out the window. "Oh."

Wiona took Emma's elbow and helped her out of the truck. "Why were you hiding from me, Mother?"

Emma jerked her elbow from Wiona's loose grasp. "Why bless your heart. I wasn't hiding from anybody."

"Then why didn't you answer when I called?"

"Maybe I didn't hear you."

"And you didn't hear the whistle?"

"I'm not one of your father's cows, Wiona."

Her mother, hugging her big black purse to her chest, had her good tweed coat tossed over her housedress.

"Let's go back in the house, Mother. You must be cold."

Emma's head dropped into a doze as Wiona refilled her coffee cup.

"You want a warm-up, Mother?"

The woman's head shot up. "Umm? I guess I do." She smiled at her daughter politely, then with lightning speed dumped three heaping teaspoons of sugar into her coffee. Before she could add a fourth, Wiona took the spoon from her hand. "That's plenty."

Emma arched a brow. "If you say so."

Wiona's teeth clenched. She worked her jaw to ease the ache there. She didn't know when clenching her teeth had become a habit. "Mother, I'm not your keeper, I'm your daughter."

"If you say so," Emma huffed, then studied Wiona for a moment. "When did you change your hair?"

"My hair?"

"Your bangs. Why did you cut them?"

She hadn't worn bangs in 10 years, maybe more, but there was no sense going into all that. "Too much trouble."

"Too bad."

Wiona started to clear the table. "What's too bad?"

"Umm?" Emma's face reddened a bit. "I don't know what's wrong with me. Sometimes it feels like I'm just waking up."

"You do sleep a lot."

"Seems to me I'm awake most of the night." Emma busied herself scraping at the dried egg yolk on her plate. "You got a good do on the eggs."

This, the highest of compliments, was something Wiona's father had often said. He might say, *You got a good do on that pie,* or *you got a good do on those reins you braided.* The mother she'd grown up with had rarely taken the time to bestow a compliment. "Thanks, Mother," she said, feeling absurdly grateful.

"Mother? That makes me feel like a relic. When did I stop being Mom?"

A thousand years ago, Wiona thought. In her head, she now referred to her mother as Emma. It seemed easier that way, so different from her old mother she'd become. Wiona smiled at the soft, round woman who had once been sharp, efficient, hard. She

piled the dishes into the sink, then ran a sponge over the worn
flowered oilcloth protecting the prized mahogany table that once
belonged to her grandmother. She couldn't recall the last time she'd
actually seen the worn wood surface of that table. The round clock
that hung above the stove was stuck on 8, but from the degree of
blue in the canyon, she knew it was closer to 7. It would be another
hour at least before Gaby would arrive to watch after Emma.

"Your programs start pretty soon, Mother. Let's get comfy in the
living room."

Once installed in front of the TV, Emma would doze off and on
through "Fellowship," "The Coral Ridge Hour" and "The Word,"
which would take her up to noon dinner. In the meantime, Wiona
could attend to chores. This morning she had to check on the stock.
Most of the cows had calved by now and she needed to check on the
few who hadn't.

She settled Emma into the lounger, tucking the old afghan
around her mother's legs. "Gaby will be here pretty soon if you need
anything."

"Where are you going?"

"Chores, Mother."

"Where's the remote?"

"In the pocket of the chair."

Emma patted her hands along the sides of the chair. "Oh. OK. I
found it."

"See you later then." Wiona dropped her cell phone inside an
old canvas pouch, which she slipped over her shoulder in much the
same manner a woman would a fine leather bag.

Out in the barn, she heaved two 50-pound molasses licks into
the little trailer her father had rigged to hook onto the back of the
ATV, then a box of sturdy trash bags, before climbing on. "OK,
girl." The dog jumped in and settled between her knees, front paws
braced on the handlebars. With any luck, she'd be back to the house
before Emma even noticed she was gone.

The first rays of sunlight bounced off the coiled razor wire capping the chain-link fence as Theodore "Stokey" Stokelund pulled his red Dodge Ram, Semper Fi etched across the back window, into the Douglas station. He was lucky to find a spot beneath a sickly mesquite. Its sparse leaves, young and still acid green, provided the only shade in the lot. Now that the sun was up, the morning would warm up fast. On the other side of the yard, rows of white and green Chevy Suburbans, the Border Patrol seal on each door, were parked in six perfect rows of 12.

He rubbed his eyes, gritty from lack of sleep. As he listened to the Texas Tornados belt out "Adios to Mexico," he considered the Peloncillo Mountains, low-slung and arid, slumping along the border and all those struggling souls who at this very moment were saying last goodbyes before beginning their journey north.

At 40, he'd already spent nearly half his life ranging up and down Highway 80, using his binoculars to "glass" those mountains and the vast, skimpy grasslands that flanked them on both sides. In a good spring the landscape would now be bright with poppies, lupine, verbena, but this was not a good spring. There were only sparse, tawny stubble and rusty creosote to rest his eyes on.

The sky, a huge unmitigated blue, promised the drought would continue. Around these parts, the word "drought" was a stoic euphemism for drier than the tit of an Egypt mummy. That dry. Hell of a place, he thought, though he couldn't imagine a life elsewhere. Cities, even pine forests, made him feel cornered, claustrophobic.

He stepped out of the cab, head gleaming like polished maple. He shaved it daily, partly for the sake of neatness and partly to disguise the fact that his receding hairline would soon merge with the bald spot at the back of his head. Tucking in the tail of the dark green shirt he'd washed and ironed the night before along with four other identical shirts, he ambled toward the main building with its half-dozen dung-brown satellites – portable buildings plopped down to handle overflow. Since California had secured its borders, and his job, the illegals had been pouring into Arizona instead, its border being slightly holier than the pope in Rome. As a consequence, staff and paperwork at the Douglas station had quadrupled.

A coffee-scented cloud greeted him as he pushed open the heavy glass door. No matter how early he got in, Florence, God bless her, always had a pot ready – no Starbucks in Douglas, nor in the whole of Cochise County. She poked her head around the corner now.

"Buenos dias, Stokey. Como esta?"

He smiled. "Muy bien, señorita." His Spanish, though hard on the ear, was adequate. He knew Florence, who was pushing 70, loved it when he addressed her in her native language, especially when he called her señorita. "Y usted?"

"Bien, gracias a Dios, pero, mis chamacos! They're driving me crazy, Stokey." She craned her neck up so she could look into his eyes. There were little pouches of fluid lingering beneath each – all that remained of the six-pack he'd purchased the night before to help him with that ironing.

"My daughter Silvia, you know the one," Florence continued. "Well, she came over last night. To stay! Husband number three out the door. And my son's no better. Forty years old and wants to borrow $10. For what?" She made a gesture then, head tilted back, thumb towards open mouth. "I told him, 'No way, m'hijo. Estas chichis son secas.' " She crossed her hands over her breasts. "You know what I'm saying? Momentito," she said, and disappeared back into her office.

Unfortunately, Stokey understood too well. His own daughter, who'd graduated near the top of her class almost two years ago, was also still unweaned, living at home, working at this or that half-assed job while attending Cochise College instead of the University of Arizona. And his son was limping through his senior year with plans to join the Marines. He was smart enough to go to college, too, but suffered from an ailment common to local youth: a serious lack of imagination compounded by an impatience to be elsewhere. Stokey was quite familiar with the symptoms.

"Bad time to be in the military," was his only comment to his son. Stokey was in the reserves and had been back from his second tour in Iraq for less than six months. What more could he say? He was not yet willing to declare the war was a pointless, miserable failure and a waste; that the kids, and they were mostly kids like his own son, who were getting blown up over there every day in that stinking desert had been wasted; and the civilians, children, women and old men, who got in the way, had been wasted. That would be disloyal to the likes of Corporal Nathan Henderson who had already given so much. Semper Fi, right?

He'd just gotten word yesterday that Nate, the tough little bugger, was back at the VA Hospital. It was one thing to die outright. It was another for your life to be taken inch by inch by the miracles of modern medicine. His face, disfigured by fire, had once been a nice, open face, almost handsome. Now? Clownish was the kindest description that came to mind. And then there was the question of the body parts. Still, he continued to fight. Willingness to put your life on the line, day after day, for your country takes courage. Willingness to fight to live when your body has been terribly transformed takes another kind of courage. Stokey had the one. He wasn't certain about the other. Most nights that uncertainty kept him awake, that and the things that filled his dreams when he did sleep.

He added two Cremoras to his coffee and a packet of Sweet'N Low, stirring it in with his index finger. When he looked up, Florence offered a platter of empanadas. He looked over the assortment of Mexican turnovers. "Which one's the apple?" he asked.

"Three little holes on top."

He helped himself to two. "Gracias, señorita."

He took his empanadas and his coffee and ducked into his cubicle to avoid further conversation. Florence loved to complain about her children. He'd gone to school with both of them and knew that they were actually doing pretty well by Douglas standards.

He set one empanada over his hot coffee to warm and took a bite of the other. From the top drawer, he took a terry rag and began to sweep yesterday's dust from his glass-topped desk, his computer, radio and the framed picture of his wife, a redhead with a lovely, white-toothed smile. On her lap she cuddled their children, 2-year-old Jackson and 5-year-old Katie. The picture was 15 years old, but he had no desire to replace it with something more recent. Finally, he squared a slim stack of policy memos and intelligence bulletins that needed reading, fished out two pens from a jelly jar and turned on his computer.

It was still early. He planned to drink his coffee and enjoy the empanadas in peace before checking the call chart. He turned on his radio to hear what was going on in the field, a mistake. A group of so-called Minutemen were holding 20 undocumented aliens – UDAs for short, wets if you were feeling belligerent or pilgrims if you were a bleeding heart – over on the Rollings place. Minutemen. In his humble opinion, they were a bunch of middle-aged dickheads playing army. For one thing, they figured they had a patent on the American flag. For another, they figured they could do his job better than he could. It irked him, is what. Worse was all the damn camouflage. He could barely stand to look at them, potbellies hanging over web belts. He considered his own belly and the empanada.

He was supposed to go through training on sexual harassment in the workplace, then take a test. He'd been procrastinating, though. Now he loaded the program. Like all mandated online training, it was just bullshit tossed together to satisfy the minimum requirements of a law dreamed up by the Washington idiofuckingocracy. Stokey figured he could skip the training and go directly to the test, which no idiot, he was certain, could fail to pass. He was just about to take a second bite of empanada, when Rudy Garza, the station's agent in charge, leaned against the doorframe of his cubicle.

Garza nodded at the empanada that was halfway to Stokey's

mouth. "Glad to see that you're still able to take nourishment."

"Just enough to keep a little meat on the bones."

Stokey liked Garza well enough. Liked his adherence to the rules of engagement, as it were. Like Stokey, Garza was a native son, but his parents had been illegals who'd gotten green cards during the last amnesty. Later, Garza had overseen their citizenship applications himself. Now they were all free to complain about the wetbacks stealing jobs and taking up tax dollars and hospital beds. Stokey didn't get it; not that it bothered him over much.

"Well, you're going to need to be fortified. The Rambos are detaining a bunch of bodies over at the Rollings place."

Stokey nodded at the radio. "So I heard."

"I dispatched Sexto, but he's going to need backup and by virtue of your sterling habit of beginning your shift early ... "

"I'm it." Stokey took another bite of empanada, dripping apple on his shirt. "Damn it." He took the dust rag and attacked the spot.

"Better hurry. The Rambos are a nervous lot. And when you're finished with that, you might as well go on over to the Flying K; you'll be halfway there anyways."

The Flying K, that caught Stokey's attention. The owner, Fletcher Hart, had been shot to death just yesterday and the news was all over the valley. Everybody pretty much agreed that Hart had had an unfortunate encounter with drug smugglers.

Garza continued. "Reese Farris was first on the scene. He says there's prints from the spot they found Fletcher leading all the way to the border."

"Fattyboy Farris? He couldn't track his own piss in the dust, let alone track a man through that rocky old mess."

"There's that. And it's what, five-some miles to the border. Somehow, I just don't see Farris and his belly bushwacking it all that way. So I want you to verify those tracks before they get blown away. Take the camera, get pictures."

"I'm all over that one," Stokey said, thinking five-six hours round trip, if in fact there were tracks all the way to the border.

"You can thank me later. And while you're at it, see if you can pump a little personal information out of the brother, if you run into him."

"Carter Hart? Like what?"

"Like who gets the ranch, the brother or the wife ... "

"Fletcher's wife died four or five years ago, stroke I think I heard it was."

"OK. And what about Fletcher's son, what's his name – Walter, Warren?"

"Wendel. You remember Wendel. He was in my class. Played baseball." Stokey took another bite of empanada.

"Yeah, Wendel," Garza said, eyes drifting to the second empanada warming on top of Stokey's coffee. "Find out. Does he get the ranch or Carter? And like who, if anybody, might have had a grudge against his brother."

"What? You don't think Fletcher was killed by a drug mule?"

"I don't have an opinion yet. That's what I'm trying to formulate. But here's the thing. Apparently, Fletcher's rifle was still in the ATV. Chew on that a minute."

It didn't take Stokey a whole minute. "Why would a mule kill an unarmed man? Ultimately, it would just interfere with commerce."

"That's kind of my thinking. Anyway, people around here are already going ape shit over this, and we better see what's what firsthand. If it turns out he was killed by a drug mule, we'll take it in the shorts, as usual. Oh yeah, be sure to express our condolences." Garza picked up the empanada warming over Stokey's coffee and left his cubicle without so much as a kiss my ass.

Damn, Garza. What a pedejo, he thought as he grabbed his coffee cup and cap and headed for whichever truck was his for the day. It didn't matter; they all came with the same equipment: a radio, a water jug, topo maps neatly curled in a cardboard tube and, most important, good air conditioning. On his belt he carried a GPS unit and another radio. Absently he patted the .40-caliber weapon in the holster at his hip. Before leaving the station, he picked up the M4 semiautomatic rife assigned to him, a 30-round clip to go with it, and he was ready to start his day.

As the sun breached the canyon wall, the cliffs flared red, then did a slow fade – rose to gold, gold to bleached lichen-patched rhyolite. It was a sight Wiona never tired of. She tied her jacket around her waist and paused to listen to the hubbub of Gambel's quail and white-winged doves calling from the brush.

One garbage bag was already full: discarded sweatshirts, plastic water jugs in makeshift burlap pouches, a blanket, a half-spent tube of toothpaste, one pair of sandals, totally useless for walking in this terrain, an Ace bandage. She spotted a pile of trash under an oak, shoved the ATV in neutral, and left it idling. Among the orange peels was a half loaf of Bimbo bread still in its plastic wrap and an empty wheel of birth control pills. She'd heard that many women who cross go on the pill temporarily to prevent a rape-engendered pregnancy. Shaking her head, she stuffed the trash in the bag. She spotted a splash of color, nudged it with the toe of her boot — a little notebook, the kind a child might have. She thumbed through the brittle pages. On the last page was a heart, cracked in two, a name written in flowery cursive in each half. Sad. Reluctantly, she put it in the bag with the other trash.

Later she'd sort out the good from the bad and add them to the growing pile that would go to Our Lady of Lourdes in Douglas. The church folks hauled a ton of used clothing and blankets over to Agua Prieta every month. She wondered how many times she had picked up the same recycled sweatshirt, say, the same blanket.

The illegals. Part of her was sympathetic – her father used to hire Mexicans who'd simply walk up to the house needing food and pocket money. They were always good workers. But a bigger part of her was resentful as hell. When it was cold, they lit fires, threatening wildfire. When it was hot, they died. Not yet on her ranch, thank

God, since it was so close to the border, less than 15 miles.

And worse were the drug runners. Some ranchers said they'd seen squads of them, dressed in black and toting canvas-covered pack frames marching military style across their ranches in broad daylight.

She swung the trash bag into the back of the ATV. Well, she didn't know who to blame for the mess and damage, the Mexicans, the Border Patrol or the damn Washington bureaucrats. But somebody was responsible and it sure wasn't her.

Wiona noticed the Texas gate sprawled in the dust. That was another thing. Those bastards never closed the damn gate! Wiona drove through. The dog jumped down to sniff at a stubby juniper as she pulled the barbed wire gate to, eased the post in the wire loop at the bottom, levered it up and tugged the other loop of wire over the top. "What's so hard about that!"

Osa trotted behind as Wiona headed for the first stock tank, with its lone sycamore. The newly unfolded leaves released a fragrance like water itself. She breathed it in deep now, hoping to untie the familiar little knot lodged just below her sternum.

The gate, the trash, the accounts waiting in the barn and this morning's adventure with Emma ground her down. She'd had to hire Gaby, bless her patient heart, to help with Emma, which meant she had to take on more accounts, which meant most days she was stuck at her desk. Not the life she wanted.

After Frankie was killed during Desert Storm, she'd had no choice but to stay on the ranch and do the job intended for her brother as well as the other job intended to make ends meet. Friendly fire, it had been. What a strange thing to call an error of that magnitude! The paired words, *friendly and fire* sounded like boys away at summer camp roasting marshmallows and singing "She'll Be Coming 'Round the Mountain."

So he'd become *one of the extinguished few*. Even after all these years, she was uncertain how she felt about that, not sure how to mourn or whether she should.

Funny how things work out, she thought. It was Emma who'd insisted she learn accounting in the first place. It was a foregone conclusion that the ranch was going to her brother and she would need to go … elsewhere. After all, a ranch can only support, and just barely, so many people: Mother and Dad, Frankie, his future wife, who would be expected to have a day job, and their children, not the old maid aunt.

And that was exactly the problem. She was alone in this grand enterprise, ranching, which was supposed to be a team effort. Where was her team?

She gazed down canyon where it widened out to the valley, scraped and clobbered by drought. No welcoming blades of green, no standing water in the creek, not one petal of orange, blue or yellow. If they didn't get an early monsoon and a good one, she'd have to think about selling some of her cows along with the steers. The monsoon was fickle; sometimes it came early, sometimes late, sometimes never.

Her cattle, some Black Angus, some Brangus, were certified organic, range-fed beef. She'd made that move – one her brother and father would have scoffed at – figuring if she got a better price per pound, she could run fewer head. If she ran fewer head, the graze would improve. Given the drought and the condition of the range, it had been a good decision, though few of the neighboring ranchers, hidebound in tradition, would admit it.

Burl Rollings, the rancher whose cattle lease bordered hers to the west was one of those. He and her father went back many years, but they'd never been friends. For one thing, Burl ran too many cattle. Nowadays, with the illegals leaving gates open and cutting fences, his cattle often strayed onto her lease.

And that was another reason why she had no use for illegals, not that she had much use for Burl, who could be mean and hateful. She knew that firsthand. He'd brag about the Minutemen he let camp out on his ranch. Sometime he'd go out with them and patrol along the boundaries. They hunted illegals down like deer, then held them, not at gunpoint, which would have been against the law, but with their rifles pointing at the ground and ready – until the Border Patrol came to take them away. It was sport to men like Burl, more than anything, and what did it accomplish? The illegals still came.

The dust rose up behind the ATV for 20 feet. If this drought continued, not just this year but into the next, she'd have to supplement graze with hay on a regular basis. No way could she afford that.

That Malpais Borderlands group was buying conservation easements to keep the ranchers from having to sell out to developers. They offered Fletcher Hart a deal and she'd heard that he was going to sign on. Of course that would mean some loss of control, but from her point of view, it would be worth it. She'd lost total control over the 20 acres she'd already been forced to sell. If it were offered, she'd sign a conservation easement in exchange for cash, but that wasn't likely. The Flying K had year-round water and some endangered species; she couldn't remember what. Her washes only ran after a heavy rain, and as far as she knew, she didn't have anything endangered on her ranch but her sanity and the ranch itself.

At the first tank, a handsome Angus bull had haremed up his cows. There were eight she could see. Each cow, save one, had a calf. One of the calves looked to have been born in the past 24 hours.

She turned her attention to the calfless cow, a rusty old Brangus she called Nana. She noted the cow's flaccid udder. Maybe she didn't calve this year; maybe she'd lost it to a mountain lion.

For this and other reasons, Wiona always carried her father's old Colt on her hip, though she'd never had occasion to take it out of its holster. She saw mountain lions from time to time, but would never shoot one unless it was attacking a calf. And from time to time there were reports of jaguars in these mountains. Would she trade a calf for one glimpse of a jaguar? Yes. Yes she would. Could she shoot a drug mule if she had to? She could only hope that she'd never be tested.

Wiona drove through a little gully and her mind jogged back to the here and now. The grass was so sparse around the tank the cows had little to eat but the sorry prickly pear. She came to a stop some 20 feet from the group. When she blew her whistle, they began to move in her direction. The whistle was another thing her brother and father would have laughed at. Before giving the stock molasses or a salt block, she'd blow the whistle. Now every time they heard it, they came willingly. Made rounding them up a lot less painful all around.

She hauled out a molasses lick, the windmill clanking and huffing like a heart with a leaky valve. As Osa trotted deliriously among the cow pies, Wiona settled back for a moment to watch the mamas and babes stroll to the lick. One cow waited calmly while her week-old calf butted furiously at her teat.

Lots of people thought cows were stupid, but those folks hadn't spent a lifetime observing them. Cows were attentive, patient mothers. Above all else, they were vigilant. Her own mother might have learned a thing or two if she'd spent a little more time watching cows. Might have learned to keep a closer eye on her offspring, for one.

She took out her birth book from the canvas pouch. The old, stained leather jacket that protected the small tablet had belonged to her father. She entered the new mama's number, yesterday's date, heifer, then remounted the ATV; Osa once again perched between her knees.

As Wiona approached the second tank, the knot tightened as she recalled afternoons skinny-dipping with Lucy Altamirano in that tank. Slick and sleek as otters, they'd been, and giddy. It all started with Lamb Chop, the name her father insisted she call her 4-H project – his attempt to keep the lamb's fate first and foremost in her mind. That year he would not buy her entry so she could keep it no matter how hard she cried. "At 16," he'd said, "you're old enough to learn the facts of life." By that, of course, he was referring to the unassailable fact that "animals – sheep, pigs, cows and the like –

were put on earth so that man could eat them, by God."

He didn't know that her boyfriend, Stokey, was trying to teach her another set of facts. But the last night of the county fair, she and Lucy were bedded down in the straw alongside Lamb Chop and Snowball, saying their last goodbyes to the lambs they'd bottle-fed and currycombed since birth. Then in a fit of tears and remorse, she and Lucy fell into each other's arms. That was the beginning of the friendship they promised would last forever and all the summer afternoons skinny-dipping in the warm, slightly slimy water of the second tank.

She and Stokey, her first and only boyfriend, had been going steady. He was good looking and tall enough that she didn't have to slump when she wore high heels to the senior prom. But mostly all they ever did was make out, and that got boring. After a few months, Wiona could no longer abide the weight of his class ring on her finger or his body upon hers as he dry-banged the bejesus out of her, so she broke up with him.

The following year Lucy went to Arizona State to become a doctor. After that, she went to practice in a little village down in Mexico someplace, was there for years, then suddenly here she was back in Douglas to begin work in the new family clinic.

Wiona had seen Lucy in town once. She'd been friendly enough in an impersonal way. Gossip was that she belonged to the Samaritans, outsiders from places like Tucson and Green Valley who provided illegals with food, water, medical attention – humanitarian aid they called it. Wiona called it encouragement. Certainly nobody wanted an illegal to die of thirst, but what the Samaritans were doing didn't seem right to her either.

Wiona turned her attention back to the cows. Now there were 10, and she took a good look at each. Three carried Burl's brand, she noted with irritation. Two of them had calves, but the third, still slick and looking forlorn, had apparently lost hers, and recently, from the look of her udders. She wasn't concerned; they'd sort those out at branding. What did concern her was that the brindle who'd been among the others just last week was missing. If she'd gone off to calve, she should be back by now. Wiona studied the cows once more.

"Damn homely old brindle." If it weren't for the fact that she had given her a calf every year for the past 12 years, she'd be hamburger. She looked at the sky, then at her watch. Both told her it was too late in the morning to hunt down the cow and her calf. Emma and the taxes needed attention.

Locally, he was known as El Camaleón, a name acquired during a short boxing career that had left him nearly blind in his left eye. But in the small town of San Martin Tilcajete in the state of Oaxaca, he was still Moises Angeles. He came from a family of carvers, but had no patience for the work. As he thought of tonight's crossing, he wondered if he was ready to learn patience, as his father had suggested a lifetime ago.

Bandy-legged and stocky as a pit bull, he stepped squinting into the glare of midday, his head bad from too much rum. Yes, soon he'd have enough money socked away and he could go home, build a house, start a little business in the city selling ... what? Maybe the woodcarvings of his brothers and father. He'd have a shop, the upscale kind where rich gringos like to go. What would his father say then? Necesitas paciencia? What had patience bought his father? A place on a bench in someone else's yard earning pennies while el jefe made dollars. Whatever he would do upon his return to Oaxaca, he was going to be boss.

Herding pollos was better, steadier money than boxing. Every trip brought in five, six hundred, sometimes a thousand dollars, depending on how many souls Corcho rounded up for him. Of course he had expenses. He thought of the delicate, pale woman he left still asleep in his bed, and smiled. And there were the cockfights. He was thinking of buying some cocks of his own. Good investment there.

From the breast pocket of his black silk shirt he took a roll of antacids, threw four into his mouth, crunched. The job was eating away his stomach.

He'd already crossed the border more than two dozen times. In the ring he'd been capable of great, unsustainable bursts of speed and power, but on the trail he maintained a steady push toward his goal, impatience tempered by his sense of accountability. For he was accountable to God, qué no, for the safety of those who put their lives in his hands. Most of them were poor indios from the south and south of that. Indios were donkeys, he should know, and family was the wagon they had to pull.

He planned to quit by the end of May. Leading a bunch of pobres pendejos through the summer desert heat? Ni madre! Let someone else take them through hell.

Before beginning this trip to the other side, he had two important purchases to make: one, a new cell phone, the other a $100 money order to send to his mother so she could keep his brothers in school. Unlike his father, she never lectured him on the virtue of patience.

While keeping one ear bent Carter Hart's way, Stokey studied the ranch yard. The Flying K was a well-run outfit, he had heard, and from the looks of things, late model F350 in the carport, nice little John Deere tractor in the side yard, what he'd heard was correct. Of course, scattered about were usual cannibalized remains of vehicles and equipment rusting into the ground. Ranchers never hauled anything away, save a dead horse.

"The irony here," Hart was saying, "Is that Fletcher let them Samaritans put water out for the wets. We butted heads over that one, I can tell you. Butted heads over a lot of things, actually, but there was no budging Fletcher once he decided what was, in his opinion, the Christian thing to do. Hell, I'm as good a Christian as any man, but I'm not a fool. And look what it got him. Got him shot in the back, that's what." He took out a red bracero scarf from his back pocket and blew his nose. "Fletcher was a good man. He didn't deserve to go that way."

Stokey waited for the older man to recover. He was a burly fellow, Hart, with a thatch of rusty hair going white and substantial paunch. Like most cowboys his age he was a bit stove up from years on horseback, but he was still powerful through the arms and shoulders. He was wearing knee-high, black rubber boots. Apparently, he'd been mucking out his brother's barn.

The temperature was kissing 60 degrees Stokey figured, but it was warm in the sun. He took off his cap and slicked the perspiration off his head with the palm of his hand. "So the place goes to Wendel now?"

"Not until I die, maybe not even then. See, Fletcher and me had this agreement, right of survivor kind of thing. If I died first, he'd get my ranch and visa versa. Either way, it would likely be my kids who'll eventually take over. Reason being my brother has, or rather had, only the one boy. Let's just say Wendel doesn't have ranching as his first priority. Fletcher knew it. My kids, on the other hand, got cow manure in their veins instead of blood. Like their old daddy on that score. Anyway, I imagine Wendel will gladly sell his share of the ranch to my kids when the time comes."

"You know of anyone who might have had it in for your brother, an old grudge or a recent confrontation?"

"You implying that somebody besides a wetback killed Fletcher?"

"No, sir."

Hart blew his nose again. "Well, my goodness. Everybody, all the ranchers, respected my brother. He was a church man, generous to a fault and honest as the day is long."

Stokey wanted to bring this conversation to a close. The Minutemen vs. the UDAs had taken up the better part of the morning and he had a long walk in front of him. "A little chilly for April."

"Yup, it is, and dry."

"Yeah, this drought." He kicked at the dust with the toe of his boot. "Well, I was wondering, do you mind it I have a look at those footprints Deputy Farris tracked to the border? Rudy Garza wants some photos."

"Go right ahead, Stokey. Just follow that road." Hart pointed to a narrow dirt lane that led out of the yard. "Fletcher's ATV is still out there about a mile, mile some after the road doglegs west. That's where I found him yesterday morning, not 20 feet from his ATV. Anyway, the tracks take off south from there. You'll see 'em easy. Fattyboy followed them all the way to the border."

"Thanks for your time, sir. And I wanted to say, well … to express our condolences. Everybody at the Douglas station, well … Rudy Garza in particular, we're all just real sorry for your loss, sir."

Carter Hart stared at the ground for a moment. "I thank you for that."

"Well, yeah." Stokey removed his cap and took another swipe at his head. "Then I'm just going to take a look at those tracks. Might be awhile. Fattyboy, I mean Reese, might have missed something. You never know."

"You never do. That's a fact."

The scene directly around the ATV was a mess of activity. Even with the sun directly overhead, he could easily pick out the imprints of Carter's treadless rubber boots and the deep impression of Fattyboy's smooth leather sole. In addition to those, there were tracks from two ATV's – Fletcher's and Carter's, he imagined – tire marks from both Fattyboy's Ram and the ambulance that carried the body away, and a swarm of prints from a variety of athletic shoes, the kind favored by EMTs and illegals. Stokey removed a small digital camera from his breast pocket and snapped a dozen pictures.

Amid the chaos of tracks he picked out one that piqued his curiosity. It had the distinct deep imprint of a narrow heeled Ariat

Packer, a lace-up work boot that used to be favored by muleskinners until the brand turned fancy and expensive. Fletcher Hart's? It seemed a strange choice of footwear for an old rancher. He studied the track. It was the left boot. The inner part of the heel print was deeper than the rest. A bit knock- kneed, this fellow. Maybe a weak ankle or an old injury. He snapped another picture.

Despite all the traffic, Stokey had no trouble picking up the two sets of tracks, worn athletic shoes and the smooth leather soles belonging to Fattyboy. They took off crosscountry to the south, just as Carter Hart had said. Stokey noted the stride and the depth of the athletic shoe. A man of medium height and weight, was his guess. It didn't appear that he was carrying a heavy load.

Puzzled, he shook his head. If this guy killed Hart, why didn't he just take the ATV back to the border instead of humping it? If this guy was a mule who'd been hauling a load of drugs, what happened to it. Certainly, he wouldn't have just ditched it. Would he even have gone back to the border? Why not just get the hell out of there and finish his business?"

He took another set of pictures and followed the tracks south. After about a mile, Stokey came to an outcropping of fractured granite where the tracks of the athletic shoes disappeared. He could almost read Fattyboy's indecision in his tracks, as they circled and crisscrossed. After a few minutes, Stokey picked up the tracks of the athletic shoes on the other side of the outcropping, but Fattyboy's were nowhere to be seen.

It was nearly dark when Stokey got back to his vehicle. Just as Fattyboy had claimed, the tracks went all the way to the border. Stocky had ducked through the fence and followed the prints another hundred feet until they disappeared into a ravine. He would have been in deep shit if he'd been caught on the wrong side of the wire, but he wanted to make sure the tracks didn't double back. Once in the truck, he radioed Garza.

"Took you long enough," Garza said.

"Yeah, well. As it turns out, a set of tracks did go all the way to the border, one set. Fattyboy gave up after about a mile."

"You get pictures?"

"Yup. At the scene and at the border."

"So, I guess that's that."

"I'd say so, except have you ever seen a rancher around here wearing Ariats?"

"Around here? Never."

"Well, we've got a first, then."

"You sure they were Ariats?"

"Sure I'm sure. The question is who was wearing them? Fletcher Hart? Carter?" He unscrewed the cap from his water bottle. Stokey could hear Garza's desk chair squeak and imagined him leaning back in his chair, feet propped up on an open file drawer.

"Hard to imagine," said Garza. "Well, Ariats or no, why would a drug mule, or any Mexican for that matter, want to kill Fletcher Hart?"

"Maybe he didn't. If you were a mule or some wily old mojado who's crossed the wire 10, 12 times and you happened on Hart's body, what would you do?"

Stokey took a deep pull from his water bottle.

"Run like hell for the border."

"So what do you think?"

"Plausible, but nobody's going to buy that. You got anything else?"

"Well, turns out that Carter, not Wendel, gets the ranch."

"So now we've got a man with a motive, but that's not going to fly with the general public either."

"I'm just saying."

There was a pause, then a sigh, more chair squeaking. "Well, I'm going home, Stokey. You should too. We'll take a look at the pictures you got tomorrow."

They were the first to be herded into the oxidized-blue panel truck. El Camaleón's hand was at Belen's elbow, urging her in. She and the children settled on one of several makeshift wooden benches bolted into the floor, but quickly found themselves wedged against the side of the truck as the other passengers squeezed in. It didn't matter. This part of the trip wouldn't take long, they had been assured.

El Camaleón took his place beside the nameless driver and immediately fell asleep. Belen closed her eyes, too, but it was airless in the truck and she was too tense to doze. Instead, to calm herself she reached for Adriana's warm, brown hand. The girl rested her head against her shoulder.

The food they'd eaten earlier lay in Belen's belly like a hot stone. Absently, she patted her chest to calm her heart as she had so often done over the course of their long journey. She thought of the green hills surrounding Los Janos. She missed the easy familiarity of her village, the laughter shared with her sisters, cousins and neighbors, even missed the smell of the chickens when she invaded the coop to collect their eggs. And how she missed her mother, felt her absence like a clot of earth lodged in her chest.

Thanks to the money Jacobo had sent each month, they'd had corn and beans and meat and lard. Her children had shoes and could attend school. But to stay in her village was to live like a widow, and as Jacobo had argued, there was no success, no joy without sacrifice. How sad and afraid she had been when she hustled the children up the steps of that first bus. And now they were about to begin the last, most dangerous part of the journey. She closed her eyes. "Ayudanos, Madre," she prayed silently.

After perhaps 30 minutes, the truck veered off the paved road onto a dirt track. By the time they came to a stop, it was nearly dark. El Camaleón and the driver hustled them out of the truck. Behind them were the cordilleras of Mexico, ahead, in silhouette, the mountains of southeast Arizona.

The truck took off in a swirl of dust, leaving her dazed by the magnitude of the task before them. Belen watched as each man ducked through the gap in the fence. When it was her turn, she hesitated. This was against the law, she knew. She'd never done anything against the law in her life. She motioned for the children to go ahead of her. Now she had no choice but to follow. Stepping through that fence felt like stepping off the edge of a deep ravine. When she straightened her back, she noted with disappointment that the mountains on both sides of the border and everything in between looked exactly the same. She had expected the other side to look different – smoother, greener, less hostile. She hefted on her own pack, then helped her children into theirs. Like penitentes, they trudged single file behind El Camaleón as he led them north across the rock-strewn desert toward the mountains.

For hours the three walked in the middle of the straggling line, El Camaleón in the lead. As they picked their way through the sandy arroyos, up muscle-burning rises and along dark mountain contours, they clung to each other's packs. Often they stumbled, and when Belen's calf was punctured by a spiny shin dagger, Adriana and Edgar suffered the same experience. Better that than risk separation.

During the few brief periods of rest, Belen always used the water from Edgar's pack to lighten his load. Adriana and she were women, and women, like donkeys, were accustomed to heavy loads.

At last, El Camaleón announced, "Estamos a la mitad."

They were at the halfway point and would stop here. When daylight came, the scrub oaks and junipers would provide shade and protection from la Migra's helicopters.

Belen piled leaves beneath an oak to cushion their sleep. She took three oranges from Edgar's pack, two from Adriana's, and from her own, this morning's tortillas. They were brittle, fit only for chickens, but that didn't matter. The only thing that mattered was to fill their stomachs and to sleep.

Before settling down she pulled her old blue rebozo from her pack and spread it across their legs. Only then did she allow her thoughts to turn to Jacabo. How proud of her, of all of them, he would be. She imagined his arms enfolding them, his cheek wet with tears of gratitude for their safe arrival. Of course they would arrive safely. Never did she permit any other thought to enter her mind. Still, she did not look forward to this new life that lay ahead, a life in a place so unlike her home, inhabited by strangers speaking a tongue that was harsh to her ear and beyond comprehension. But these thoughts were not permissible either. She tried to turn away from them, force a blankness upon her mind so she could rest.

She closed her eyes, surrounded by the scorched-cotton scent of oak. When she opened them once more, a slim crescent moon was rising above the canyon, backlighting its torn edges like paper lace. To Belen, the moon was the embodiment of la Virgencita. Her light, and the warmth radiating from the children pressed to her sides, brought her comfort and allowed sleep to come at last.

Day 2

By the time she awoke, the sun was filtering through the oak leaves, warming her aching bones. The children, still deep in sleep, had rolled away from her side. Around them fellow pilgrims sprawled. Loosened by sleep they looked like so many piles of rags. Only El Camaleón, his back against a boulder, was alert like the coyote he was. He glanced at her, then quickly turned away. It struck her as delicate, a consideration of her modesty. She rose quietly, straightened her twisted clothing. Normally, she would greet him. Buenos dias, she would say. But under the circumstances, such niceties struck her as intrusive, ridiculous. Instead, she went in search of a little privacy, for she felt a sudden pressure, a foot or an elbow perhaps, pressing against her bladder.

On the way back to their makeshift encampment, Belen noticed a strange arrangement of rocks, forming a small grotto of sorts. She peered inside. Amid pools of sooty candle wax were worn prayer cards, one of Santo Niño de Atocha, many others of the Virgin of Guadalupe, several pesos, a plastic rosary, a child's hair clip. Someone had made a cross of twigs and grass. Mentally, she went over her own meager belongings. What could she spare that had any value at all?

Belen pulled up her pant leg and felt for the cloth coin purse secured just above her knee. She unpinned it now and removed a small crucifix on a delicate silver chain.

"Ayudanos, Madre," she whispered, digging a small hole toward the back of the shrine where it would go unnoticed. She placed the crucifix in the hole, then smoothed the dirt over it. With the Virgin's help her family would be reunited.

When she got back to the camp the rag piles were beginning to shake themselves alive. Her children were rummaging through the packs, setting out all their food on a flat rock to determine how best to ration it. Edgar, so serious now, no running, no laughing, no teasing, seemed to have grown from child to man overnight. It made her proud, but it made her sad as well.

She sat against a large rock next to her children, belly resting on her thighs. The warm rock eased the ache that was beginning low in her back. Throughout the day, they would rest, drink and eat to prepare for another long walk through the night. She'd been told it would not be more than 30, 35 kilometers total. That would leave perhaps only 15 kilometers or so to go. If they left at dusk, they might be in Phoenix by tomorrow night, the following morning at the latest. Fifteen, even 20 kilometers they could do easily. She closed her eyes. For a moment she could almost feel Jacabo's arms around her.

In the late afternoon they went into the bush to take their second suppository. Belen quickly relieved herself. Almost immediately, she felt a different kind of pressure, and for the second time since leaving the village, she was deeply afraid, and worse, she felt humiliated, a failure. For a few minutes, she simply walked around in a tight circle, hands pressed against the small of her back as she tried to gauge the depth of her trouble.

If they failed, all the money and hard work would be wasted. Could they start again? How long would it take Jacabo to save up another 6,000 American dollars? Would he be angry? He had wanted her to wait until after the baby was born, but then there would have been the heat, and a baby to carry and nurse. She'd heard stories of women, children dying in the heat. No. They must succeed.

She took a deep breath and began to calculate. With Adriana, the sun rose and set and rose again before she was born. Edgar took some 18 hours. Last night they had only walked eight, maybe 10 hours at most. How long could she continue to walk while in labor? Perhaps if they got started right away rather than waiting until dark, she might make it. There was a chance she might make it still.

El Camaleón was dozing in the sun when a shadow passed over him, cooling the air. He opened his eyes. "Qué necesita?"

"I need to talk with you," the pregnant woman said.

He rose and the two distanced themselves from the rest.

"Can we start early?" she asked.

"No señora, es imposible. Travel in daylight is too risky." He started to return to his place under the juniper.

The woman put her arm on his to stay him.

He pulled his arm away. Reconsidered. "What is it?"

Gazing down at her shoes, she whispered, "My labor has begun early, but if we start now, I think I can make it."

His lips paled. He turned his head and spit in the sand, looked at the sun, then his watch. He should just tell the woman to go to the devil; any other coyote would do just that. It was her mistake, not his, to make this trip in such a condition. And what about the others? He had a responsibility to them, too, qué no? He glared at her, hating her face. The color of madrone, it was plump, pleasant, a face like so many women from his village. She could have been his aunt, cousin, neighbor. He looked at the sky again. The sun had just begun its western descent. "OK, pues."

In another hour it would be dark and they would be safe. She had divided most of the contents of her pack between Adriana and Edgar. Some things she decided could be left behind. A bag of oranges they could do without, two liters of water. The contractions were still far apart, not so bad, and Belen could clearly see the last of the men only eight or 10 meters ahead.

They were picking their way down the steep slope of yet another canyon. Below was a canopy of bright, spring green where a little stream might be running. How nice to wash her face in cold water, Belen was thinking. Suddenly she felt a rush between her legs, and halted. "*Ay!*"

"Mamá?" Adriana, turned, saw the wet ground at her mother's feet.

"Hush." Belen, said and kept walking. How stupid she had been. She would not make it, that was clear, but her children …

"Adriana," she whispered. "Repeat your father's telephone number." She had made both of them memorize it.

Adriana repeated the number.

"Muy bien, mijita." Belen continued down the slope, praying that her feet would not slip out from beneath her. She would not stop until they reached the bottom of the canyon, not until she reached the slender band of green.

It hadn't been easy to convince El Camaleón to take the children without her. She'd had to take an extra hundred out of the little purse pinned inside her pant leg to persuade him. But the children had been worse, especially Adriana.

"Be brave, mijita," she'd told her. "You can do this for me and your brother. She gave her daughter the little package of saladitos she'd been saving for an emergency. "Tienes cuidado, mijita. I love you. And don't worry about me. I'll join you in a few days, you'll see."

And it might still be true, she thought, watching them walk away. El Camaleón had promised to send someone for her. Quien sabe, maybe he would. And if he didn't? Well, she couldn't think of it now. Now her baby was coming.

It was so dark beneath the trees and there was no water, as the green had promised, and no midwife but herself. For comfort, she took out her rosary and her rebozo from her pack. "Please, holy mother of God, not before daylight," she prayed and tried not to bear down as the next contraction pounded her like a crushing wave. She wanted to scream, but held back out of fear of what might be hiding in the black night.

They'd reached the pickup spot hours early. El Camaleón had called his ride, and soon they would be on their way.

The cocaine he'd been periodically snorting to stay awake was gone and he was suddenly spent. He closed his eyes, hoping sleep would wipe out the image of the woman beneath the oak and the cries of her children as he dragged them away. It was what she wanted, qué no? Paid him extra to do just that, drag them away. Hell, in a few hours he'd be rid of them all. The kids would be with their father. And the mother? She could go to the devil.

The night was cool. To the west the mountains, showered with light from the rising moon, stood in contrast to the pools of black beneath the yuccas, creosotes and mesquites. In each of a dozen dark pools huddled a man too tired to care about comfort.

The kids sat with El Camaleón. He tossed them a plastic bag with two slices of Bimbo bread inside. The girl shook her head, but the boy accepted the offer.

El Camaleón pulled up the hood of his sweatshirt, then wrapped his arms across his chest and closed his eyes. He was a professional. He'd done his job and deserved his rest.

Within the hour he heard the sound of a car on blacktop. "Stay where you are," he whispered to the bushes. Crouching, he hurried to the edge of the asphalt and peered toward the oncoming lights. They blinked once, twice. "OK, amigos. This is it." Rubbing his gut, he opened a fresh package of antacids and tossed half a dozen into his mouth.

Everyone stood at the edge of the road. The ride, an old utility truck with a flaking sign advertising termite control, pulled up and within less than a minute he had the men loaded. He motioned to the children. "Hurry up."

El Camaleón tossed his cell phone into the brush before climbing into the back with the others. If la Migra stopped them, he would blend in with the pollos like the chameleon that he was.

The driver, a paunchy guy called Tito, started to slide the door closed.

"Wait!" El Camaleón jumped out of the truck.

"Qué pasa?"

"Give me a minute." He located the cell phone with his foot. "I have to make a call."

"You have to make a call? Ay pinche indio! Where do you think you are? Fucking McDonald's?" The driver looked up and down the dark road. "Make it quick, pues."

El Camaleón suppressed a fierce urge to punch the fat son of a whore in the face. Stepping behind the truck, he dialed 911. Let la pinche Migra deal with the stupid bitch.

Back inside the truck, he motioned to one of the pollos to move over so he could see out the front window. The road, a darker ribbon in the dark, unspooled east to Interstate 10. I-10 would take them west, then north to Phoenix. In four or five hours it would be over once again. With a deep sigh, he settled his back against the seat.

He awoke shortly to bright lights shining in the back window. "Chingado," he hissed. "La Migra."

Tito sped up, the worst thing he could do. Every coyote knew somebody who'd been killed in a rollover trying to escape la Migra. "Pull over, buey! Pull over, you dumb fuck!"

The white lights were blinding, then three rapid explosions.

"Hijo de puta! Pull over before they blow out the tires."

Tito slammed on the brakes and the truck rocked to a stop in the middle of the road.

The car, not the Chevy Suburban of la Migra, but a white Chrysler 300 pulled in front. They were going to be robbed, or worse! He'd heard about loads being jacked, all the pollos trucked down to Florida or someplace where they were guarded by men with AK-47s, and never paid. He didn't want to spend the next 10 years of his life cutting cane or picking oranges. Trying not to panic, he rubbed at the pain gnawing at his belly like a hungry rat. At least he had very little money on him. Cooperation, he figured, was his best option. He slid the door open and motioned everyone out of the truck, including the children, who were hugging their backpacks to their chests.

Two men got out of the Chrysler. Guns in hand, they entered the rectangle of light cast through the open doors of the truck. Though both were Mexicans, one was a güero, light-skinned, freckled, slender. The other, in new jeans and white ostrich-skin boots, was blocky and barrel-chested, with sleepy green eyes.

With the muzzle of a 9mm Glock semiautomatic, Boots motioned for everyone to line up along the pavement. El Camaleón took his place at the end of the line, hoping for a chance to slip away into the desert.

"Donde esta la embarasada?" Boots demanded of the driver.

Tito shuffled and shrugged.

Boots struck him with his gun. "Where is the pregnant woman?"

Hand on bleeding cheek, Tito whined, "Believe me, jefe, no woman, pregnant or otherwise, got into this truck."

El Güero entered the van, flashed a light around. Shrugging his shoulders, he jumped out. Each man grabbed a child by the upper arm, and they hustled them into the back of the Chrysler. The rest, they left standing on the side of the road, unmolested.

As they drove off, El Camaleón noticed a magnetic yellow ribbon stuck on the trunk of the car with the command "God Bless Our Troops."

The car sped down the blacktop. In the back, Adriana and Edgar were still and stiff as rods. They could see nothing through the smoked window glass. When Edgar began to whimper, Adriana put her arm around him and pulled him to her.

The man turned around then. His teeth were so large and white that when he smiled Adriana could see El Muerto.

"Don't worry mijitos. We're friends of your father's." He

popped the lids on two Pepsis. "Here." He handed each a soda. "Bienvenidos. Welcome to the other side."

Day 3

Wiona awoke to the shrill of the alarm. She groped for the off button, pressed, but the alarm persisted. She gazed at the red numbers, 4:10, for a moment before she realized it was the whistle of the teakettle that had jerked her out of sleep. Massaging the hinges of her jaw, she got out of bed.

In the kitchen, Emma was setting the table for four.

"Morning," she said cheerfully.

"Morning, Mother. How come you're up so early?"

"Early?" She pointed to the clock whose hands pointed to 6:35. "Go wake your brother."

Wiona started to remind Emma that Frankie was dead, but reconsidered. It was 4 in the morning. "Didn't he tell you he was staying over at the Hartford's? They're castrating their calves this morning. Why don't you go back to bed? Sleep in a bit. I can get my own breakfast."

"I'm up now. Might as well fix breakfast. Two eggs or three?"

"Two."

She should have gone after the brindle cow and her calf yesterday, but had gotten caught up a bit on the bookkeeping instead. So today was the day, and it looked like she was going to get an early start. For the hundredth time, she made a mental note to buy a new kitchen clock.

Keeping his eye on the scrub mesquite thickets along each side of the road, Stokey didn't let up on the gas pedal until the speedometer hit 90. It wasn't that he was in any hurry to get to the Douglas drag, a swath of dirt road running just north of Highway 80. It was just that speed distracted him from the goldfish that began to circle in his stomach every time he got behind the wheel. A little residual from his second tour.

Every few days, a Border Patrol agent would attach five tires chained together to the back of a truck and sweep the drag. On a clean drag, fresh tracks made by undocumented aliens going north stood out like neon.

More than once, he'd cut sign from the drag right up to a dead body. More often you found them alive and well, running through the brush like a bunch of jackrabbits. In summer, though, when temperatures on the desert floor hovered at 110 degrees and they were lost and drinking their own piss, the UDAs welcomed you like Jesus Christ himself. It was one of the perks of the job, saving the occasional soul from dying of dehydration.

Ahead two ravens pulled at some now undistinguishable roadkill. They flapped away at his approach, wings shining blue-black in the brittle morning sunshine. He looked out over the valley, brutal in drought. Two dust devils rose in great scouring spirals of grit 300 feet into the air, then careened through the scrub like a couple of drunks. Stokey shook his head. "Poor fucking bastards." Still, if they all stayed home, he'd be out of a job.

His thoughts turned to Fletcher Hart. The locals weren't wasting any time. Ranchers, folks in Douglas, Rodeo – even Portal and Paradise – were contributing to a reward for any information leading to an arrest. It was already posted in Rodeo, Douglas, Agua Prieta and Naco. So far, they'd collected more than $2,000, he'd heard. Didn't sound like much, but for folks south of the border, and even some north, it could be a life changer.

Garza and he had studied the photos he'd taken of the tracks, then turned them over to the sheriff's department. See what they might make of those damn Ariats. Out of curiosity, he had called Carter Hart himself. Turns out Wendel might have had a pair of Ariats, but Wendel was up in Phoenix working on some kind of real estate deal, shopping center or something, Hart wasn't certain exactly what. It wasn't hard to imagine Wendel Hart in a pair of Ariats. He was that kind of guy, a bit flashy and arrogant, as Stokey recalled.

Then again, maybe he'd been wrong about the Ariats; maybe they were just plain old cowboy boots after all. Could have been Fletcher's or Carter's. But there was another niggling little detail. Garza had talked to Fattyboy Farris. It seems the weapon used to kill Fletcher was a 410-gauge shotgun. The weapon of choice for any self-respecting drug mule would be a semiautomatic of some kind. Peculiar, is what it was. Well, it was off his plate now.

Stokey let his mind wander to his garden. There was always a lot to do in April. He needed to work compost into the beds. The poppies were about to bloom, and there were a few pansies and Johnny-jump-ups that had reseeded, but all the perennials and bulbs had died of neglect while he was in Iraq and needed to be replaced. He'd spent hours looking through catalogs, studying the mostly naked beds and making lists. He'd never tried lavender, for instance, and there were a dozen varieties of salvia that would be nice. If he planted them along the periphery of the garden, they'd ward off ground squirrels and pack rats, then he could tuck the zucchini, tomato and bell pepper plants in between. The runner beans, cantaloupe and such, he'd plant inside chicken-wire cages. Next fall, if he didn't get redeployed, he'd put in a drip system, though he always enjoyed hand watering.

Back in Iraq, when he couldn't sleep, he'd visualized himself watering the garden. In this vision, it was always summer after the heat had abated, but before the sun had set. The air was gold with pollen, the tomatoes bursting out of their cages and waist high.

Sometimes he could fall asleep.

He was about to turn off the highway when Rudy Garza's twang cracked from the radio mounted between the front seats. "What's your 10/20?" He wanted to know. "We got a situation this morning."

A "situation" was never good. Stokey turned up the radio a notch. "Still on 80, about five miles from the Cave Creek drag. What's up?"

"Got a call from the 911 dispatcher in Douglas. Someone, pollero would be my guess, called in to report a woman in labor out there on what, according to his description, might be Frank Rutherford's place. Course could be some other place. But he said they crossed about 30 miles east of Agua Prieta and then proceeded pretty much northwest, 15, 20 klicks, before she got left behind. According to the topo, that would put her pretty close to Rutherford's second tank. Course it could be some Josés messing with us, but go on up there and check it out. Let me know if we need to call the BORSTAR to helicopter in."

"Ten-four," he answered. Turning on his flashers, he made a U-turn.

The Rutherford place. Stokey knew it well. He and Frank Jr. had been buddies and, of course, he'd dated Wiona in high school. Dated her again for a bit the summer before he and Frankie shipped out to Camp Lejuene for basic.

Wiona. It'd been years, really, since they'd exchanged anything other than the occasional muttered greeting. That was his fault, of course. If he hadn't … well sort of forced himself on her, they could have remained friends at least. He regretted that, especially after what happened to Frankie. He'd wanted to go over and say something to Frankie's mom and dad about how it was in Kuwait, how Frankie had been a good soldier and all, but he couldn't face Wiona.

He remembered that night, their last. He and Wiona had been over to Douglas for a dance. Wiona was a good dancer, light and easy. She'd been wearing a pair of ass hugging jeans. And a turquoise shirt that practically glowed in the dark, he remembered that. Plus her smell. She always smelled like almonds. Was he in love with her back then? Probably not, or maybe just a little because she'd been so hard to get.

If he'd been more patient, things wouldn't have gotten so messed up between them, maybe. He drew a hand down one side of his face and across his jaw.

They'd been splitting beers for awhile in the back of his pickup and both were a little drunk. He eased her down on the horse blanket kept handy in case he got lucky. Hadn't gotten very far, when she rolled him off with her hip.

"Ah, Wiona," he'd said. "How long you gonna keep me waiting?"

She sat up then, started to button her blouse. "I just don't want to, Stokey. What if I got pregnant?"

"I'd marry you."

"You're leaving next month."

"Exactly. Who knows what might happen?" He kissed her neck. "See what you do to me?" He took her hand then, placed it on the bulge in his jeans. "Don't be a such a damn prick tease."

"I'm not a prick tease."

"OK then." He began unbuttoning once more. She let him. She let him unbuckle her belt, let him kiss her breasts and belly. When he pulled his cock out, she panicked though.

"Hush, honey. Relax. I won't do a thing you don't want me to." He hadn't intended to lie.

Stokey pulled off onto the dirt road south of the Rutherford's cattle lease. If he wanted to cross over the Peloncillos, this is the route he'd take. There were fresh tire tracks. He got out of the truck. Not a dozen paces up the road he saw a mess of footprints. By the multitude of mice and quail that had run over them since, he figured they'd crossed the road a day or at most two before, probably early evening. Must have been 12, maybe 15 UDAs heading north. He studied the prints. Standard footwear – tennis shoes, boots; one poor bastard was wearing huaraches. Several sets of tracks stood out because of the newness of the soles. Nikes or, more likely, cheap knockoffs. By their size he'd say a child, maybe two, and a pregnant woman? Could be, they were pretty deep for being so small.

Back in his truck he radioed the station.

"What's your 10-20?" Garza asked.

"South end of Doubtful Wash. There's plenty sign. A bunch of 'em crossed the road some 36 hours ago. A woman and maybe a couple of kids. I'm going up the road a ways and see what's what."

Stokey got back in the truck and climbed slowly up a cut alongside the wash that was more boulder-strewn cow path than road. When he could go no farther, he got out and took a GPS reading. Before heading out on foot, he radioed in his position, then loaded a pack with a gallon of water, a quart of Gatorade and a half-dozen protein bars. He figured he was not more than 10 miles from the second tank. If he hurried, and he would hurry, he'd be there in two, two and a half hours.

Wiona was out in the barn when she heard Gaby's truck pull up. She paid Gaby practically nothing to come over twice a week to stay with her mother for a few hours. Gaby'd offered to do it for nothing, but like most ranchers, she and her husband, Beto, were struggling to make ends meet. Gaby was unloading her 2-year-old daughter, Susana, from the back seat. She put the child down and Susana hit the ground running, jet pigtails corkscrewing just above her ears.
"Ona!" she cried. Her arms flapped like a little penguins.

Wiona scooped Susana up, swung her around, then bounced her into the house.

"Ona spoils you," Gaby said, smiling. She tugged Susana's jacket off and hung it on the hat rack in the hall, then turned serious. "Did you hear about Fletcher Hart?"

"Fletcher? No. Not another heart attack."

Gaby shook her head. "He was shot in the back not two miles

from his house."

"Is he … ? How bad?"

"He's dead, Wiona. They say he confronted some illegal, drug runner most likely. There were footprints all the way to the border."

Fletcher and her father had been of an age, and on friendly terms. For years, they helped each other at roundup and branding. On automatic, Wiona poured two mugs of coffee and set them on the kitchen table. "When's the funeral?"

Gaby accepted the mug. "Haven't gotten that far yet, I guess. Carter's offering a reward. Number of ranchers and folks are contributing."

"I can help with that."

"You sure you want to do that?"

"Money's tight, but not that tight." She put down her mug and went to the old breadbox on the counter where they'd always hidden the emergency funds. From behind a loaf of Wonder Bread, the only kind Emma would eat, she pulled a worn leather wallet that had belonged to her father. She parted the various folds, but the wallet was empty. "There was $78 in here. Damn it." She stomped out of the kitchen.

As expected, Emma was dozing in her recliner. She studied the woman a moment. How best to proceed. By experience, she knew a direct accusation would bring out her mother's stubborn and the woman could be wily mean when she felt cornered.

"Mother," she said softly. "Wake up, Mother. I need your help."

The woman's eyes fluttered open. "Wiona, you're blocking my program."

"Sorry, Mother," she said, but didn't step aside. "I need $50 to give Gaby. Do you have any money in your purse?"

"Why does Gaby need $50?"

"She's short on her groceries this week. It's just a loan until Beto gets his pay on Friday."

"Well, she can wait to get her groceries until Friday, just like everybody."

"She can't do that, Mother, not with the baby."

"Baby! What baby?"

"Susana. Hang on." Wiona marched into the kitchen where Susana sat in a high chair before a small pile of Cheerios. "Come here a minute, sweetie." She pulled the child out of her chair then marched back into the living room.

"Say hi to Nana," Wiona said, and plunked the baby onto her mother's lap.

"Nana." Susana opened her fist and presented Emma with a Cheerio.

"Why thank you," Emma said, looking confused but delighted.

"Mother, you remember Gaby's little girl, Susana."

"Why of course I do." Emma gave the child a big kiss on the cheek. "Susana."

"Well, Gaby needs $50 dollars to buy groceries for Susana."

"Let me go look," Emma set the toddler on the floor. After a few minutes, she came back with a $20 bill."

"Gaby needs $50, Mother."

"Twenty's all I've got. Besides, $20 should buy enough Cheerios and milk to keep Susana until Friday. People have to learn how to live within their means, Wiona."

She handed her the bill.

Wiona plucked Susana up off the floor.

"What?" Emma settled back into the recliner. "No 'thank you, Mother,' no goddamn grateful as hell?"

"Thank you, Mother. You can get back to your program now."

Exasperated, she carried Susana back to the kitchen. She handed the bill to Gaby. "Fletcher and my dad were good friends. It's not much, but I guess every little bit helps."

It would be faster and easier to take the ATV or the truck for that matter. But the old road ended a quarter mile from the second tank and Wiona suspected that the brindle cow wouldn't be easy to find.

Besides, Link hadn't been out in a week and she owed him, owed herself, a leisurely, quiet trip up the canyon. When she strapped on her chaps, Link pricked his ears knowing that meant he had a job to do. Thunder poked his head out. He brayed once, reconsidered, farted, then disappeared.

Osa waited patiently as Wiona hefted the saddle onto Link's back. She snugged the front cinch, tightened the back, then led Link around a bit. When she heard him expel pent-up air, she quickly tightened the front cinch once again. As she rode out of the yard, the moon, no more than a pale lash, still hovered, midsky.

By the time she reached the second tank, the canyon walls were a blue silhouette against gray. There was no breeze to turn the windmill and only the thrasher's little opera broke the silence. Cows and their calves stirred as the trio passed, no brindle among them.

Feeling edgy, Wiona patted the Colt on her hip, then circled the tank. She continued along the edge of the canyon for a ways, then dropped down into the wash, alert for tracks, both cow and human. She didn't want to end up like Fletcher Hart.

It was then she heard the oriole, it's liquid song unmistakable. Staring into the brush, Osa came to a halt. Wiona looked toward the source of the song. There at the base of an Emory oak sat Wade Spalding. He had a device in his lap that was sending the oriole's call into the canopy.

Shortly after her father's death, she'd sold Wade 20 deeded acres along the creek. Even in times of good rain, it only ran a few months out of the year, but it was lined with oaks, cottonwoods and sycamores, prime birding habitat, according to Wade. She'd been reluctant to do it, but two funerals in two years had put them way behind and the house had needed a new roof.

Wade was one of those California types who get rich, retire early and then try to find something to fill up time. He'd chosen birds, which seemed a good choice to Wiona. With his pointy nose, protruding belly and spindly legs, he sort of resembled one. From what she gathered, birding was an expensive pastime, necessitating lots of fancy cameras, recording devices, binoculars and spotting scopes, as well as several trips each year to exotic places to find new birds to add to his life list. She didn't get it, but allowed him to come and go on her property as he pleased in search of new additions to his yard list. Wade considered much of her ranch as his back yard, apparently. She didn't begrudge him.

She waved. "Working on your list, Wade?"

"Hey, Wiona." He turned off the birdsong. "Just trying out some new equipment."

"Sorry to have interrupted."

He looked at his watch. "No worries."

"You hear about Fletcher Hart?"

"Fletcher? No. What about him?"

"Shot dead. They say it was an illegal. Say there's tracks all the way from the body to the border."

His eyebrows shot up. "When was this?"

"Day before yesterday, day before that. I'm not quite sure."

He stood, dusting the dry leaves off his pants. "Fletcher dead, I can't believe it. I just saw him last week. You know he's got a trogon nest along his creek and I was out looking. ... I can't believe it."

Wiona was surprised and a bit embarrassed when Wade took out a handkerchief and dabbed at his eyes. "His brother, Carter, is collecting for a reward if you want to make a contribution."

"I'll do that, Wiona," he said still patting his eyes. "Fletcher dead. I can't believe it."

"Me neither, Wade. He was a good man." She adjusted herself in the saddle. "Well, I've got a mama and baby to find, so I'll see you later." She headed Link to the other side of the canyon, Osa out in front, scouting.

She hadn't realized that Wade was so soft-hearted. It wasn't that she didn't mourn Fletcher Hart's passing, but she wasn't moved to tears over it. There wasn't much anymore that moved her to tears.

Seemed Wade was turning out to be a pretty good neighbor.

Quiet and just friendly enough, she didn't regret selling him that 20 acres. And she sure did like the new roof. Green metal, it was more expensive than shingles, but it was what Emma had always wanted. Wiona knew that it was seldom in life that a person gets just what she wants, and a metal roof was a good investment. They lasted, and if there was a fire in the canyon, and this could be the year, it sure wouldn't burn. For a while, Emma had been real excited about that roof.

Intuition sent her up a draw where, in better times, there had been a year-round seep. It would be dry after so many months of nothing more than God's spittle, but there might be some grass up there still, something to eat at any rate that would tempt the cow to linger after giving birth. She blew her whistle and waited, scanning the buff and decomposed granite for tracks. There they were, fresh and plain as day. The damn cow was here someplace. She blew the whistle again. Link picked his way up the draw, Osa out front looking for a little something, fox scat possibly, to hold her over until her next meal. As far as Wiona was concerned, shit eating was the dog's only shortcoming.

She heard the lowing before she saw them. Let her come to me, she thought, and dismounted. Taking the chunk of molasses lick from her saddlebag, she blew the whistle again. Finally, the cow led her calf, black and shiny, down the draw. "Hey, mama," she called softly.

Sometime past dawn, Belen found herself hurrying down the narrow road to San Pablito, dust powdering her feet and ankles. The air, full of the scent of iron and dry leaves, was chilly. For hours, it seemed, she'd been fighting her way though canyons and arroyos to get there and she was very tired.

At last she stood before her grandmother's whitewashed casita with its tin roof bleeding rust. Sweeping back the flowered curtain that served as a door, she stepped inside the room where her grandmother was laid out on a wooden table surrounded by flickering votive candles and red hibiscus. Her long braid wrapped round her head like a silver crown, and she wore her most beautifully embroidered apron.

This sight of her dead grandmother did not surprise her, nor did it make her sad, for her grandmother had died long ago. As she gazed upon the withered face, hardly more than a skull after so many years, the old woman opened her eyes and smiled.

"I've been waiting so long for you to come, my little daughter," she said in Otomí, the only language she knew. "I have something very important to tell you. Come closer so I can whisper in your ear."

Belen leaned forward, the heat of the little candles warming her cheek, but she could hear only an insistent buzzing, as if a hive of bees had taken residence within the bony cage of her grandmother's chest.

"Grandmother," she said, suddenly frantic. "I can't understand. What are you trying to say?"

The grandmother grew frantic, too, repeating the message again and again, but all Belen heard was the sound of bees. Suddenly, her grandmother started to wail, thin, mournful. "Ay, Grandmother! Tell me."

Belen's eyes fluttered open, her infant son swaddled in the blue rebozo, red-faced and screaming, beside her.

Osa was at the heels of the brindle cow and her calf, encouraging them along. They proceeded down the canyon single file. Link, plodding along the familiar track, rocked Wiona into a doze. She was startled alert by a thin wail. Hair on her arms and the back of her neck rose, and her teeth and stomach clenched simultaneously.
"Stay, Osa," she commanded, while she tried to quiet the blood-rush and pound of her heart. Again the wail. Wiona's hand found the butt of the gun at her hip. What the hell was it and where was it coming

from? The wail stopped abruptly.

She urged Link off the path towards the creek bottom. Her eyes scanned the dry bed and the opposite slope, Osa sniffing her way among the rocks and brush. Barking furiously, the dog halted beneath an old black walnut where a woman held a blue bundle to her breast.

The two women eyed each other nervously, while Osa continued her alarmed barking. Wiona glanced around. Surely there were others, but no.

"Shut up, Osa, and lay down." The dog did as told and Wiona dismounted. She took the canteen from her saddlebag, and held it toward the woman. "Necesita agua?" she asked, conscious of her stiff gringa tongue.

The woman nodded her head.

Wiona passed the canteen to the woman, watched her drink half of it straightaway, all the while searching her brains for remnants of high school Spanish. There'd been three years of it some 20 years ago, plus some ranch Spanish she'd picked up along the way. "Como se llama?" was all that came to her.

"Belen," the woman said softly.

Wiona held her palm out stiffly, a gesture meant to convey: Don't be afraid. Stay where you are. "Momentito, Belen."

"Espera, señora." She pulled the blue bundle from her breast so Wiona could see. The baby was tiny, but managed a mighty wail of protest. Like an offering, she held the baby out to Wiona. "Por favor. El nació en los Estados Unidos. Es un cuidadano. Cuidadano de los Estado Unidos! Me entiende? Tengo dos otra niños qui estan con sus padre en Phoenix. Nos debemos juntarles. Por amor de Dios, ayudame."

Wiona got United States, two children, father, Phoenix and for the love of God. She nodded slowly, struck by the open desperation in the woman's dark, round face, in her exhausted eyes. Kneeling, inadequate, she took the woman's hand.

"Muy bien," Wiona said. She would help, but at the moment she didn't know just how she might go about doing that, since this woman was clearly an illegal.

Before remounting she again made the palm gesture. Kicking Link's ribs to hurry him along, she headed back up the draw to the ridge where her cell phone might work if it wasn't windy. Who to call, who to call? She could simply call 911. The Border Patrol would send a helicopter, and that would be that. At least they would be safe. But what about the children waiting with their father in Phoenix, waiting and not knowing what had happened to their mother?

At the top of the ridge, she took the cell phone out and dialed. After two rings, she heard Emma's voice. "Speaking."

Wiona nearly laughed. "Mother, put Gaby on, OK?"

"Gaby?"

"Yes, Mother. She's probably in the kitchen. Tell her I need to talk to her."

She could almost hear her considering. "You mean Gaby?"

"Yes, Mother. Gaby."

"Why would she be here? You must have the wrong number," Emma said, and hung up the phone."

Wiona dialed again, waited. She could imagine Emma's stubborn glare as the phone rang again and again.

"Hello?"

"Gaby. Thank God."

"Sorry, I was changing the baby. What's wrong?"

"Where's Mother?"

"It's the 'Coral Ridge Hour,' isn't it?"

"Listen. I need you to sneak out to my office. Load the mattress into the back of the truck and meet me at the second tank."

"What's going on? Is somebody hurt?"

"I'll tell you about it when you get here. Just hurry."

It would be another hour at least before Gaby could get there.

"Puede caminar? Puede caminar un poco?" Wiona rehearsed the phrase as she rode back down the draw. Somehow, either on foot or by horseback, she had to get Belen and the baby to the second tank. Surely walking would be easier than riding for a woman who'd just given birth in the bottom of a wash. Could she and Gaby carry her to the truck? Probably not without a stretcher. And what would she do with mother and babe once they got to the house? Should she take them to the hospital or could she let them rest for a few days and then … ? And then she would just drive them up to Phoenix. She pictured a happy reunion, small brown children jumping up and down, the father's tears of joy and relief and gratitude. Of course that would be totally illegal. Maybe once she got them to the house she'd just call the Border Patrol.

Well, I don't have to decide right now, she thought. In this kind of situation, bringing them down to the house would certainly qualify as humanitarian aid. Perfectly legal. Besides, a lot would depend on Gaby.

Stokey had lost their trail in the bottom of a rocky wash but picked it up again as he dropped down from the ridge, following a contour where years of foot traffic had cut a narrow swath between shin daggers and prickly pear. Here sign cut in the finely decomposed granite was clear even in the glare of midmorning. The new Nikes were now superimposed on the others. Mother and children walked at the end of the line.

He upped his pace.

She had left Link and Osa up canyon. Now Wiona was carrying the sleeping infant in the soiled rebozo slung across her chest and knotted at the shoulder. One arm was around Belen, who leaned into her for support. Both women were sweating.

Wiona saw the dust before she heard the truck laboring up the track to the second tank. "Solamente un poco mas."

Belen, white around the mouth, said nothing.

Before they reached the second tank, Gaby trundled up the steep path toward them. Despite the young woman's girth, she was quick and strong. Between the two of them, they half-carried, half-dragged Belen the remaining 100 yards.

"Help me get her into the truck."

"Give me the baby first," Gaby directed. "El es tan pequeño."

"Pequeño, pero fuerte," Belen said.

Gaby lay the infant in the front seat next to Susana. The toddler was crying, red-faced and outraged, as she struggled against the confines of her car seat.

"Baby." Susana pointed and settled back, suddenly placated.

With the aid of an old paint bucket, they got Belen into the back of the truck and settled on the mattress. "Aqui esta su nene, señora," Gaby murmured as she placed the infant in her arms.

Susana was howling again, now for want of the baby. Gaby ignored her. With both hands, she pushed back the dark curly hair clinging to her damp forehead and cheeks, then blotted them on her broad backside. "Phew!" She turned to Wiona and asked, "What now?"

"I don't know."

"You don't know?"

"Let's just take her to the ranch, I guess. Get her settled in my office. And for God's sake, don't let Mother see her."

"Wiona, you are loca. This is totally illegal."

"Humanitarian aid."

"Humanitarian aid, mi culo."

"Please just take her to my office."

"But ... "

"She's got two more kids. They're in Phoenix with the father."

"Shit ... "

"I know. We'll talk about it when I get back. I got to get Link and the dog and bring that damn cow and calf down." She turned and hurried back up the canyon.

Osa was under the walnut tree, just as she had left her. She picked up Belen's backpack. Then out of some guilty need, she kicked dry leaves over the birthing place, though the chance of someone coming here before ants and scavengers removed the evidence was zero.

Determined to finish the business of the brindle cow, she mounted Link and blew her whistle.

Stokey could tell they had stopped to rest here because the tracks dispersed in various directions before proceeding down canyon. He followed one set of tracks until it led him to the spot where they re-formed their single line. Over the human prints were cow tracks and the tracks of a horse. "Hmm." he said, though there was nothing unusual about horse and cow tracks on a ranch. Still, they were fresh. And here were several nice canine tracks, with a perfect little pyramid of dust x-ing the center of each. Dog, horse, cow, calf. Nothing strange about that, except ... He followed the dog prints until he lost them in the leaves under a walnut. Peering beneath, he noticed a disturbance in the duff.
"Hmm."

With the toe of his boot he pushed some leaves aside. "So where is she now?"

He followed their tracks, the Nikes and a pair of cowboy boots set so close together one was likely supporting the other. Close to the second tank they were joined by a third set of tracks, small, formless, deep, possibly a heavy woman in sandals or moccasins. At the second tank, the footprints ended where a fresh set of tire tracks began and the boot tracks reversed course.

He took off his hat and splashed water from the cattle tank onto his face and naked head. "Hmm." For a moment he just stood letting the water drip down his neck and into his shirt while he considered the story told by the tracks. What would the rules of engagement require here?

It was late afternoon when he knocked on the Rutherford's screen door, a small, scruffy Aussie growling at him from the bottom of the stoop. Wiona appeared behind the screen, smiled. "Well, Stokey," she said, not bothering to call off the dog. "I didn't hear you drive in." She pushed the screen door open, held it ajar with her booted foot. "So what brings you out here?"
"Looking for a mother and a baby."

"How'd you hear about that?" She said without hesitation. "I left them up at the second tank."

"What?"

"My brindle cow and her calf. Isn't that what we're talking about? I found them up canyon and brought them down to the second tank this afternoon." She looked around him then, wide-eyed. "Hey, Stokey. Where's your truck?"

"Left it at the bottom of Doubtful Wash. Got a call that some illegal was having a baby somewhere out by your second tank. Been looking for them."

"Well, I was all over there. Didn't see anybody, though. You look beat. Why don't you come on in? I just made a pot of coffee and I think there's pie. Gaby?" she called. "Didn't you make a pie this morning?"

There was no answer. "She must be changing her daughter's diaper. Well, come on in. Say hello to Mother."

Stokey took off his cap and ducked into the dark hallway. To the left was the living room where a woman dozed beneath a crocheted lap blanket, her lounger in full recline.

"Don't be surprised if she doesn't remember you. After Frankie and Dad died she had a bunch of little strokes and she's … well, not quite herself," she whispered, then raised her voice to a near yell, "Mother? Look who's dropped in to say hello. Stokey Stokelund, Frankie's old high school buddy."

"Nice to see you again, Mrs. Rutherford."

Emma pulled a lever at the side of her chair and sprang to a sitting position. "Stokey? Well, Stokey Stokelund. You didn't used to be so bald." She patted her own scattered hair in place and added, "How's your mother?"

In the kitchen Wiona slipped a piece of berry pie onto a Melmac plate so old the once bright turquoise geometric pattern around the edge was little more than a pale smear. She set the plate before him. "Ice cream with that?"
"This will be fine, thanks."

Wiona looked around the kitchen for something to do so she wouldn't have to sit at the table with him. She put a little soap on a dishrag and began to swab down the counters.

"Noticed you got some posts that need replacing in the corral," he said around a mouthful of pie. "Good pie."

"I can't take any credit for that." She tossed the dishrag into the sink. "And yeah, there're the posts and about a half-dozen other things need doing before I bring in the calves. But it's the end of tax season, you know. Can't do everything at once."

"Nope." He took a sip of coffee. "You know, I'm sitting here eating this nice pie, but I can't quit thinking that maybe there's a woman and a baby out there someplace that need help, or maybe it was just a false alarm, and I'm thinking, to be on the safe side I should call BORSTAR in. Ever heard of 'em?"

Wiona had not.

"BORSTAR stands for Border Patrol, Search, Trauma and Rescue. They're the guys we send out when we've gotten word some illegal is out in the middle of nowhere in the process of dying. Man, now those guys really know how to cut sign. They can look at a set of tracks and tell you not only which pocket the guy keeps his wallet in, but whether he's wearing Levis or Wranglers. Spooky, they're so good."

Jaw aching, Wiona retrieved the dishrag and went over the stovetop. "I guess it's like a sixth sense, tracking."

"Yup. That's it, a sixth sense. If she's out there someplace, they'll no doubt find her. The thing is, I hate to call 'em if there's no emergency, know what I'm saying? I mean, if she somehow made it out to the road and somebody gave her a lift, well … what can I do about that? But I can't just leave it be unless I know she's safe."

He scraped the last of the pie off the plate. "Man, that's some good pie."

"Another slice? Maybe some more coffee?"

"No thanks. I better radio the station. Can't take the chance she's still out there, unless … "

"The mama and baby are safe."

"We talking about the cow and her calf now?"

"They're safe. Can we leave it at that?"

He studied her a moment. "I think we can. I just hope you know what you're getting into, is all."

"You need a ride back to your truck?"

"Been a long day. I'd appreciate it."

"I'll get Mother," she said, trying to find a way to feel less vulnerable. "I'm sure she'd like to come along for the ride."

"Now, Stokey," Emma was saying from her perch in the back seat of the truck. "I want you to tell your mother I apologize for not making it to the church potluck. I haven't been all that peppy lately. My arthritis, for one thing."

Wiona hadn't seen Emma as sharp or congenial in months, though the reference to the church potluck was out of the blue. Emma hadn't been to church in over a year, preferring to get her dose of religion daily from the televangelists.

The wind was kicking up, and Wiona gripped the wheel as Emma went on and on about Frankie, Frankie as quarterback, Frankie as bull rider, Frankie so handsome in his uniform, on and on. But what else could she expect? Frankie was always at the center of Emma's little world. Wiona figured that was why her father seemed to favor her a bit. It was a chicken or the egg kind of question. Did her father favor her because Emma favored Frankie or did Emma favor Frankie because her father favored her? Not that it mattered anymore.

Wiona shut Emma's voice out and turned her thoughts to the current predicament. Could she trust Stokey? Did she have a choice? Oh, she should have handed Belen over right there and then, but she couldn't do it. She felt sorry for the woman, but mostly it was the baby that had gotten to her, so tiny yet so solid he had been in her arms. She thought of that other baby, the secret one. Helping Belen and her baby – would that take off some of the weight she'd been carrying around all these years?

"Wiona," Emma was saying. "Since we're already halfway to Douglas, why don't we go to the store and pick up a nice shoulder of pork."

"It's too late to go all the way to Douglas. Besides, Gaby's already made us a beef stew," she said flatly, trying to stay in neutral.

"Beef stew. All we ever eat is beef."

"Well, that's because we're ranchers. Besides, last night we had chicken."

"Chicken and beef, beef and chicken. That's all we ever eat," Emma complained, Stokey and her role as sane and spunky widow totally forgotten.

"I'll ask Gaby to get some pork chops when she shops next week."

"Pork chops," Emma sighed, dismissing the whole idea. "Well, bless your heart."

After a few minutes her head fell back and she was snoring softly.

"By now I guess you heard about Fletcher Hart," Stokey said.

"A terrible thing. And why Fletcher, of all people?"

"I think that's a question on everybody's mind. Say, you don't know anybody around here who wears Ariats do you?"

"Ariats? What's that?"

"A type of expensive boot. Kind of a hybrid cowboy boot/work boot thing that laces up the front. When I was a kid it was mule drivers who favored them."

"I don't pay much attention to footwear, Stokey. Why do you ask?"

He shrugged. "No particular reason. Just saw a track that looked like it was made by an Ariat and was wondering."

"Where was this track? My ranch?"

"Hart's."

"So what are you thinking?"

"I'm not paid to think, but if I were, I'd say an Ariat's an unusual kind of boot for around here. Curious to know who would be wearing that kind of foot gear, is all."

Wiona considered that. "So folks are saying there were tracks that went all the way to the border."

"That's what I heard, too."

Wiona figured that was about all Stokey was going to say on the matter. The valley was a wind factory, especially in spring when the alfalfa and chili farmers were disking their fields, filling its length and breadth with a great wall of pale dust. The sun hovered low over the Chiricahua Mountains now, turning the dust to gold. Wiona concentrated on the buffeting wind, and they drove the rest of the way in silence.

There was a fire in the stove, and the remains of a plate of beef stew sat on the desk next to the aged Mac she'd purchased cheap from Cochise College when they upgraded. Belen and the baby were asleep on the little bed. Wiona recognized the T-shirt she was wearing. Oversized, with the Marine's insignia across the chest, it had been given to her by her brother before he shipped out to Iraq. She had never once worn it. Seeing it now made her slightly queasy. "Hope you don't mind," Gaby whispered, Susana sleeping in her lap. "She needed something to put on after her shower. I gave her a couple of your mom's house dresses and your dad's old bathrobe, too." She nodded to the place where they hung on the back of the door.

"She wants to phone her husband, make sure the kids arrived safely," Gaby added. "Let him know she's OK."

"Here's my cell. If she can get a signal in this wind, she can call when she wakes up. Otherwise, we'll have to wait until Mother is in bed for the night and use the house phone."

"One more thing. Is there any way we can get a birth certificate for this little guy? Something to prove he was born in the good old USA."

"That might be problematic."

"It would mean a lot to her."

Wiona shrugged. "Let me think."

She glanced out the window. The dust filtered into the canyon like pulverized sulfur. By the glow, she reckoned that it was around 6. The clinic in Douglas probably stayed open until 6 or 7 to accommodate working mothers and their kids who were the bulk of the clients.

"I hate to ask, Gaby, but could you stay until we get a few things straightened out with Belen?"

"I've already called Beto to let him know I'd be late."

"Thanks." Wiona leaned in over the sleeping Susana and kissed Gaby on the top of her head. "I couldn't survive without you."

As Wiona walked toward the house, she was working up a pretty good case of the jitters. Appealing to Lucy Altamirano seemed like the only reasonable option. Worst thing that could happen would be that she'd say no. If that was the worst thing, what might be the best thing? It was this notion of *the best thing* that was making Wiona's stomach fill up with jackrabbits and sparrows.

She poked her head into the living room. Satisfied that her mother was sound asleep, she stepped into the kitchen. Quickly she located the number, dialed, then waited as the recording ran through a list of options. Wiona punched zero and after several rings, a human voice answered.

"Is Lucy Altamirano there?" Wiona asked.

"She's around here somewhere. I'll put you through to her extension."

Lucy's recorded voice told her to phone 911 if this was an emergency, to leave a name and number and a brief message after the beep if it wasn't.

She wanted to hang up. Instead, she took a deep breath. "Lucy. This is Wiona Rutherford calling. I have a woman out here on the ranch who's just given birth. Baby and mom … "

"Hello? Wiona?"

"Oh! You're there." She took up a broom and started sweeping the linoleum to calm herself.

"For the moment. What's up?"

"Well, it's complicated. A woman gave birth here on the ranch. Baby and mom seem fine, but I'm concerned. Seems he, the baby, came early and … "

"Bring them on in. I'll check them out."

"Well … it's not that simple. I was hoping you could come out here. The issue is, well … travel is an issue right now, and the mom really needs a birth certificate. I was hoping … "

"What are we talking about here?"

"She had the baby out by the second tank, alone."

"I see. Does this woman work for you?"

"No."

"I see."

"You do? Will you help?"

"The clinic closes at 7. I'll be there by 8."

"Thank you, Lucy. I hate to put this on you, but I don't know anyone else I can ask."

When she hung up the phone, it was slick with sweat. She wiped her palms on the back of her jeans, then swept up a little pile of bits and pieces into the dustpan.

Leaning on the door jamb, Emma asked, "Who were you talking to just now?"

"Oh! I didn't see you standing there," Wiona said, feeling like she'd been caught with her hand in Emma's Christmas box of See's assorted chews and nuts.

"Ready for supper?" she asked, changing the subject.

"What is it we're having?"

"Stew."

"I thought you said we were having pork roast."

"No, Mother. It's stew tonight."

"Well you said. So who were you talking to just now?"

Wiona busied herself in the freezer while she tried to think up a suitable lie. "Doc Glutterman. I think Link's got something going on with his leg, maybe a pulled ligament. I was hoping Doc would come out and have a look. Would you like broccoli or peas with dinner?"

"What else have we got?"

Wiona made a big production of shoving things around the freezer. "There's corn."

"Make it corn then." She stepped into the kitchen. "You must think I'm stupid, deaf and blind."

Wiona slapped the package of corn on the counter and considered her options. She could continue to embellish the lie, she could continue fixing supper as if Emma weren't standing right there waiting for an answer, or she could tell Emma some of the truth and hope she'd forget it. "I'm letting a sick friend stay in the office, and I just called a doctor to come see her."

"Since when do you make friends with wetbacks?"

"Mother, why don't you go into the living room? I'll call you when supper's on the table," she said, then watched amazed as Emma did just that.

Unable to see the road for the dust, Stokey pulled the truck onto the shoulder and turned off the engine. After he radioed in his 10-20, he unwrapped a power bar and settled back to wait for the visibility to improve. It might be minutes, could be hours.

He considered his decision to pretend that Wiona was not harboring an illegal alien. Of course he could still get a search warrant to verify what he already knew. The law required him to do just that. But what did the rules of engagement require – the rules that he occasionally applied in cases where the law was clear, but the merit of abiding by it was not? There were larger issues here, and he figured he owed Wiona.

The air smelled like powdered iron filings, as dust seeped into the truck coating the inside of his nostrils, settling on his hairless head. He swiped at the grit with his handkerchief then blew his nose. A case of moral ambiguity, that's what it was, having nothing to do with the fact that Wiona's looks were improving with age. Contours that were unyielding when she was 18 seemed softer, the wrinkles at the corners of her eyes, the way her cheeks folded when she smiled made her face ... what? Kinder, maybe, more tolerant, probably. Accepting. Stokey would like to feel accepted once again. Mere acceptance didn't seem like so much to ask for.

He thought of his wife. Most people probably suspected that Becka had run off to be with another man. Not so. She didn't want somebody else, or at least that's what she claimed. She just didn't want him. Period. And that made it worse, somehow. Up until the very day she walked out, Becka had been the only one he'd ever, ever really wanted. She was up in Tucson now, working at Kinko's part-time and living in a dump – he'd seen it himself. And she preferred that to living with him.

And the kids! Jackson's only crime was that he wanted to fire a .50-caliber machine gun out the window of a chopper like his old man. Stokey hadn't encouraged him in this desire, but there it was. As for Katie, well, she was a girlie-girl, a little pig-headed, but a good, bright kid who simply had not yet found herself. Becka had never invited Katie to join her on this grand venture of what?

Emancipation? Now why was that?

"Damn good thing that she hadn't," he muttered as the dust continued to powder the hood of his truck, his dash, his head.

In front of the bathroom mirror, Wiona unbraided her hair, brushed it, then rebraided it. She pulled it over her left shoulder and considered the effect. Too girlish. She swung it back to its customary location between her shoulder blades and was starting to brush her teeth, when she heard the doorbell. "Shit!" She splashed water in her mouth and ran to the front of the house.

As Wiona rushed down the hall, wiping her mouth on her sleeve, Emma was saying, "Lord, look at what you've done to your hair!" to a petite woman in purple scrubs, a nubby, green sweater thrown over her shoulders.

Wiona reached for the woman's hand and gripped firmly, hoping Lucy wouldn't notice that her own was shaking. "Thanks for coming."

Lucy's dark eyes were smudged beneath with fatigue, but otherwise she was small and tight and mostly unchanged except for her hair. Once it hung black, glossy and straight to her rump. Now it was short, spiky and flecked with white.

"My friend is out in the barn. Can I get you a cup of coffee first?"

Lucy looked up at Wiona and offered a smile full of straight, white teeth. "I'd like that. Maybe after I see her."

Emma grabbed the corduroy jacket from the hat tree. "I'm coming, too."

"It's cold out, Mother. I think you should ... "

"Nonsense." She said, and strode out the door.

They heard the howling as they crossed the yard. When they entered the office, Belen, the baby and even Susana were sobbing.

Gently, Emma took the baby out of Belen's arms. "There, there, sweetheart," she said, patting him quiet. She looked at Wiona then, arched her brow as if to say, *I knew it all along.*

Wiona turned to Gaby. "What's wrong?"

"The kids. Belen just spoke to her husband. They never got there."

Part 2

The Other Side

Day 4

As the Chrysler cruised through the blue-white haze of halogen street lamps along Camelback Road, the man El Camaleón called Boots checked on the children sleeping in the back seat. Satisfied that they'd be out through the whole transaction and into the middle of the next day, he looked at his watch. It was nearly 4 a.m.

His name was Francisco Ochoa de Mejia, though his friends and family, even his mother, called him Dutch. His wife was from an old established family whose wealth accrued traditionally from the trafficking of cocaine and heroin. As a resident alien, he had long enjoyed legal access to the United States. Only recently had he expanded the family business into trafficking of a specialized nature, working the border both ways.

His dentures, the result of a very bad encounter with the federales, were paining him, but he was too vain to take them out.

The driver turned off the thoroughfare onto a darkened avenue, then pulled into a lane that was darker still. He stopped in front of a low, sprawling ranch-style house; its front yard was covered with glowing white quartz rock.

Dutch stepped out of the car and onto a brick path leading to the entry. Before he could ring the bell, a burly man in a Hawaiian shirt and white pants opened the door. The man, known to him as James, smiled broadly, revealing small, perfectly even teeth. The two shook hands briefly.

"I'll open the garage door," James said. His bright blue eyes contrasted nicely with his hair and mustache, which were white and thick. An expression of pleasant anticipation gave him the appearance of a grandfather waiting for his grandson's soccer match to begin.

Once the Chrysler was safely in the garage, James clasped his hands together over his heart. "Let's see what we've got."

The driver opened the back door, and James peered in at the sleeping children. "Where's the pregnant woman?"

"She wasn't with the children. I suspect that the coyote left her behind."

"I'm disappointed."

Dutch shrugged. "What can I say?"

From his pocket James extracted a wad of bills. He pealed off 20 and handed them over.

Dutch quickly counted. "What's this? The rate is $10,000 *each*."

"They're too old and too dark."

Dutch's green eyes narrowed. "This is no department store two-for-one. There are other buyers."

"There are other providers. Besides, you really let me down."

"How so?"

He slicked his fingers over his mustache. "Have you ever had veal so tender you know its feet never even touched the ground?"

"On occasion."

"Well, you didn't deliver the veal."

"And the mother. What did you have planned for her?"

Mouth downturned, James shrugged. "There's always someone who'll buy someone for something."

Dutch didn't bother to disguise his loathing, but what could he do? It was late. His wife would scream at him if he brought the children home with him, and he was too tired for that. Telling himself that he would probably never have do business with this son of a whore again, he accepted the money. Tomorrow he had a transaction of a different nature to make, and any delay would be costly. If that went well, he'd soon be out of this end of the business for good.

Belen, eyes red and puffy, stood alongside Wiona in the cool, blue morning. Absently, she smoothed the front of the loose, flowered housedress over her swollen belly as she watched Gaby and Beto drive away.

The plan was for the couple to go down to Agua Prieta and pretend they wanted to cross. "It will be easy," Beto had promised. "All you have to do is stand at the bus station. The contractors come to you."

They would let it be known that they'd heard of a man, un muy buen guía with a drooping left eyelid who called himself El Camaleón. Once they found him, they would demand answers. They had money, five crisp $20 bills provided by Señora Emma, to pay for them if necessary. Belen could only pray that soon she would know where her children were.

In the meantime there was nothing she could do but attend to the immediate needs of her son, who lay sleeping in the house. For the sake of the birth certificate and without consulting her husband, she had named him Jesús Milagros Verales de Jimenez. He weighed only 2.6 kilos, but la doctora still had declared him a fit and healthy citizen of the United States.

Though Belen had thanked her sincerely, the pronouncement did nothing to relieve her deep dread. Where were her children? Had they been caught by la Migra and sent back to Mexico alone? She'd heard of other things that could happen – people stolen and held for ransom. If that were the case, Jacabo might hear from the kidnappers soon. Maybe Edgar and Adriana were being kept in hiding somewhere until it was safe to take them to their father. "Blessed Virgencita. Keep them from harm," she prayed silently.

When the two women came into the kitchen, Emma was standing at the stove.

"We've got to get some diapers for the baby," she said, without turning away from the pan of frying bacon. "I'm near out of dishtowels. And we need other things; I made a list."

"I'll go into town after breakfast. By the way, where did you get that money?"

"What money?"

"The five brand-new $20 bills you gave to Gaby and Beto."

"From my purse, of course."

"Well, do you have any more so I can buy all that stuff on your list?"

"Nope. You'll have to use your own money."

While she digested that, Wiona bent over Susana, who sat in her high chair plucking at a pile of Cheerios, and kissed the toddler on both cheeks. Susana offered a Cheerio. Silently commending herself for her restraint, Wiona popped it into her mouth. "Yum."

Belen stood over Jesús. He was temporarily snuggled in bath towels inside his makeshift crib, an old plastic washtub, which sat in the middle of the kitchen table. Wiona could sense that the woman wanted to wake him so she'd have something to occupy her.

"Tiene hambre, Belen?"

Belen shook her head.

"Belen's not hungry, Mother."

"Tell her she has to eat some eggs at least, for Jesus' sake."

Wiona smiled. Emma's pronunciation made it sound like Belen needed to eat her eggs for Christ's sake, a blasphemy Emma would never consciously utter.

"It's pronounced *Hey zeus* in Spanish," she offered.

"We live in America, Wiona, and it's pronounced *Gee zus*!"

This was so much like her old mother Wiona had to smile again. Still, Emma actually seemed to be taking to her role as Samaritan.

The old mother would never have allowed an illegal in the house, much less put her up in the bedroom that she'd maintained as a shrine to Frankie.

Her smile quickly faded as she thought about last night's conversation with Lucy. Wiona had wanted to call Stokey, but Lucy talked her out of it.

"Stokey's Border Patrol," Lucy had argued. "Once he's officially alerted he won't have a choice. He'll take Belen and the baby into custody and ship them back to Mexico."

"What about her other children?"

"If they're already in custody, that's one thing. But what if they're not?"

"What do you mean? Of course they're in custody." Wiona said.

"Not necessarily so. There are these turf wars. One rival gang will steal a load of UDAs from another at gunpoint. It happens all the time along I-10. Sometimes a coyote will lock them in a safe house and demand more money before he turns them over. For an extra, I don't know, 500 bucks, Belen could get the kids back. That would be the best case scenario."

"What's the worst case scenario?"

Lucy had looked at Belen then. "You don't want to hear about worst case scenarios," she had said.

Dear God, Wiona thought, I hope we're doing the right thing. She began setting the table. Like Belen, she needed something to do to keep herself from thinking about worst case scenarios.

Stokey set out the boxes of cereal: raisin bran for himself, granola for Katie, Captain Crunch for the would-be Marine. He thought of his son, blond, mostly hairless, no meat on his long bones. Captain Crunch for breakfast! The Marines will eat *him* for breakfast!

From under the table came a persistent thumping. Stokey took a handful of cereal and dropped it in the dog's bowl. Shorty, a mix of pit bull, dachshund and some unidentified other that provided him with a thin pelt of long wiry hair, ran to his bowl, toenails skittering on the linoleum.

Stokey went to the hallway, yelled. "Hey! You guys up?"

Katie was the first to appear. "Morning, Pop." She kissed him on the cheek.

"Morning, Sissy." He took a moment to appraise her. "What's up? You're already dressed."

"I told you last night I have a job interview. How do I look?"

He noted the nylons, the skirt just nicking the top of her slender knees, the navy sweater that made her blue eyes bluer. Her red hair, a gift from Becka, was held away from her face with twin, silver barrettes. "Very pretty," he concluded. "But professional."

"Thanks." She smiled and poured a small pile of granola into the bottom of a bowl. "Any yogurt?"

Stokey opened the refrigerator, scanned the selection. "Peach, vanilla, strawberry, blueberry, pineapple or lemon custard, all nonfat, as requested."

"Peach, please."

"Hey, Jacks," He yelled down the hallway once more. "You up, son?"

He poured a bowl of cereal for himself, floated it in 2 percent. "I was pretty tired last night. So tell me again about this interview."

"You were pretty sloshed last night," Katie said flatly. Stokey winced. His daughter never did hold back. "It had been a tough day."

"Most every day's a tough day," she observed. "Anyway, it's at the Women's Clinic. Front desk, some record keeping." She reached beneath the table and slipped Shorty a raisin.

"Don't feed the dog at the table."

"It was only a raisin."

"Bad precedent." He sipped his coffee, reflectively. "So this sounds like a real job. Hope you've been practicing your Spanish."

"What's that supposed to mean?"

"Supposed to mean that most of the folks that go to that clinic speak Spanish, that's all."

"Oh. I can probably manage. So you going to see Mom today?"

"I suppose. She asked me to."

"I know."

"How do you know?"

"She calls most days after you leave for work."

"Hmm. Imagine that!" He felt oddly let down. As the injured party, he expected … what from his daughter? Sympathy? Loyalty? Did he expect her to refuse to speak with her own mother? Stop being childish, he told himself. He put a large spoonful of cereal into his mouth to preclude further speech, chewed, swallowed.

Stokey rose from the table and yelled down the hall. "Jackson? If you're not out here in one minute, I'm coming in with a glass of ice water, which I will pour on your bone head!" He looked at his watch. Just as the second hand was about to complete its sweep, a lanky, blond boy in T-shirt and boxers with large, very white bare feet entered the kitchen.

"Morning, son." Stokey said, without looking up from his cereal.

"Morning, Pop. Morning, Doofus."

"You're the doofus," Katie said. "Anyway. I really want this job."

"Well, good, Sissy. I'm glad to hear it."

"What's that supposed to mean?" she said, putting down her spoon.

"Supposed to mean I'm happy that there's something you really want. My you're tetchy this morning."

"Sorry. I'm just nervous. Do I really look OK?"

"Honey, to my old eyes, you are a sight of rare beauty."

She smiled. "But professional."

"To the core." He set his dishes in the sink then poured the remaining coffee into an insulated Red Cross mug that had cost him five pints of blood. "Your ups at dishes this morning, Jacks," he said. "Jacks?"

"Right, Pop."

He kissed his daughter on the cheek. "Break a leg, Sissy," he said, then patting his son on the shoulder none too gently, he added, "Be good, be smart, be safe."

Shorty's tail thumped the linoleum loudly. "Sorry, boy, can't come. It's your turn to guard the house." The thumping stopped. Stokey reached under the table, scratched the proffered belly.

Though he had the day off, Stokey needed to stop by the station to do some paperwork before going to Tucson. As he got into the truck, he spotted the juniper posts he'd been planning to use to shore up his back fence. He snapped his fingers and hopped out of the truck, thinking he'd drop by the Rutherford's place in the next day or so, use the posts to fix that sagging corral instead, maybe see what's up.

Light sluiced through the open louvers of the shutter. El Camaleón felt its heat on his face and smooth, bare chest. He started to rise, but fell back against the pillow. Once again his head was bad, very bad. He didn't recognize the naked woman lying next to him. Coarse, dark hair hid her face, but her flaccid breasts and belly told him that she was some five-buck whore. Chingado, he thought, trying to reconstruct the previous night. Since his last run, he'd been partying nonstop, though it no longer felt like a party. He couldn't remember what happened just last night, but he couldn't forget those kids, the look on their faces as Boots led them away. El Camaleón could guess what was probably in store for them. It made him sick, in fact, but what could he have done?

He put his back to the sleeping woman. There was a run scheduled for tomorrow evening. Corcho had rounded up 20 pollos. Lots of money there. But it wasn't money he needed now. He needed his mind to stop taking him back to those kids. He needed to go home, needed to see his mother.

His gut twisted when he remembered that Corcho still owed him for the last run. How had he allowed that to happen? From the bedside table he took the roll of antacids, put a handful in his mouth and chewed as he evaluated the situation.

Corcho would be mad, would try to cheat him out of his money, but Corcho could fuck himself. Slowly he rose. Tomorrow he'd get a bus heading south. He'd had enough of this life.

Corcho was sitting in the hotel office, feet propped on his desk. "Hola, compadre," he said when El Camaleón appeared at the door. "Come in, friend. You look like hell." He pulled a bottle of tequila from a drawer.

El Camaleón nodded, thinking this pinche cabron would smile as he stuck a knife between the ribs of his own brother. He was pretty certain that the man was somehow involved with the kidnapping; how else had Boots known when and where he and his pollos would be?

Corcho splashed tequila into a cup and pushed it across his desk. El Camaleón tipped it back. The fat man offered a refill, but he declined.

"My mother's sick," El Camaleón lied.

"I'm sorry to hear this. After the next trip north maybe you should go see her."

"She's very sick. I'm leaving tomorrow and I need my money."

"I'll pay you when you return."

"I need it now."

"But when you come back, you'll need it more. Fighting cocks are an expensive hobby and a man like you should have some of his own, qué no? I have several I'd be happy to let you have for a reasonable price."

El Camaleón smiled then, recalling how much money he had already squandered on cockfighting. "No, hombre. You give me my money now and then we'll see about fighting cocks when I return," he said, though he had no intention of ever revisiting this little part of hell.

"I don't have it right now, pues. After the next run you'll be paid."

The pain in his head and stomach were making him impatient. "You disrespect me," he said quietly. Stepping forward, El Camaleón smashed his fist into the exact middle of the man's face. Despite the force of the blow, the man's center of gravity was so low he didn't fall over. El Camaleón pulled him out of the chair. From his pants pocket he extracted a thick wad of bills. Again he punched him, this time in his soft gut, and the fat man sagged to the floor. El Camaleón dragged his dead weight into the middle of the room where he could keep an eye on him as he counted the bills.

"You're $200 short, puto," he said. He slipped the fat man's gold watch from his wrist, then backed out the door.

Feeling a little better than he had been lately, El Camaleón headed back to his room to gather his things. He picked up his pace then began to jog. Now it would be necessary to leave town immediately.

Gaby and Beto stood in the bus station. Gaby wore Belen's Diamondbacks cap, pulling her hair though the opening in the back. Slim and lean-muscled, Beto was half a head taller than the other men standing around. Still, in their dark sweatshirts, jeans and worn running shoes, the couple did not stand out among the others. It wasn't long before a young man approached them.

"Buenos dias, amigos," he said. "Do you need a guide to the other side?"

They nodded and followed him out of the station.

El Camaleón took his Stetson from its box and placed it on his head. The rest of his belongings – clothes, jewelry, toilet kit, the blender he had bought as a gift for his mother – he quickly packed in two cardboard boxes and secured them with jute twine. He stared at the boxes. This is all that my life in the north has amounted to, he thought with disgust. He caressed the gold watch on his wrist. It would make a fine gift for his father.

Snoring softly, the whore slept through it all. There was a knock on the door. El Camaleón froze for a moment then moved quietly to the louvered shutters. A kid he knew from the streets stood on the step with two pollos. Why had he brought them here instead of to Corcho? Was it a lure to get him to come out so he could be shot? Even if it wasn't a trap, why should he open the door?

The boy knocked again. "Abre, Camaleón, I've got business for you." The boy turned to the pollos. "I guess he's not here."

"Knock again," the woman said.

The boy knocked again.

The whore opened her eyes. "Qué passa?" she whined.

El Camaleón silenced her with a look.

"Abre, amigo," the man said. "All we want to do is talk to you. We'll pay."

El Camaleón considered his options. He could wait for them to leave, or he could climb out the bathroom window into the alley.

"Por favor," said the woman. "Just tell us what happened to the children."

The children. He opened the door.

The woman awoke for the second time to a pounding at the door. What now, she wondered. The pounding became blows. Suddenly afraid, she wrapped the sheet about her as the wood splintered around the lock and the door gave way. Two men stepped into the room, one young and nervous, one older, calm. Both had guns pointed at her.

"Where is El Camaleón?" The nervous one demanded.

She could only shake her head.

"Tell us now. You don't want to waste our time," the older one said quietly.

"But I don't know where he is."

The nervous one ripped the sheet from her body, and began to hit her in the breasts and belly. She rolled from the bed to the floor, drawing herself into a ball as he kicked at her legs and buttocks.

"I don't know, I don't know," she screamed.

"Stop," the calm one said. He helped her to her feet and led her to a chair. Slowly, he drew the handcuffs from his pocket, gently cuffing first one wrist, then the other behind the back of the chair. As the nervous one watched, a grin splitting his face, he took a small sheet of coarse sandpaper from the pocket of his jacket.

When they were finally convinced that she truly knew nothing, the nervous one started to unzip his pants.

"What are you doing, pendejo? He's probably at the bus station by now, besides, this woman is too ugly."

The nervous one shrugged. "No woman is too ugly."

"Later then. First we have the other business."

At the bus station, the two men separated. The nervous one went to look in the men's room, the calm one went to the counter. He pushed a 100-peso note across the counter. "Have you sold a ticket to a man, young, muy indio, left eye drooping."

"About half an hour ago."

"Where was he going?"

The ticket seller pulled his mouth into a frown and shrugged. "I've sold many tickets today."

The calm one produced another 100-peso note, waved it between his two fingers.

"I think it was to Oaxaca. That bus will arrive in Chihuahua City about 4:30, si Dios lo desea."

"Muchas gracias," the calm one said, letting the note slip from his fingers.

The nervous one was waiting for him by the door.

"Call El Gallo in Chihuahua," the calm one ordered. "Tell him to meet the 4:30 bus from Agua Prieta. "Tell him to bring that son of a whore back here one way or another."

Susana's head lolled in her car seat. Wiona couldn't rely on Emma or Belen, in her current state, to watch over a 2-year-old who took such glee in climbing everything in sight and running in the opposite direction whenever summoned, so she'd packed her into the truck for the trip into town.

Now Susana's eyes fluttered in an attempt to resist sleep. Before Wiona had gone five miles she was out. Wiona sighed, relieved. She loved Susana but was grateful for the quiet.

For some minutes, her mind was a pleasant blank as she took in the Chiricahua Mountains, its apron of rolling hills transformed by morning light from flat blue-gray to golden relief. Beautiful, though there should be wildflowers skirting the roadside where the crowned asphalt directed the least rain their way. Not this year. Some folks were talking global warming. She didn't have an opinion about that. All she knew was that whatever it was, it was breaking her heart. Well, her heart had been broken before.

She braked slightly to avoid a roadrunner that took to reluctant flight inches from her bumper. Homely predators of innocents – baby quail and lizards mostly – even these, she conceded, had their place in the larger picture. The larger picture. Where was her place? Things might have been so different if it hadn't been for Frankie, she thought for the thousandth time. If Frankie were alive the ranch, Emma, everything would have been on him. That would have served him right. Then she'd have been free to do … what? Get married? Go off to college. Get a job in town. She never wanted any of those things. Maybe she was meant to be alone, though there was Emma. Was taking care of her mother better than being alone? She'd have to give that some thought.

Wiona slowed as she approached the Douglas exit. Just as she passed the Border Patrol station she noticed a truck on her bumper. Irritated, she tapped the brake, then realized it was Stokey. "Damn," she whispered.

He sped in front of her then motioned for her to follow as he swung into a defunct Esso station.

She pulled over abruptly. Braking harder than necessary, she hoped Susana would start screaming. The child slept placidly on as Wiona rolled her window down.

"Morning, Stokey."

He bent to look in the window. "Hey, Wiona. You babysitting today?"

"Just taking Susana for a ride to the grocery store. Give Gaby a little break."

"That's nice." He glanced in the back. "Cute when they're asleep."

Wiona looked at the sleeping child through the rearview mirror and smiled her agreement.

"Listen, I've got some juniper posts. Was thinking you could use them to fix your corral. Tomorrow's Saturday. I could drop them by in the morning."

"That's really nice of you, Stokey, but this Saturday's not good for me. I'm way behind on my accounts."

He nodded his head. "Maybe next week then. So how's mama and baby?"

"I haven't been back up canyon to check on them. I'm sure they're fine, though. Range cows are pretty good at taking care of themselves."

"Right." He tugged on the beak of his cap. "Maybe I'll see you sometime next week, then. You have a good day, now."

"You bet, Stokey. You, too." She started to roll up the window then stopped. "Hey, anything more about Fletcher Hart?"

"Nada. But come to think of it, I got a question for you."

"Shoot."

"Carter mentioned that he and Fletcher didn't always see eye to eye on things. Aside from letting the Samaritans onto his ranch, you know what those things might be?"

Wiona considered this for a moment. "Is Carter a suspect?"

"Nope, just wondering."

She shrugged. "It's pretty common knowledge that Fletcher was about to sign over a conservation easement to the Malpais Borderlands Group."

"What group is that?"

"Basically it's an organization that wants to keep ranchers from having to sell out to developers."

"Why would Carter oppose that?"

"Some of the ranchers around here, Carter being one of them, have a basic mistrust of eggheads and urban environmentalists. They don't want to give up any control over their lands. I guess I understand that, though personally, I'd be thrilled if the Malpais group offered me a deal."

"So they pay for these … "

"Conservation easements. Sometimes. Anyway, that's what I understand. How much depends on the ranch, I guess. I imagine an easement on a place like Fletcher's might be pretty pricey."

"Interesting. Conservation easement. Well, you learn something new every day if you can afford to pay attention."

"That it?"

"That's it."

"Take care then." She rolled up the window.

As soon as she pulled back onto the road, Susana woke up screaming. "Big help you were," Wiona said. She felt around in her bag for the half of a banana she'd brought along in case of emergency, peeled it, passed it back to Susana.

" 'Nana," the child observed.

"Banana," Wiona agreed.

Ordinarily she'd have been grateful for Stokey's offer, but she'd heard that his wife was living up in Tucson with some guy. Stokey didn't deserve that, but Wiona had no interest in filling in for Becka, if that's what he had in mind. More likely he just wanted an excuse to snoop around for the mama and baby. Well, in a couple of days, she hoped both would be on their way. Belen's husband would be coming for them soon, she figured.

Susana was making a contented mess out of herself and everything within reach. "Happy, happy," she sang, holding out banana sticky hands for Wiona's approval.

"Good for you, sweetie."

The sheet of plywood over the window made it difficult to know the time of day. A little light leaked around the edges and Adriana guessed it might still be morning, the second in this place. Through the walls, voices of other children rang over the sound of cartoons on a television. Occasionally, she heard her brother's voice. Once in a while someone would rap quietly on the locked door. She suspected it was Edgar's way of telling her that he was OK.

Someone had taken her clothes and she lay naked beneath a plaid quilted bedspread, which she'd pulled up to her chin. Her stomach rumbled. She hoped that girl would come soon to take her to the bathroom.

Except for the bed, the room was bare. Earlier she had tried to pull back the plywood on the window, just a little, so she could peek outside, but it was bolted to the wall.

She reached under the bed for her backpack and took out a bottle of water and an orange. For a moment, she considered opening the package of saladitos, but thought better of it. These she would save for Edgar. She took a sip of water and started to tear at the skin of the orange.

Maybe today she would see her brother. She pulled off a thick section of orange, and put it in her mouth. Maybe today they would be taken to their father. She wouldn't allow any other thoughts to enter her mind.

When she finished the orange, she pulled the cover back up. Turning her face to the wall, she closed her eyes and hoped for sleep to make the hours pass more quickly.

At the click of the bolt, Adriana opened her eyes. The girl, pregnant, with heavy makeup and white-blond hair was standing in the doorway. "Get up," the girl said.

Adriana wrapped the spread around her. She noticed a small, brightly colored bird perched on the girl's shoulder. Pointing to the bird, she smiled.

The girl plucked it off her shoulder and scratched its throat where a patch of pink down parted the sleek red feathers. "His name is Romeo," she said, turning it in her hand to show off the brilliant green and blue of his wings, back and tail. "He's a peach-throated lovebird."

Adriana understood the words *bird, name* and *love*. She followed the girl to the bathroom, mouthing the word bird. Quickly she relieved herself, as the girl looked into the mirror. "You can take a shower," she said, tugging bits of mascara from the brittle lashes surrounding her pale, blue eyes. "But make it quick."

"*Mande?*" Adriana asked.

"Shit," the girl said. "You don't speak any English?" She pulled the shower-curtain back and turned on the water. "Get in."

After she had showered, the girl handed her a pair of pink Lycra shorts and a tight, pink and white polka-dot tank to wear. Adriana pulled on the shorts, then the top. Her nipples made little inverted dimples in the cloth. She plucked the fabric away from her body but it snapped back against her chest. The girl handed her a comb and Adriana pulled it through the thick, black hair that fell just beyond her shoulders.

"Come on," the girl directed. She led Adriana to another room. This one had lavender floral curtains at the window, a white dresser with a large mirror. There was a canopy-covered bed. Scattered over a bedspread that matched the curtains, there were cloth dolls and plush teddy bears – the perfect bedroom for a little girl.

"Que bonita." Adriana's smile was hopeful.

"Whatever," the girl answered, and closed the door.

In one corner of the room Adriana noticed a video camera on a chair. Two computers sat on a table inside the closet where a little girl's clothes would normally be hung. Adriana went to the window and peeked through the curtain.

Another sheet of plywood was bolted to the wall.

Stokey rang the doorbell once, twice, waited. Along the windowsill was a blue metal window box filled with old soil and a few cigarette butts. Red geraniums would look nice with that blue, he thought and rang again. He was about to leave when Becka, in baggy gray sweatpants and one of his old T-shirts, opened the door.
"Did I get you out of bed?" he asked.

She nodded. Pushing her tangled hair away from her face, she stepped aside so he could enter. "I didn't expect you so early."

"It's almost noon, Becka."

"Oh. Sorry. Thanks for coming. Coffee?"

"That'd be nice." He looked around the apartment. It was in the same unembellished state as the day he helped her move in three months ago. Not even a picture of the kids on the television set, he noted.

He watched as she put the filter into the Mr. Coffee he'd bought her. "So how have you been?"

"Better."

"Better than what?"

"Better than dead, I guess."

"What's that supposed to mean?"

She shrugged, then lit a cigarette. "Have a seat."

Stokey sat on a wobbly stool at a small dinette table shoved tight against the wall. When they started trying for another baby, Becka had stopped smoking. That was two years ago, and now she was back up to a pack a day or more, he figured. He hated the smell of smoke. He especially hated it when Becka smoked. Focusing on the smell of coffee, he tried to keep his mouth shut about it.

Becka put a carton of milk, sugar bowl, spoon and a paper towel in front of him. She drew smoke deep into her lungs, exhaled slowly. "How are the kids?"

"Good."

"And you?"

"Fine."

"Well, fine." She sighed. "This is just real awkward."

It's a hell of a lot more than awkward, he thought. Well, whatever it was she had on her mind, he had no intention of making things less awkward.

"You know, Stokey, you've been really good through all this. Did Katie tell you I've started seeing a therapist?"

He pointed to the Mr. Coffee with his chin. "Coffee's ready." He had no intention of pleading for explanations either.

Becka poured them each a cup. "So what are you thinking?"

He added milk and sugar to his coffee. He drew his mouth into a neutral frown. "Not much." And neither was he going to make it easy for her to say whatever it was she wanted to say.

"OK," she said, nodding her head. She took another deep drag off her cigarette, then stubbed it out. "So, I'm seeing this therapist. And I'm taking Prozac. You know what people take Prozac for, Stokey?"

"Nerves?"

"Depression."

"What have you got to be depressed about?" He asked, forgetting that he wasn't going to ask any questions.

She stared at her hands for a long moment. In a whisper harsh as a rasp, she said, "Why do you have to make this so hard for me?"

"Like you're splitting is not hard on me, on the kids?"

"This isn't about you and the kids."

"What's it about then, Becka?"

"We've been through this." She lit another cigarette. "OK, let me try to explain again." She looked at the ceiling as if the reason might appear there. "You know I wanted that baby."

He nodded as he thought of the baby. They'd picked out such a pretty name for her, Anne Marie. In his mind he'd already started calling her Annie. *Come to Papa, Annie.* For a moment, he couldn't trust himself to speak. "Me too, honey," he said at last.

She nodded slowly as you might to encourage a child. "You know why I wanted that baby?"

"Well … "

"Cause I needed a change, needed to think that there was something else that could still happen in my life. And a baby … well babies are so totally dependent. I guess I wanted someone to love who really depended on me. Stupid reason to have a baby, I know, but I wanted her real bad, Stokey." Tears pooled and slid down her cheeks. "Sorry." She wiped her eyes with the paper towel, took a sip of coffee, frowned, then pushed it away.

"I was still dealing with that and then when you went off to Iraq again," she continued, the edge in her voice getting sharper. "Jackson was what, 15? I'd tell him something and he'd say, 'Yes, ma'am,' just like you taught him. Then he'd go out and do whatever. I don't know who I was scared for most, you or Jackson."

"You never told me you were having trouble."

"What was I supposed to tell? You're in Iraq facing roadside bombs and helicopter crashes, and I'm supposed to tell you how stressed out I was because I wrote a check I knew would bounce and Jackson had seven unexcused absences in first period?"

Shaking her head, she took another pull on her cigarette. "Anyway, I managed to keep things together, took the job at Safeway so I could keep up with the mortgage, went in to talk with the school counselor, took the car in when it needed to be serviced, did all the things I usually do and most of the things you usually do. And when you got back, did you appreciate how normal everything was? No. You went straight out to your precious garden, the only thing I didn't keep up with while you were gone, and accused me of killing it. But you'd just gotten home, so I couldn't tell you how pissed I was about that. I knew I was just supposed to be thankful that you weren't killed. Well, I was thankful, of course I was. But I was also really, really pissed."

She took two little puffs of her cigarette, and snuffed it out on her saucer. "Anyway, I looked around and saw how powerless I was to … I don't know … change how things were, couldn't change how I felt about them. And all I could see was years ahead of me dragging on, like walking through a tunnel that was getting darker with each step I took. When I try to put it into words it all sounds so stupid, not an explanation at all, but … and yes I do know how much that garden means to you … "

"Can you forget about the fucking garden, Becka? Jesus, I mean, I'm sorry I didn't realize. Can't you just come home. We can figure it all out if you come home."

"No, Stokey. I'd just bring the tunnel with me. Listen. I know what I've had to deal with, call it stress, anger, depression. Whatever, it doesn't begin to match what you were facing over there every day – I read the newspapers. And that just makes me feel worse – incompetent, a failure, and a bitch for resenting you so!"

"I'm sorry."

"What are you sorry about?"

"About the garden? I don't know. Can't I just be sorry?"

"I guess, but it would mean more if you could be a little more specific."

"I'm sorry. I should have … noticed things."

"Yes you should have." She shrugged. "All I can say is that I feel I'm about to fly apart and I'm just trying so hard all the time to hold myself together."

"Can't I help hold you together."

"I need to fix this myself, Stokey." Her voice was thin, weary. She blotted her eyes on the paper towel again, blew her nose. "Besides, right now I can't stand the pressure of anyone's needs but my own."

Pressure? He figured he hadn't pressed his needs at all lately. He rubbed his closed eyelids for a moment so he wouldn't have to look at her. The sight of her was making him physically sick. He looked out the window. "Well, I don't know how long I can go on supporting a woman who's no mother to my kids, no wife to me."

"The kids don't need a mother anymore. And you? What do you want? You want to screw me? You can, if that's what it takes."

The words were a slap that snapped his head back in her direction. "That's not what I'm saying, and you damn well know it!"

"Then what?"

"I want you to come home, damn it!"

"You want! When I was there you paid no attention to what I wanted."

"For instance."

"For instance, I asked you to get rid of the gun."

"I see no reason for that."

"There you go." Her hand shook when she poured milk into her cup.

"Give me another for instance."

"I don't know. It's just that in so many ways you told me the things that were important to me didn't matter. When I'd ask your opinion, let's say about what to have for dinner, or maybe about repainting the living room, you'd say, 'It makes no difference to me' or 'suit yourself.' Sometimes you wouldn't even answer, just shrug your shoulders. It made me feel that my life was stupid, trivial."

"Hmm. Trivial."

Her eyes narrowed to angry slits. "Yes, Stokey. Trivial! And how many times did I wake up in the middle of the night and find you out in the living room watching television? Come to bed, I'd say. In a minute, you'd say. Later I'd wake up again and you'd still be out there with the damn television. Do you have any idea how *trivial* that made me feel?"

"I'm sorry. I didn't mean to make you feel that way. Come home. I want you to come home."

"And I need you to help me stay here."

He got up from the table. "How much longer?"

"I don't know."

"I'll put the check in the mail when I get home," he said, one hand on the doorknob.

"Thank you, Stokey." She reached out and touched his arm. "So, do you hate me yet?"

He shook his head. He didn't think so. All this would be lots easier if he did. "You'll get a check early next week."

Wiona spotted Lucy's green Highlander the moment she drove into the yard. She lifted Susana out of her car seat and tried to will calm. Screeching happily the moment her feet touched ground, Susana waddled for the porch.

Lucy met them at the front door. "Need some help?" She asked, nodding towards the plastic bags Wiona had looped over her arms.

"There's more in the bed of the truck." Smiling her thanks, Wiona swept through the front door, grateful for all the busy little things that would occupy her for the next 10 minutes.

In the kitchen, Emma was keeping vigil as Belen nursed the baby. Immediately, she began going through the grocery bags, sorting out diapers, lotions, swabs. She pulled the pork roast from a bag then set it aside like a box of laundry soap, the longing for pork apparently forgotten.

"These will come in handy," Emma said holding aloft a packet of tiny white singlets Wiona had bought at Kmart, along with seven pairs of tiny blue socks, two yellow footed jumpsuits, seven receiving blankets, three cartons of baby wipes, 12-packs of disposable diapers, all purchased with some calf that hadn't even been weaned yet, much less sold. Like an offering, Emma set each item on the table in front of Belen.

"Muchisimas gracias, Wiona, Emma y todas." She smiled for the first time since speaking with her husband. As she touched each package, the smile faded.

"All the clothes have to be washed before you put them on the baby," Emma directed.

Lucy set the other grocery bags on the counter. "I just stopped by to check on Belen and the baby. Any news yet?"

"Beto and Gaby should be back anytime."

"I'll make coffee," Emma offered with an air of celebration. She opened several cupboards. "Where in the devil did you put the coffeepot, Wiona?"

"Where I always put it," she said, pointing to the coffee maker sitting in plain sight on the counter. Wiona saw the familiar cloud of confusion cross on Emma's face, and realized she was referring to the old percolator that they used to set to boil on the stove. "You want me to make the coffee?"

"Well, bless your heart. I guess you better. I don't know what on earth you did with my coffeepot."

Teeth clenched, Wiona pressed a palm against her temple. "Why don't you all go sit in the living room?" She needed a moment to order her thoughts.

Lucy lingered. When they were alone, she reached out and touched Wiona on the shoulder, smiled sweetly. "What you're doing … you are so kind." She indicated the array of packages spread over the table with a cock of her head. "And generous." Then Lucy stood on her toes and kissed her on the cheek.

Wiona's face flushed. "What else could I do?" she managed. And it was the truth. Given the extent of Belen's need, she could have done nothing differently. Despite the expense, she didn't regret a single blue sock.

From the porch, the dog started barking as Beto's truck pull into the yard.

The moment they stepped through the front door, Wiona could see that the news wasn't good. "Let's all sit down," she said.

Beto sat on the edge of a ladder-back chair. Gaby perched on the arm of the couch beside Belen and took her hand. Reluctantly she began to tell her everything they'd found out.

"What's she saying?" Emma whispered, clearly anxious and irritated.

"Hush, Mother. I'm listening." But Gaby continued in her rapid Spanish and Wiona gave up trying to follow. "We'll find out soon enough. I'm going to get the coffee."

Emma followed her into the kitchen. "I don't understand why they can't just speak English."

Lips pressed tight, Wiona turned to get the milk out of the refrigerator. When she closed the door, Lucy was standing by the table. Eyes wide and shining, she held her thumbnail between her teeth.

"They found the coyote," she said. "The children were kidnapped."

"Kidnapped! Well, then Belen's husband should hear from them soon, like you said. How much money do you think they'll need to get the kids back?"

Lucy took a deep breath, exhaled slowly. "It doesn't sound like that kind of operation."

"What do you mean?"

"Some guys with guns forced them over on Highway 80. According to what the coyote told Gaby and Beto, it was probably set up by the man who operates the hotel in Agua Prieta where Belen and the kids stayed while they waited to cross."

"So how much are they demanding?"

"It's not that simple. It seems that the kidnappers knew there were two children and that there should have been a pregnant woman in the van. The worst is, they didn't take anyone but the kids. Had come expressly …" She took another deep breath.

"Expressly for Belen and the kids."

"What does that mean?" Wiona said, though her stomach had already digested the information and was turning over. "Dear God, Lucy. I'm calling Stokey."

Although Negra Modelo was Stokey's beer of choice, the beer that he could afford was Budweiser. Beer in hand, he stood in the middle of the third garden bed – there were four. He swept the spray of water like the beam of a searchlight, slowly, evenly over the soil until every inch was black and glossy. The process lasted approximately one beer per bed.

Several green tips of errant Bermuda grass poked between the dark clods. He stooped and gently teased each young blade from the ground. Stokey considered weeding a Zen kind of thing. You couldn't yank a weed. No, a weed needed to be eased out. Too much tug and you leave the root intact to grow again. It took just the right amount of attention, keeping him firmly in the present. He scanned the soil for another weed, but it was clean for now.

He drained his beer. Before moving on to the fourth bed, he fished for a fresh one in the ice-filled red plastic bucket that served as cooler.

It was Katie's week to make dinner and he imagined her inside the warm kitchen, looking so much like her mother it was unnerving. Yet she was nothing like Becka, really. Practical, a bit stubborn and thick-skinned, smart – he liked to think she got those qualities from him, not that Becka wasn't smart. But smart by itself didn't cut it in this world. You had to be tough-minded, pragmatic, solid.

Take Wiona. Dad and brother dead, left to take care of a half-batty mother and a mostly worthless ranch. A hard row, but she wasn't folding or whining about stress or tunnels and such. And needing a change? Who the hell doesn't need a change?

He trained the hose on the rosemary he'd planted because it was hearty and smelled good. It was getting late. Cold and wet pressed through his shoes. He scanned the garden. There was still no sign of the seeds he planted last month that by June should become neat rows of tomato plants, peppers, green beans, squash and cantaloupe, but his violas edged each bed in alternating splashes of yellow, white and blue and there were random clumps of Mexican gold poppies, the only spontaneous event he allowed in his garden. He stooped to examine a clump of violas that seemed to be fairing poorly, noted nipped leaves and blossoms. He scrutinized the periphery of the garden for a pack rat hole. It was there in the corner of the third bed. Damn destructive nuisances, pack rats. He'd have to come back after dinner with a flashlight and his .38 and nail the little fucker. He thought of Becka, then, and her objection to the gun. She would not approve of him shooting a pack rat, but then there wasn't much he did, it seemed, that she approved of. Fuck her approval. He didn't need it.

He turned his attention back to watering. When he was satisfied that each bed was uniformly doused and clear of weeds, he screwed his Bud into the wet soil and began to arrange the hose in tight, uniform coils by the spigot. Katie would have dinner ready soon. Gathering the three empties, he tipped back the last of the fourth, crushed each in his fist, then made his reluctant way back to the house.

At the back door, he dropped the cans in the recycle bin and pulled off his muddy boots. Katie was at the stove pouring a jar of tomato sauce over ground beef and something less obvious. He kissed his daughter's warm cheek. "Spaghetti?"

"Stuffed bell peppers. You smell like beer."

"Had one out in the garden. Will Jacks eat stuffed bell pepper?"

"That bratty a-hole! Who gives a poop?" She said stirring. She lifted the lid on a pot of steaming water, added salt.

"Hmm," he said, now sniffing the bubbling mixture with curiosity. "Do I dare ask how the interview went?"

She turned down the heat and replaced the lid. "Dare! I start my training tomorrow."

"Sweet! Congratulations, Sissy."

"Thanks, Dad," she said, fanning steam. "So how was Mom?"

He glanced through the mail on the table. "Who gives a poop?"

"Dad! Seriously."

"Seriously. But I guess she's finding herself or something."

"Don't trivialize her like that."

"Trivialize is it? Sounds like you've been talking to your mother." He separated out the junk mail, then opened the telephone bill. "Why didn't you tell me she was seeing a therapist and taking..."

"Prozac. Because I thought it was her responsibility to tell you herself." She poured rice into the now boiling water. "I found this recipe in the newspaper. It's got green olives in it."

"Hmm." Stokey marveled how his daughter could transform herself from child to a woman in less time than it takes to boil water. "Smells good."

"Thanks. Oh. You're supposed to phone Wiona Rutherford. Something about a mama and baby."

"When'd she call?"

"Sometime this afternoon, I guess. She left a message on the machine."

"I think I'll just go on over there. I got some posts I want to drop off at her place anyway."

"Dinner's at 6:30."

"If I'm not back by then, just stick a plate in the oven for me."

"Dad!" She gestured at the steaming pots like a practiced housewife.

"I won't be too late. Promise."

"Dad."

"Sissy?"

"You're starting to get a beer belly."

"I only had one."

Before leaving, he ducked into the bathroom to brush his teeth. Standing before the mirror, he sucked his gut in until it was flat.

Wiona had just finished mucking out Link's pen when she heard Osa putting up a fit in the yard. This time she was relieved to see Stokey's truck. She waved. "I'm over here."

He followed her into the barn and back to her office. "It's chilly," she said, "I'll have the stove going in a minute."

Stokey watched as she rolled sheets of newspaper into tubes, layering then them with kindling. She stuck a match to the pyre, waited till it caught, then added two small split juniper logs.

"You're pretty good at that," he said.

"I've been doing it for a few years."

"So you wanted to talk with me?"

"Have a seat." Motioning to the bed, she squatted in front of the stove, holding her hands out to the young flame. As the stove heated the room, she became aware of the aroma of fresh manure rising from her boots. "Sorry. I guess I stink."

"Actually, manure's not such a bad smell as bad smells go. So what's up?"

"We're in big trouble here, Stokey."

"Not so big. Humanitarian aid, as I see it."

"It's way bigger than that," she said. "Bigger and so scary. I don't know what's to be done."

He leaned forward, elbows on his knees. "Well, why don't you tell me about it and then we'll figure it out."

Taking a deep breath, she studied his face for a sign of disapproval. "God, I hope there's still time to figure it out, Stokey." She dropped into her chair, scared for herself, and terrified for Belen and her children.

When Wiona got back to the house Emma was standing in the middle of the living room singing and swishing her housedress while Susana tripped around the floor, giddy and way too tired. She had a nice voice, Emma. For a time she sang in the choir of the First Methodist. Now Wiona was taken aback.

"I'm going to go where you go," Emma crooned happily.

"Do what you do,
be where you are and I'll be happy.
I'll lift up my dress,
show you my best.
you do the rest,
and I'll be happy."

"Where on earth did you learn that song?" Wiona was trying to decide whether she should be embarrassed or tickled.

Emma arched an eyebrow. "I wasn't always married to your father, you know."

This was definitely not the woman she knew. Still Gaby, Beto and Susana seemed to be enjoying the diversion.

"Where's Belen and the baby?"

Gaby tilted her head towards the kitchen where Jesús lay snug within the plastic basin. "Before she left, Lucy gave Belen something and she's napping, too. What did Stokey have to say?"

"Said they could stay here for now. He'll get back to us after he's talked it over with his boss, Rudy Garza."

"Rudy Garza is a son of bitch," Beto said in thickly accented English. "He stopped me one time out on 80. Even though I showed him my papers, he made me get out of the car and sit on the ground while he got on the radio. Took his time about it, too, as if my time was worth nothing. Didn't apologize, neither, when he finally decided to let me go. Sometimes the Mexicans are the biggest hard-asses."

Wiona didn't like the sound of that. Lucy had tried to get her to call some group called Derechos Humanos instead of Stokey. Now she hoped that she'd made the right decision. "We'll just have to wait and see." She looked at Susana, who would soon go into meltdown mode. "In the meantime, take Susana home. You two must be dead. I know I am."

Gaby got up, gave Wiona a hug. "I put the pork roast on. Should be ready in, she looked at her watch, 45 minutes or so."

"I forgot about the roast. You want to stay for dinner?" She offered, hoping they'd refuse.

Gaby shook her head. "It's been a long day for everyone. We're going home."

Wiona walked them to the front door, kissed each cheek, then waved them out to the yard. When she got back to the house Emma was sitting at the kitchen table, running her finger through a pile of sugar.

"Didn't Stokey used to have the hots for you?"

Despite herself, Wiona laughed. "Where'd you get that expression."

"I wasn't always your mother. Used to be a boy who had the hots for me."

"You mean dad?"

"Not dad." She put the sugared finger into her mouth and sucked on it pensively. "Some other boy. So how come you and Stokey didn't get married?"

Wiona swept the pile of sugar into her palm and dumped it in the sink. "We didn't love each other, Mother."

"I didn't love your dad all that much and we've managed well enough all these years. Besides, if you'd married Stokey, we'd have another hand around here. Your dad could use another hand."

Wiona didn't correct Emma. "It's not help we lack, Mother. It's money."

"Well, Stokey could have helped out with that, too. He's some kind of a job, doesn't he?"

"Stokey works for the Border Patrol, remember?"

"That's right."

"And he's married with two kids."

"Oh. That's too bad. We could use a new roof."

Wiona was about to remind her mother of the almost new roof, the green metal one of her mother's dreams, but Emma was suddenly dead asleep in her chair, chin resting practically on her chest, as though a switch had been thrown somewhere inside her head.

Wiona peered into the plastic tub at the sleeping baby. The puffy look of the newborn was gone and he was simply beautiful with his red, rosebud mouth and fine black hair. With one finger she stroked the round cheek, wondering what kind of a mother she would have made had she married Stokey.

El Camaleón stepped down from the bus. Already he was anticipating the homecoming. His mother would make him a party, that was for certain. People would crowd in close, admiring his boots, his brand new Stetson. He put it on his head now to keep the sun out of his eyes. Smiling to himself, he imagined how it would be when his mother opened the package with the blender, her expression wide-eyed with surprise and pride.

He rubbed his stomach, popped a few antacids. Home would cure his stomach, too. He hadn't eaten all day and wanted a plate of something. There were many choices. Across the street a woman painted big yellow ears of elote with red chili and lime, another offered cones of fresh watermelon, pineapple, avocado, cucumber, and yet another filled little tortillas with slivers of carne de cabeza, cabbage and jalapeños. He started to cross the street.

He would have an ear of corn, then a plate of tacos. He took the gold watch out of his pocket. He only had 20 minutes before the bus was to leave. He would take a cone of watermelon with him, and maybe buy a bottle of rum to help him sleep.

He searched his pocket for change as the woman held out an ear of corn. Suddenly, from the corner of his good eye, he detected a green uniform rapidly approaching. El Camaleón started to run.

"Parate!" the federale ordered, drawing his gun.

El Camaleón picked up his speed. Better to be shot in the back than end up in the hands of El Corcho and his crew. He was nearly to the other side of the street when he felt fire enter between his shoulders. He stumbled a few paces then fell against the stand of the fruit vendor. Slowly he slipped to the ground, where he lay amid the crumpled cones and wasted fruit, wet and sticky against his cheek. He didn't even feel it when the federale held the gun to the back of his head and fired.

Belen and Emma had gone to bed right after dinner. It was still

early. Wiona figured she might as well go out to the office to work –
time better spent than listening to the worry that was playing in her
head.

Link nickered at her as she passed the corral. She stopped, ran
her hand over his whiskered muzzle. "Sweet boy."

Once in her office, she switched on the desk lamp. Punkin was
asleep on the bed. Wiona poked up the coals in the stove, added
kindling and a fresh log. She sat at her desk and stared at the blank
computer screen as if she expected some reassuring message to
appear there.

Emma, a strict Methodist of the old school, allowed no alcohol
in the house. Her father had stashed his Old Crow in the tool chest
in the barn, *in case of emergency.* Wiona kept her emergency bottle
of Jose Cuervo in the bottom drawer of her desk. Though there'd
been any number of emergencies in the past few years, she had yet
to encounter one that afforded the leisure to drink tequila.

Wiona considered the still sealed bottle now. She really was too
tired to work and this was an emergency. She unscrewed the top,
and took a sip directly.

"Whoof." Her eyes teared. A coffee cup sat on her desk. She
poured some tequila over the dried residue in the bottom, sipped
again, winced as the burning liquid slipped down her throat. She
turned the desk light off and settled back. The fire from the stove
bounced shadows on the wall. Wiona kicked her boots off and
propped her feet on the cot. Punkin jumped onto her lap and settled
into a small warm coil.

What would her father have done if he'd been the one to find
Belen and her baby? Or Frankie? What if he had found them?

There used to be a time when border crossing was a casual
thing. When a Mexican stopped by the ranch, her father would offer
him work. After a few days the man would leave with a full
stomach, clean clothes and a little money in his pockets. As often as
not, he'd be wearing one of her father's old shirts or a pair of his
worn but still serviceable boots. Things had changed so drastically

in the past 10 years. She had no clear understanding of why.

Still, Wiona knew her father would have taken Belen and her baby in, but with Frankie there was no telling. He was a harder man than their father had been. She had no clear idea how that had happened either.

When they were young, she'd worshipped Frankie. Followed him around when he allowed it, often with mixed results. Sometimes he would tease and torment her. Once he'd actually pinned her down with a pitchfork leaving four bright red points on the white flesh of her stomach. Sometimes he'd spare her a spanking by taking the blame for something she'd done. She'd loved him without condition back then, thought him so handsome with that dark hair hanging over his smooth forehead and eyes blue as a jay's wing.

As they grew older, things changed between them. By the time she was 12 the teasing turned into something else. Sometimes he'd pin her arms back, press his body against hers so she could barely move. Laughing, he'd finally release her as if it had all been a joke.

Even after his death, he continued to dominate her thoughts. Only recently had she come to understand that Frankie, for whatever reason, had wanted to crush her.

She inhaled the smoky aroma of the tequila. Closed her eyes. After all this time she was still unable to determine how exactly she felt about Frankie and the way things turned out.

Dawn was the name she'd chosen for herself when she first came to live with James. She never thought of herself as Nola anymore, a name that never suited her. Somebody by the name of Nola would never have a matching suite of Hollywood style furniture. Some Nola would not have this dresser with its oval mirror surrounded by lights, its matching bench was upholstered in the same red satin as the bedspread and curtains. There were framed posters on her wall of Britney Spears and Pink. Dawn had picked out everything in the room herself. A girl named Nola wouldn't have a lovebird named Romeo. She opened the door to Romeo's cage, placed a sunflower seed between her lips and offered it to the bird. He plucked it from her lips and she closed the door.

Adjusting her iPod, she stood before the mirror rolling her pelvis to a Jessica Simpson tune. "My heart is my possession, I'll be my own reflection," she sang, thin arms waving above her head. Turning sideways, she ran her hands over the pale slice of belly protruding below her cropped, black T-shirt. She pressed her thumb down hard on her navel. Bulging, ugly, it reminded her of a snail shell.

On the bed there were several magazines from which she'd been cutting pictures for her fashion album. She picked up the scissors. They were special Japanese scissors, long and sharp enough that she could slice a perfect line without a single jagged edge along each picture. James had bought them over the Internet especially for her. She pressed the point down her arm. It made a satisfying red streak, along which tiny beads of blood surfaced. She licked them away with her tongue.

Dawn put aside the scissors and magazines then scooped up the pictures she'd clipped from In Touch's picks for "Best Dressed of the Week." Her personal favorite was Jennifer Lopez in a red, practically see-through, micro-mini. With a sweep of her arm, she dumped everything onto the floor. Turning the volume up on her iPod, she flopped on the bed, rolling onto her side away from the muffled cries coming from the set, coming from the new girl.

She'll get used to it, she thought, clutching a white plush bear almost as tall as she was. James bought it for her the last time he took her to the mall. She could make James buy her almost anything.

Last fall he'd taken her to see *The Lion King* – not the movie, but the stage production! It was awesome, with all the music and the dancers dressed as animals, but it made her sad when the little lion, Simba, got blamed for his father's death and ran away from home.

Dawn could relate. Because of her, her father – well Daryl wasn't her real father – but because of her he was sent to jail, which is a little like dying, she supposed.

Dawn hadn't told on purpose. Her teacher just sort of found out. Dawn couldn't even remember anymore what it was she had said, exactly, that made the teacher call the cops. Everybody was really mad at her except for her little sister, Lynny.

Well, she didn't miss her mother and wasn't sorry that Daryl went to jail. It was his own fault anyway. He'd always said it was just another part of the body like a hand or a foot, talked about how it was God's gift. Yeah, right. And even after she had put her hand on the Bible and sworn she was telling the truth, her mother wouldn't believe that she hadn't told.

"Liars go to hell," was all her mother said.

Lynny just stood there, eyes drilling holes into the floor. Dawn wondered if Lynny knew about what Daryl did to her at night. She always seemed to sleep right through it. One thing Dawn felt good about was that Daryl never touched Lynny. She always stayed awake to make sure of that.

Just before Dawn ran away, Lynny kissed her on the cheek and said, "I don't think you're going to hell." So maybe she did know.

She missed Lynny. Hoped she'd be all right without her. Dawn had almost taken her along when she left, but a 9-year-old kid? They probably would have both been caught and sent to juvie.

After the performance of *The Lion King*, James bought her a stuffed Simba for a souvenir, but she had given it to a little boy who was getting adopted. That's the way it went. Either you stayed here and made movies, or you got adopted. Personally, she didn't want to be adopted. She and James were partners. She took care of the place, of the kids, and he took care of her. Plus there was her acting career to consider.

After she made her first real movie, she'd bring Lynny out to Hollywood to live with her. She'd have a nice house and a swimming pool. In Hollywood, the weather was always perfect, never cold or stinking hot like Phoenix. You could swim every day if you wanted. Lynny loved to swim.

Dawn started to sing along with Jessica Simpson – "I gotta let you know before I let you in …." Her voice trailed off. It used to be her in that room, but James hadn't used her since she started showing, not that she cared. It was nothing. It was so nothing compared to what went down when she was out on the street.

After the baby, James promised to help her get an acting job. How much longer, couple of weeks, a month? She didn't know, but this baby was taking forever.

"Ouch!" She rubbed her stomach just below her ribs. It was always kicking and punching now. She didn't mind that much. When it kicked, she felt less lonely. But it would be gone soon. James had already found a couple who wanted to adopt it, a couple who had a big, two-story house, slides and swings and a swimming pool. After it was over, James promised he'd take her to the mall and buy her a whole new wardrobe, inside to out.

Dawn pulled the pod from one ear, popped it back in place. She hoped they'd be done with the girl soon. She was getting bored. Whenever James was making a movie everybody was supposed stay in their rooms. The door to the boys' room was bolted from the outside, but not hers. She was on the honor system.

She closed her eyes tight and straddled the bear, biting down hard on the its soft, white ear while she rocked back and forth until she saw big bright stars.

Belen awoke to Jesús' thin wail. She was disoriented by the newness of her surroundings and the medicine la doctora had given her. Sitting on the side of the bed she looked around the room, illuminated by a small nightlight, noted the cowboy hat sitting on a wooden chair, the boots tucked neatly beneath. A flag folded into a triangular box sat on the dresser. She wondered who usually slept in this room, then wondered where Adriana and Edgar were sleeping. It took a moment before the meaning of their absence came to her, pressing down so hard upon her that she couldn't rise to feed her baby.

By the time Señora Emma came into the room, she was shivering with cold and Jesús was screaming, outraged to be kept waiting.

Belen watched dully as the old woman reached into the plastic basin, watched her fumble with a clean diaper, then wrap the baby tightly in a fresh blanket. La señora threw an afghan around Belen's shoulders, then placed the baby in her arms. Murmuring something that sounded comforting to Belen's ears, the old woman touched the back of her hand to Belen's forehead, then left the room.

Belen lifted her shirt. Only then did her tears begin to flow again, warm and urgent as the milk from her breasts.

When Wiona came in from the barn, the teakettle was shrilling. Emma stood at the counter and poured scalding milk over a piece of buttered toast.

"I thought you were asleep," she said, afraid that Emma might catch a whiff of tequila on her breath.

"The baby woke me up. I think Gaby's got a fever."

"Gaby?"

"Yes, it got to be late so I invited her to spend the night. Good thing, too. She's sick as a dog. I'm going to take her a cup of throat dope and some milk toast."

Milk toast and throat dope – hot water poured over lemon juice, honey and a zinc lozenge. Wiona almost envied Belen.

As a child Wiona liked to be sick. It was the only time she didn't have to compete for her mother's attention. Once she determined Wiona was truly sick, which she did by placing the back of her hand against her forehead and scrutinizing her eyes to determine if they were rheumy, she was allowed to spend the day on the couch, wrapped in the old afghan. Her mother would bring her cups of scalding throat dope and steaming bowls of milk toast glistening with dots of butter and so much pepper her chest burned.

"Fight fire with fire." Emma's cure for most of life's ills.

When she was sick, Emma was never impatient or short, and there was her hand, competent, tender even, sweeping her bangs aside to see if another dose of throat dope was in order.

The drawback to being sick, of course, was that she couldn't ride her pony, Wooly, a Shetland her father had gotten her when she was 4. On about the third or fourth day of any illness, the conversation always turned to the pony.

"No, you can't ride Wooly until you've done your chores."

"But I'm excused from chores because I'm sick."

"Yes, and when you're well enough to do your chores, you'll be well enough to ride Wooly."

Back then Emma's logic had been perfect. Wiona watched her put the steaming cup and bowl on a tray, feeling tender and nostalgic for the mother Emma had become every once in awhile when Wiona was little and sick. "Need help with the tray, Mother?"

"I can handle it," she said, brusque and efficient. After all it wasn't Wiona who had a fever.

Wiona opened the spice drawer and dusted her tongue with ground cloves. At the sink, she scrubbed the tacky film of milk from the pan, rinsed it and put it on the drainboard, then looked around for something else that needed doing. Seeing nothing dirty or out of place, she turned off the kitchen light.

She plucked her jacket from the hall tree. Out on the porch, she eased herself down on the old glider, its metal slats cold right through the thick corduroy. Immediately, she heard the little tap, tap of toenails on wood, as Osa hurried up the steps. Sighing, the dog settled her head on Wiona's boot.

The moon had yet to rise over the canyon and the stars were so bright in the brittle air, it almost hurt her eyes to look at them. Orion was beginning to slide south, soon to be replaced by Scorpio, which would bring the summer heat with it. Wiona crossed her arms. With the slightest push of her heel, she set the glider in motion. Back and forth, back and forth she glided to the rhythmic skree, skree, skree of rusty hinges. Lulled, she closed her eyes and soon the baby was hungry at her breast. Each tug of his mouth seemed to pull on something deep inside her and she felt a moment of hot joy. The door opened and Wiona startled awake.

"What are you doing out here in the cold?" Emma asked.

"Just letting it soak in, I guess."

"It's true. Soon it'll be hotter than Satan's own tail. Move over, dog." Emma nudged Osa with her foot and sat beside Wiona.

For a few minutes, the two women glided in companionable silence as if it were their habit to sit like this, side by side. A dark shape trotted across the yard, paused, stared in their direction. Outraged, Osa leaped from the porch. The coyote issued a few rough coughs, then took off, the little shepherd hard on it.

"Aren't you going to call her back?" Emma asked.

"Wouldn't do any good." Wiona heard them pounding though the underbrush. "She'll be OK." Wiona gave a push with the heel of her boot and the glider recommenced its soothing motion. "How's Belen?"

"Who?"

"Belen – the woman with the baby. She's staying in Frankie's room."

For a long moment, there was only the protest of the rusty hinges. "Sleeping," Emma answered at last. "Do I smell cloves? Every time I smelled cloves on your father, I knew he'd been drinking down in the barn."

Wiona didn't know whether to confirm or deny this observation. "Yeah well," she conceded. "It's just that everything is such a big scary mess." This she tossed off to the brilliant sky as much as to the woman rocking beside her. "I don't know what I should do."

"Bless your heart." Emma patted her knee. "For one thing, you should oil the hinges on this glider."

Part 3

Into the Hands of God

Day 5

Haze bunched up against the mountains like dirty cotton sacking. Belen was dozing, head against the cool window glass. In back, Jesús was secured in the infant seat on loan from Gaby.

First thing that morning, Emma had tested Belen's forehead with the back of her hand and declared her still feverish. Right after breakfast, Wiona loaded mother and baby into the truck for the trip to the clinic in Douglas. Though they had passed three Border Patrol trucks, a white woman driving a brown woman in an open pickup didn't seem to fit any profile and not one of the agents did more than turn a head.

That morning the sun had risen an angry red. Now as the valley warmed, dust devils danced across the creosote flats. One spun beside the road, threatening to skip into her path. She didn't know whether to brake or accelerate. She did neither and the wicked little funnel spun itself out.

Wiona would be glad when the farmers finished disking the fields. She checked her appearance in the rear-view mirror now, smiled at her reflection. A bit of bacon was wedged between her molar and eyetooth. She worked it out with her tongue, smiled again. Should have brushed my teeth, she thought, suddenly on edge. Though she showered daily, Wiona was out of the grooming habit. She fumbled in the compartment between the two seats, extracted a tube of Johnson and Johnson's and rubbed lotion on her face, neck, hands.

The baby began to fuss in the back seat and Belen roused. Reaching back, she patted him, hushing him momentarily with a little song. Wiona thought the song was about a cat.

"Llegaremos en un poco," Wiona said. They'd be there in a few minutes. She hoped Jesús could wait.

A pretty girl with bright, shoulder length red hair sat at the front desk next to an older, very pregnant woman. Wiona stepped up to the counter. "May I help you?" the girl said, smiling encouragement. "Is Lucy Altamirano in?"

"Do you have an appointment?" The pregnant one asked.

"No, but my friend here..."   She gestured to Belen. "Dr. Altamirano examined her yesterday. Now she's running a fever and I hoped maybe Dr. Altamirano would have time to see her again."

"And what is her name?"

"Belen..." Wiona tried to recall the name on the birth certificate. "Belen Verales."

"Insurance?"

"None."

"Have her fill out these forms," the woman said, shoving a sheaf of papers across the counter. "Be sure she signs everywhere there's a big red X."

Nodding, Wiona collected the forms, noted that they were all in Spanish.

While Belen filled out the forms, Wiona paced up and down the length of the waiting room, clutching the fussy Jesús to her shoulder. A shoulder was not what the baby wanted. She bobbed up and down, then side to side. "Hush now," she whispered into his wispy, black hair.

Finally, Lucy came into the waiting room. "Here, give me the little guy," she said, holding out her arms. Wiona was happy to comply. "Let's go back and see what's what." She took Belen by the elbow. "Vamos a ver que está pasando con usted," she said.

Wiona pressed her hand to her throat, as if she could cover the flush that was rising from her collarbones to her scalp.

"We won't be long," Lucy said. "Oh yeah. Katie? I want you to meet someone."

The young redhead at the front desk poked her head through the window.

"This is Stokey's daughter, Katie," she said as she hustled Belen and Jesús into an examining room.

Wiona extended her hand. "Wiona Rutherford. I haven't seen you since you were a little girl."

The girl took a loose hold of Wiona's hand, smiled,

"Your dad and my brother were buddies."

"Oh, yeah. You left a message on the answering machine."

Nodding like a bobble-head doll, Wiona pasted a smile on her face and wished she were elsewhere. "Yup. That was me. Well, it was nice to meet you, Katie. Say hi to your father for me."

She took a seat and picked up Healthy Living. Feeling oddly let down, she flipped blindly through the pages. Get over yourself, Wiona, she commanded silently. It was clear that Lucy had forgotten how close they'd once been.

Could she blame Frankie for that? Recalling that day, she wanted to.

It had been one of those afternoons, air fresh washed and heavy from a storm the night before. And it was hot, gnats buzzing in their ears and eyes and everything so green. Sideoats grama was thick and the sacaton tall and top-heavy, like it gets in late summer when the monsoon's been good.

She and Lucy were skinny-dipping in the tank, just floating side by side, holding hands, not saying much. Wiona had stood for a moment, warm water lapping at her belly. That was when she saw him. She hadn't heard him, had no idea how long he been standing there in the thigh deep grass peering down into the tank from a little rise not 20 feet away. Reflexively, she pulled Lucy to the edge of the tank.

"What is it?"

"My brother. He's been watching." They both hunkered down. After a moment, Wiona peeked over the rim of the tank, but he was already gone.

And that had signaled the end of their forever friendship, hers and Lucy's.

Lucy opened the door to the waiting room. Come on back for a minute."

She followed Lucy to the examination room where Belen was nursing Jesús.

"Sit down," she gestured to the examining table.

Wiona climbed up, feeling all knees and elbows. "So what's going on?"

"Belen has a fever, but because of Jesús I'm reluctant to give her an antibiotic. I took some blood. Until we get the results of the blood work..."

"We just do nothing?"

"Tylenol is all for now. I'll have the lab do the blood work ASAP and call you with the results tomorrow. I'll give you a prescription for antibiotics, just in case. If her fever goes up past 102, start the antibiotics and call me."

Wiona nodded.

"So what do you hear from Stokey?"

"Nothing so far."

"Well, no news is good news, probably."

"You think?"

Lucy shrugged. "I really have no idea." She opened the door to the office.

Wiona gathered this was their signal to leave.

Dawn looked around the kitchen and living room. The TV was

blaring Pokémon cartoons in the boys' room, and of course the parrot was screeching at her. She supposed James might be out, or he could be in his bedroom. It didn't matter. As long as he wasn't making a movie, she had the run of the house.

As she passed by the parrot's cage, she glanced in to see if he needed water. The bird was named Pancho Villa. Dawn didn't like him. He was noisy and dirty. She was always cleaning up poop and scattered sunflower seeds. Still, the bird hadn't asked to be locked in a cage and she took good care of him.

In the kitchen, she sliced an orange and put a pan of water on to boil. From the cupboard she selected a package of Top Ramen. The cupboard was filled with jars of peanut butter, boxes of cereal, mac and cheese, and dozens of packages of Top Ramen. It was just about all she ever ate. That was OK with Dawn; she could eat Top Ramen three times a day. The boys preferred mac and cheese and peanut butter and jelly sandwiches. Sometimes James sent out for pizza or brought home chicken and fries from Church's.

She emptied the little envelope of spices into the boiling water and added the noodles – something she'd been doing since age 6. When the noodles were soft, she divided the soup into two mugs. On the way to the girl's room, she stopped by the parrot's cage. "Pretty girl," she prompted.

Pancho glared at her and screamed. He'd been pulling out his feathers again, one leg looked like raw chicken.

She dropped the orange slices in the cage, taking care not let her fingers get too close to the bird. Unlike Romeo, Pancho was a biter.

The girl was in her room. She wouldn't be allowed to go out with the rest of the kids until she'd finished her period of adjustment. According to James, every new kid needed a period of adjustment. Dawn couldn't even remember her own.

Technically, she was breaking the rules by going into the new girl's room without permission, but mostly James' rules didn't apply to her. After all, she and James were partners. Sometimes that's what he called her, only he said it *padna*, all cowboylike.

Holding both mugs in one hand, she unbolted the door. The new girl lay still on the bed, bedspread pulled over her head.

"Hey," Dawn whispered. "You need to pee?"

The girl didn't stir.

She closed the door behind her. "Are you hungry? I brought you some Top Ramen."

She set the mugs on the floor, then pulled the spread from the girl's face. "Wake up."

The girl opened her eyes then. They were red and crusty. Dried snot glazed her upper lip, and her gaze was unfocused as if she were alone in the room. Dawn pulled her by the arm until she had no choice but to rise. "You'll feel better when you get cleaned up. Then we'll eat."

The girl's knees buckled and Dawn caught her beneath her arms, supporting her as they made their way to the bathroom.

While the girl sat on the toilet, Dawn went to her own room and gathered up a pair of pink sweatpants and matching hoodie. A gift from James, the hoodie had *Daddy's Girl* in sparkling magenta letters across the chest. She took Romeo out of his cage and set him on her shoulder.

The girl hadn't moved. Dawn turned on the shower. When the water was hot, hot, she pulled her to her feet and gently shoved her into the steam.

For a long time the girl stood motionless in the shower, dark hair washing over her face. "Take your time," Dawn said, and sat on the toilet seat to wait. She placed Romeo on her head. Dawn liked the tickle of his little feet in her hair.

When they got back to the room, Dawn put Romeo on the girl's shoulder.

"Bird," the girl said.

"His name is Romeo."

"Romeo," she repeated.

The ramen was cold. It didn't matter; it was just as good cold as hot. They ate directly from the mugs, sucking up the long noodles with great slurps and smacks. It was the girl who laughed first.

When the laughing at last subsided, the girl asked, "You name?"

"I thought you didn't speak English?"

The girl waggled long, slim fingers in the air. "A little. I learn in school." She pointed to her chest. "Am Adriana."

"Am Dawn."

"And she is Romeo," she said, stroking the bird with her index finger.

"He. It's a boy."

Adriana nodded her head. "A boy." She pointed to Dawn's belly. "How many?"

"How many what? You mean months?" She shrugged then held up eight fingers. "Ocho, maybe almost nuevo." she said.

"You speak Spanish?"

"Only uno through diez."

Just then the baby began kicking. Nobody but she had ever felt the baby move. Dawn took Adriana's hand and placed it on her belly.

Adriana smiled. "Era fuerte."

"Whatever that means," she said, returning the smile. She was feeling good, now, motherly, superior, like with Lynny, but when she looked up at Adriana, the girl's face collapsed and she began to cry and babble words whose meaning Dawn could only guess.

She patted Adriana's shoulder then picked up the mugs. "Your brother's OK.

Do you understand? Brother OK." There wasn't much more she could do or say.

Crying was all part of the period of adjustment.

"You can keep Romeo for awhile," she said, then left the room, bolting the door behind her.

Emma poured coffee into Stokey's cup, nudged the milk and sugar his way.

"Thanks, Mrs. Rutherford."

"You're welcome young man. Now tell me all about your dear mother."

"She's just fine, ma'am. Sends her regards."

"Anyone else need a warm-up?" She looked around the table, poised, and gracious.

"No thanks, Mrs. Rutherford," Lucy said. "I've still got half a cup."

Emma waved the pot toward Belen. The woman shook her head. "No gracias, señora." Belen's chest rose and fell visibly beneath the blue rebozo. She pressed a corner of it over her mouth and took a deep breath through her nostrils.

"Mother, I think your program is on."

"Bless your heart, Wiona. My program can wait." She refilled her own cup, then sat at the kitchen table next to Stokey.

"Here's the deal," he said, making eye contact with each woman. "We can go one of two ways. I can get her ..." He raised his brows towards Belen. "What's her name again?"

"Belen Verales."

"I can get Señora Verales a snitch visa or …"

"Snitch visa?" Wiona asked.

"It's really called a C.I. parole – confidential informant parole – it's only temporary, but it would allow Belen to stay in the U.S. during the investigation. Trouble with that is, from what I understand, she didn't witness the load-jack."

Lucy arched an eyebrow. "We are talking about children here, not cattle or television sets."

"Hmm." Stokey took a sip of coffee. "You're absolutely right. Beg your pardon. Anyway, from what I understand Belen wasn't present during the abduction. I don't think I can justify a snitch, I mean, a confidential informant parole when she wasn't a witness to the crime."

"She can describe the coyote," Wiona said. "And Gaby and Beto even talked to him."

"That's all good information that may help in the investigation, but we're not after the coyote here. We've already reported the case to the FBI. We'll certainly be talking to Gaby and Beto, but that doesn't do anything for Belen's case."

"What's the other option?" Wiona asked.

"We can go for a humanitarian visa. I'm sure I can get one for the husband, too. If we go that route, they both have to go to the Douglas Port of Entry and turn themselves in. I could take them there myself."

"So how does a humanitarian visa work?" Lucy asked.

"Same deal. As long as there is an active investigation, that is until we find the kids or give up, they can remain in the U.S."

Emma started to get up from the table. "Anybody need a refill?"

"Everybody's fine, Mother." Wiona patted her hand. "And after you find the children?"

"If we find the children, if we don't find the children, the Verales will eventually be deported." He took another sip of coffee to let that sink in.

Lucy and Wiona exchanged looks and Stokey continued. "Belen really doesn't have much choice in the matter. Frankly, I could just take her into custody right now, probably should, under the circumstances."

"Where will she stay?"

"She can continue to stay here if that's all right with you."

"Let me take a moment to explain all this to Belen." Lucy began in rapid Spanish. Belen listened, eyes intent upon Lucy's face, as her fingers wove through the fringes on her rebozo.

After a few minutes, Emma turned to Wiona. "Are they talking about me?"

"No, Mother."

"Then what on earth are they yammering about?"

"Lucy is just telling Belen what Stokey said."

Stokey listened to Lucy's translation carefully. He was relieved when Belen agreed to turn herself in. At this point, he'd feel like a real asshole if he had to take her into custody. He turned to Belen and asked, "Tiene fotografías de sus hijos?"

"Si. Momentito."

Shortly Belen returned with two small photographs. As she handed then over, she began to cry.

Stokey studied the photographs. One was of a boy with the gap-toothed smile of a 6-year-old, dark hair pressed carefully across his brow. The other child, a girl, looked to be about 9 in the photo. She had large, shining eyes and a shy, sweet smile. Two neat braids fell over the front of her narrow shoulders. Each was tied with a red ribbon. Becka had combed Katie's hair in the exact same way when she was that age.

Belen wiped her eyes on the corner of her rebozo. "Las photos son viejos."

He cleared his throat. "It's OK. We can do a computer update on them. I'll copy these and return them, OK?" This time he waited for Lucy to translate.

Emma shook her head. "Well bless their hearts, never in my wildest dreams would I have guessed that someday a foreign tongue would be spoken at my mother's precious table." She turned to Stokey then. "So tell me about your dear mother."

Stokey was driving south on Highway 80 when he spotted a truck with a cab-over camper. From the amount of dust on the vehicle, it'd been driven off-road. That captured his attention as well as the fact that the driver was going too slow. But there was something else about the rig that tickled his sixth sense. When he looked in the rearview mirror, he saw that the license plate was smeared with mud. Mud? It hadn't rained in months. He executed a U-turn and put his flashers on.

The two youngish white guys in the cab were grubby, unshaven and sporting camouflage, he noted, with some satisfaction. It was always nice to nail a couple of bastards in camouflage. There was a

.22 on the rack behind the seat. Reflexively, Stokey patted his sidearm.

"Morning," he began.

When they finally agreed to open the back of the camper, Stokey was knocked back by a powerful animal stench. An easy dozen coyotes in a large wire cage, some stony-eyed and close to death, all shocky, lay amid the shit and pee.

"You got a permit for these?" he asked, matter-of-fact.

The one who'd been driving, pulled out his wallet. After a bit of fishing, he produced a much-folded piece of paper.

Stokey examined it. "This was issued in California. You are in the state of Arizona."

"So?"

"It's illegal to transport wild animals across state boundaries." If these guys had shot a deer in Arizona on a California permit, he would be sympathetic. But the sons of bitches weren't hunters, at least not in any normal sense of the word. They'd live-trapped the coyotes, he was pretty sure, for the purpose of transporting them to a game ranch, probably in some southern backwater a thousand miles away, so rich bastards could shoot them.

After he'd cuffed them, he pointed to the side of the road. "Have a seat over there, boys."

"On the ground?" The driver seemed offended.

Stokey took him firmly by the arm to a spot back from the road and sat him down hard. The other man eased himself down, first one knee then the other.

Stokey radioed Fish and Game. This kind of apprehension made his work a pleasure. These guys were not only assholes, they were stupid assholes. Another day in the back of that truck and every one of those coyotes would have been dead. No profit in that.

He walked back to his truck to get his water jug. Though the coyotes would be euthanized, he could at least relieve their thirst.

By the time he'd finally relinquished custody of the coyotes and their captors to a deputy from Fish and Game, he figured he might as well head in to the station. Once back on the road, he gazed out into Mexico, now only a few miles to the south. The folks in Washington seemed to be losing their determination to string a giant fence along the entire border. From San Diego to Brownsville, the border was at least 2,000 miles long. Hundreds of those miles were currently roadless – a good deterrent to illegal activity in itself. But to build the fence, they would have to build roads. They'd started a section of it all ready out of Sasabe. "Idiots," he said aloud. Which Washington toady got that contract, he wondered.

He had just two questions to ask the damn bureaucrats who thought up this boondoggle. If two oceans couldn't keep folks out of this land of opportunity, what made them think a fence would? And just how high would that fence have to be to keep out people like Belen Verales? He considered what circumstances would make a pregnant woman with two kids attempt a border crossing. Desperate circumstances, he concluded.

Stokey pulled into the station. Rudy Garza would definitely have an opinion about his reasons for not bringing Belen Verales into the station with him.

While Belen spoke to her husband on the phone, Wiona busied herself about the kitchen. From the long, one-sided conversation, she understood only that no, he had heard nothing from the children or their kidnappers, and no he would not turn himself in to la Migra. But yes, he would come to the ranch tonight to see her and the baby. And yes, she agreed they were all in the hands of God and would be reunited if that was what God desired. He would pray. She would pray.

Belen passed the phone to Wiona. "El quiere hablar con usted."

"Bueno?" she said into the receiver.

"Thank you for the keeping of my wife and son," he said in halting English.

Wiona heard the emotion in his voice, imagined tears. "You're welcome. How can I help you?"

"Can tell me, las direcciónes ..."

"A mi casa?"

"Si, señora."

Slowly Wiona gave him directions, supplementing her Spanish with English, then asked him to repeat them. When she was satisfied that he knew how to get to the ranch, she said goodbye and handed the telephone back to Belen. She went into the living room so Belen could finish her conversation in privacy.

As usual Emma was dozing in the recliner. Wiona took her hand and squeezed it gently until she opened her eyes. "Belen's husband is coming to see her tonight."

"What on earth are you talking about?"

"Belen, the woman with the baby who's staying in Frankie's room."

"Who?"

"Belen."

"I don't know any Belen."

Wiona tried another approach. "You know Belen. She's Gaby's sister."

"Oh yes, Gaby's sister. Her husband is coming tonight?

"Yes. Isn't that nice?"

"If you say so."

"Well, it'll probably be late. He's coming all the way from Phoenix."

"Gaby's husband?"

"He'll be here later."

When Stokey walked into the kitchen, Shorty at his heels, Katie was staring at the microwave.

"Hi, Sissy. What's nuking?"

She nodded toward the empty packaging on the counter. "Turkey or lasagna. Grandma called to see if you could take Papa to the VA next Wednesday for his colonoscopy."

"Wednesday? Umm." His mother, who had macular degeneration, no longer drove. Increasingly his parents needed someone to play chauffeur. "What time?"

"They have to be there at 8. I'd take them, but I'd have to take the morning off from work and since I just started …"

"It's OK, Sissy. I'll take care of it. Anybody else call?"

"That's it. Oh yeah, there's one other thing. I think you need to have the little talk with your son."

"The little talk?"

"Ye-ah?"

He noted the way she broke it into two syllables, e and ya, underscoring his cluelessness.

"It's supposed to be his week to cook."

"And he's not here …" He looked in the refrigerator. There were only three beers left. Should have stopped on the way home, he thought.

"He's not here because he's banging his girlfriend."

"Jacks has a girlfriend?"

"Yeah!"

Again the two syllables. "And he's …"

"Yeah!"

"How do you know?"

"He's showing all the signs." The microwave dinged and Katie removed two TV dinners.

"How do you know the signs?"

"This isn't about me, Dad. Mom and I already had our little talk."

"You did? When was that?"

"A long time ago."

Well, of course, he figured at her age, Katie was … what? Sexually active was the most antiseptic term he could think of for it. Still, he didn't like being confronted with this information, no matter how obliquely. "Hmm."

"Is that all you have to say?" Her tone was so much like Becka's, he had to smile.

"What's so funny?" she said, hand on hip.

"I'm not laughing."

"You're trying not to."

"I was just thinking about the increase in the water bill," he lied, though the thought had occurred to him.

"The water bill?"

"Yeah, all the showers. This development might explain the recent up-tic in Jacks' hygiene. He's even started doing his own laundry. That's a good thing, right?"

"Dad, I don't think you're taking this seriously. If this were about me, you'd be apoplectic."

"Apoplectic? I don't recall ever being apoplectic in my life."

"Casey Hampton?"

"Oh. Is that what apoplectic means?"

"More or less. Besides, this isn't just about Jacks. Don't forget there's a girl involved, too. If Mom were here …"

"Right. I'll talk to him when he gets home."

"Turkey dinner or lasagna?" Hands in oven mitts, she proffered two plastic plates.

"You're the chef. You choose."

When she choose the lasagna, he was surprised and a bit chagrined, thought she'd probably done that just to get his goat. He took his plate to the table and peeled back the lid. Steam rose. The smell reminded him of Iraq and his appetite vanished.

"Oh, and another thing. Since I'm taking classes and working this new job, you'll need to help out more with the cleaning."

"I wash and iron my clothes, pick up around the house and take my turn doing dishes and cooking."

"Big whoop. There's a lot more to do around here than that. You might, for instance, clean your toilet. It's disgusting, by the way, and I refuse."

He peeked under the turkey. Stuffing would be his guess. "Good for you."

"Yes, good for me."

"So is that why your mother left? I didn't clean the toilet?"

"No! I don't know."

"I thought you knew everything."

"Sorry, Dad." She got up from the table and scraped her lasagna, barely touched, into the garbage. Rinsed the plate and threw it in the recycle bin.

Stokey regarded his dinner: turkey, peas and carrots, a blob of translucent potatoes, stuffing, all awash in a sea of a yellow-green. Gravy he supposed. He would have gladly finished Katie's lasagna for her had she offered.

"I've got to go." She brushed her lips across the dome of his head. "Got a date."

"With who?"

"I'm not ready to discuss it yet."

"Must be serious." He grabbed her hand, pecked a kiss on the back. "Have fun, Sissy, but not too much fun."

He thought of the boys Katie had dated in high school, dim-witted thugs, in his estimation. It occurred to him now that in the estimation of the parents of this girl his son was ... having sex with, he'd probably raised a dim-witted thug of his own. He would corner the lad tonight and have that talk.

He scraped the turkey into Shorty's bowl. At the dull thunk, the dog shot out from under the table, tail setting his whole back end to wagging.

"Live it up." Stokey retrieved the beers from the refrigerator. The sun had already set, but there was still enough light left to weed by. He might have to wait another week or two for his tomato plants, but he could pull up Bermuda grass any time of the day or night, turn around and pull up some more. And there was the matter of Mr. Pack Rat. He went to his bedroom to retrieve his flashlight and the gun he kept on the top shelf of the closet. He thought of Becka with irritation. What was the point of having a gun if you didn't keep it handy?

When he stepped out the back door, a pale moon, one day past full, was just clearing the Peloncillos. The sight caused a ping of loneliness to ricochet around his ribcage. "Damn."

After a cursory weeding, he poked the hose into the pack rat hole and turned it on full blast. "That should do it." Stokey settled down on the cool ground Indian style and directed the flashlight on the hole. It didn't take long before the rat emerged, a handsome little guy, as rats go, but before he could get a bead on it, it scurried back down the hole.

Gun poised now, Stokey sipped his beer. What was wrong with her, anyway? He did appreciate her, appreciated every goddamn thing about her. Appreciated her skin, her hair. Sure, the sex part was important; he'd appreciated the hell out of that. But he also appreciated all the little things she'd accused him of dismissing. He missed coming home to find her in the kitchen. Becka had never served him a goddamn TV dinner in all the years they'd been married. He missed the way she'd tell him about the kids. He missed the way she might do all the talking so he wouldn't have to, but he also missed the way she listened when he wanted to talk. Granted, that wasn't often these days, but when he did talk she'd been a good listener. Should have told her about all the ways he appreciated her every fucking day.

The rat reappeared. This time it was carrying something in its mouth. Stokey squinted down the flashlight beam. "Shit. Looks like Mr. Pack Rat has given birth," he whispered when he realized she was moving a baby to dry ground. He hesitated a beat too long and mother and baby disappeared into the rosemary.

Belen heard the car pull into the drive. She eased the sleeping Jesús from his plastic washtub and went to the front door.

Moonlight poured over the yard like milk skimmed of its cream. For a moment she stood on the porch unable to move, such was her relief now that Jacabo was here. She took in his smooth, dark face. Though he was not much taller than she, his chest and rounded belly were well muscled. She'd somehow forgotten how handsome, how strong he was. Gray hairs had sprouted in his thick mustache and at his temples. She reached out to touch the ones just above his ear.

Jacabo grabbed her hand. Turning it, he kissed her palm. "Ay mi vida," he said. It was nearly a sigh. He took the infant from her arms. "Qué nombre le daremos?" He asked.

"I already named him," she said, holding the rebozo in front of her mouth. "It was necessary for the birth certificate."

"Ah, yes. So what did you name our little American citizen?"

"Jesús Milagros Verales de Jimenez." Belen had waited so long for this moment, but now she had trouble meeting his eyes.

"Such a long name for such a little baby."

"Pero, qué piensas? Do you like the name?"

He nodded. He stroked the tiny palm with his finger and the baby enclosed it in his fist. "He's little, but he's strong."

"Like his father." She took his arm then and led him into the living room.

"Are you hungry?" she asked.

"Just tired." He sank down onto the sofa. Baby cradled in one arm, he patted the place next to him and Belen entered the circle of the other.

"I want you to stay here," she said, still not daring to look at him. "We could turn ourselves in to la Migra. They promise to give us visas so we can stay while they look for Adriana and Edgar."

"Who promises this?"

"A man from la Migra."

"And you believe him?"

"What choice do I have?" She sat up straight and faced him then. "How can we find our children without their help?"

For a moment Jacabo was silent. Jesús began to fuss. Reluctant to let his tiny son go so soon, he gave him his knuckle to suck on. "I don't trust la Migra. What does la Migra care about our children?

What if they arrest us and send us back to Veracruz? Here at least we have money coming in."

"What good is money without our children?"

"What good are we to our children if they send us back to Veracruz? Better that you turn yourself in and I go back to Phoenix. The children know my phone number. How many days has it been?"

"Five."

"Only five? Perhaps they will still call."

Belen shook her head. "So what am I to do without you?"

"Pray."

"It doesn't seem like enough anymore."

"What else is there?" He placed his lips on her temple and inhaled deeply.

Stokey turned the television off when he heard the front door open. "Jackson?" he called. "Come in here, son. I want to talk to you."

Jacket in hand, the boy slouched against the doorframe. "What's up?"

"My question exactly. Your sister fixed dinner tonight. It was your turn to cook, and I was wondering where you were."

"Went out for pizza with the guys."

Stokey eyed his son. He had a certain sheen on his face, part oil, part dried sweat, that suggested some earlier exertion. "Your sister tells me you've got a girl."

The boy shrugged, nibbled at the cuticle of his thumb.

"Was she one of the guys you had pizza with tonight?"

"She was there."

"Was anybody else there?"

"What are you trying to say?"

Stokey took a deep breath. "If you have a girlfriend, Jacks …"

"Listen, Dad. I need to grab a shower. I still have homework …"

"Sit down a minute, son."

Jacks perched on the arm of the sofa, cocking his head in an eloquent manner Stokey understood to mean, *Whatever you have to say, I could give a rat's ass.*

"I'll be blunt, here, Jackson. Are you sleeping with her?"

The boy shot up from his perch and stormed down the hall.

"I take that to be an affirmative," Stokey called after him. Reluctantly, he got up from his chair. There were parts of being a father that he hated. He tried the door to the bathroom. It was locked. Stokey shoved it with his shoulder, something he hadn't had to do since Katie was 12. It easily gave way. His son was leaning against the sink, head in hands. "Don't shut the door on me when I'm talking to you, son." He stepped into the small room, aware of the sweet, slightly fetid aroma of sex.

"Jesus, can't you just leave me alone?"

"I can after I'm finished talking to you. So do you use a condom every time?"

"She's on the pill."

"Well, son, you can't always trust them when they say that."

"Them?"

Stokey saw the hatred on his son's normally blank face and realized that the boy was in love. "Hmm." He nodded his head. "OK, Jacks. I see how it is. All's I'm saying is that a man protects his woman. You know what I mean?"

"Like you protect Mom?"

"If I knew how to protect your mother, I certainly would. You have any suggestions?"

Tight jawed, the boy delivered a silent glare.

Stokey glared back. Why do I bother? He thought. No one around here seemed to appreciate the fact that it was Becka who walked out, not vice versa. He shifted his gaze to the tile floor then and took a deep breath while considering his next step. He was the father, goddamn it. This was his goddamn son. What he said to him mattered, so he better say it right. His expression softened.

"Well then, if you have no suggestions to make on the my marriage to your mother, let's get back to you and your girl. What's her name?"

"Sara."

Stokey eased himself down on the rim of the tub. "So how long have you and Sara been … in love?" He saw his son's jaw relax, thought he caught a bit of a smile.

"A week from Friday, it'll be two months."

"Love's a fine thing. When I first met your mother, it was like … I don't know, like some kinda high. My heart felt like it was being squeezed every time I saw her. Know what I mean?"

Jackson, nodded, smiled. "Sara's really beautiful, well, not that beautiful, but … I don't know, pretty and sweet and she makes me laugh. We laugh all the time."

"Laughter's good. So when do I get to meet her?"

The house was quiet and dark when she knocked on James' door, waited, knocked again. Dawn was pretty sure that earlier she'd heard him leave. When there was still no answer, she went to the boys' room and unbolted the door. There were only three now, a tall, slender black boy that she'd sometimes worked with on the set, named Dante, a 4-year-old they just called Honey because his speech was so bad, no one understood him when he'd said his name, and Adriana's brother, Edgar. They were piled on the naked mattress like puppies. She shook Edgar's shoulder. "Adriana," she whispered.

The boy rose, pulling up his saggy Jockey's and followed her in silence.

Dawn unbolted the door to Adriana's room. "Shush," she said, and pushed Edgar ahead. Adriana threw back the covers and opened her arms.

For a moment, Dawn stood there watching them hug. Watching made her feel both good and bad: good because it was nice that they had each other, bad because it made her miss Lynny. She had James, of course, but now that she was so big he never took her anyplace, mostly just left her alone to watch over things, which was so totally boring. There was the baby, but it didn't really count since it already belonged to somebody else. She shut and bolted the door.

In the living room, Dawn shuffled through a stack of DVDs – *Snow White, Cinderella, The Little Mermaid, Ants* – there were dozens. She selected one and slipped it into the player. She'd seen *The Lion King* a hundred times, maybe more. Now she settled back on the sagging sofa, legs sprawled, fast-forwarding. She stopped toward the end, after Simba defeats Scar and returns to his pride, a hero.

Someday that will be her. After she's a famous actress, she'll go back home. Once her mother sees how rich and famous she's become, she'll be all sorry. Dawn will be kind, like she is to everyone, even the lady who cleans her bathroom, but she won't stay any longer than it takes to get her sister. Lynny won't have to pack because she'll buy her a whole new wardrobe, inside to out. The two of them will live in her big house with 10 bedrooms, a home theater, a yard full of swings and stuff and a big swimming pool and water slide. She'll adopt some children, three boys and three girls. Everyone will have their own bedroom with a closet full of clothes that they pick out themselves, and the maid will come every day to clean the house and do the laundry. There will be a chef to fix the food, which will be home cooked, like fried chicken and biscuits, real macaroni and cheese from scratch, and pizza, not the frozen kind.

Settling back, she started *The Lion King* from the beginning. Dawn never slept at night.

When Adriana saw Edgar, she didn't cry. He looked so little in his baggy underwear, she knew she had to be the strong one.

"Come here," she whispered, opening her arms wide. She didn't ask any questions. Didn't want to know the answers. It was enough that he was here in her arms and that they were together.

When Dawn closed the door, Adriana smiled, remembering the

gift she had for him. She retrieved her backpack from under the bed and presented him with the package of saladitos. "I saved these for you."

He ripped open the cellophane, put one into his mouth, then held one out for her. She made a pillow for him in the crook of her arm. Sucking the sour-sweet, salty plums, the two lay back and gazed at the ceiling.

"Don't worry," she said, stroking his head like their mother had when he was hurt or afraid. His hair was lank and had a nutty, unwashed smell. "Maybe tomorrow Papa will come for us." She tucked the cover around them. "Tomorrow, or the next day. If God wants it, he will."

Day 6

On the other side of the cluttered desk sat a very black woman in an electric blue suit. The thick column of her neck rose out of a pair of shoulders young boys dream of. In contrast, her head was delicate, with sculpted cheekbones and hair braided close to her scalp in a complicated pattern of rosettes. A series of diamond studs ascended, large to small, from her left lobe to the point where her ear began its curl. In her right ear a single half-carat diamond winked.

Last year Stokey had assisted Agent Rosamond Beauxchamps on an FBI case involving baby smuggling. As her appearance suggested, she was a tough, well-respected agent, attentive to detail, and as formidable as a fullback. And it didn't hurt that she had a law degree from Tulane.

"So, Rosy, you look like life's been treating you well." Stokey said, stirring a packet of Splenda into the coffee she'd offered the moment he'd sat down.

"Well, thank you, Stokey," she drawled. Smiling, she gave her jacket a little tug so it lay smooth over her prow of a bosom. "I am doing well, real well. How are those kids of yours – Katie and Jackson, right?"

"Right." He was impressed that she remembered. "Well, Katie's doing pretty good, just got a new job at the local health clinic, and she's going to the J.C. Jackson, on the other hand, is going through the awkward stage."

"How's that?"

"Too old to spank and too young to kick out of the house, plus he's in love."

"I've been there. Both my boys thought that they were hot shit on a real cold day." She laughed. "But they do grow up."

"That's what they say. I hope I'll live long enough to celebrate the day."

"I hear you." She took a sip of tea. "And your wife?"

"Becka."

"Yes, Becka."

"She's doing all right." Stokey understood that Rosy was being polite, not inquisitive, so he spared her the details.

She pulled out a BlackBerry from the pocket of a black patent leather briefcase, indicating that the real conversation could now begin. "So Stokey, tell me what you got."

He handed her copies of the photographs Belen had given him, along with ones that had been age-enhanced by computer. "There was a load-jack, or I should say kidnapping, on April 10. These two children, only the children, illegals aged 9 and 12, were taken at gunpoint and loaded into a white, late model Chrysler 300. The vehicle had one of those yellow ribbon things, "God Bless Our Troops," on the back. The kidnappers are Hispanic – Mexicans probably, or perhaps Mexican-Americans, one thin and light-skinned, the other heavy-set, dark with green or blue eyes. The burly guy has a penchant for fancy boots. On the night of the kidnapping, he was sporting ones made of white ostrich skin.

"No license plate number?" she asked without taking her eyes off the photos.

"Nope."

"Got the coyote in custody?"

"Nope. What we got, we got secondhand from Gabriela and Roberto Chavez, both legal. They went over to Agua Prieta and found the guy, somebody who calls himself El Camaleón, just before he went south."

"What's their interest in this?"

"Ranchers, neighbors and friends of the woman who found the mother, Belen Verales."

"Back up. Where's the mother now?"

"The mother went into premature labor and sent the children on with the pollero, this El Camaleón, to join their father in Phoenix, so she didn't witness the kidnapping. A rancher, Wiona Rutherford, found mother and child. Both are in her custody on a C.I. parole."

"OK. We'll want to talk to …" She looked down at her notes. "The Chavezes. What about the rancher? She see anything?"

"No. At the moment, we've got only one lead. The coyote seemed to think the load-jack was a setup by some guy who operates a safe house in Agua Prieta, Hotel Las Palomitas. Might be something we can do with that."

Rosy made a few notations on her BlackBerry.

"Nobody's contacted the father in Phoenix or asked for ransom, so I guess we're looking at child porn, child prostitution," Stokey suggested.

"That would be the best case scenario."

"There's a worse scenario?"

"I guess that depends on your point of view. There have been any number of cases involving children and organ harvesting, children and snuff films."

Stokey nodded. Pinched his nostrils. Took a sip of the coffee. "So now what?"

"Might send a couple of our Hispanic liaisons to talk to the authorities in Agua Prieta. They might convince the federales to haul the operator of this Hotel Las Palomitas in for interrogation. … Do we have a name?"

"Not really."

"Not really?"

"Just El Corcho."

"We could try to get Corcho hauled in by the federales for interrogation, but that's not likely to yield much info. If he were to tell us anything significant, the Mexican Mafia would know all about it before we left the building. So he's not likely to cooperate."

"Or," she held up an index finger and continued. "The federales could stake out the hotel. Might ask them to get a search warrant."

Stokey was nodding. "Search warrant would be good."

"Trouble is, I've never known a single case in which the federales actually obtained a search warrant. Oh they say, si se puede. But in reality it's no can do."

Stokey continued to nod. This investigation was looking like it was going to be a short one. "What can we do from this side? What about car registrations? How many late model Chrysler 300s can there be in Arizona?"

Pity or perhaps it was scorn caused Rosy's smooth brow to furl. "These guys were driving a car registered to them? How likely is that?"

"Right," he said, his face changing from tan to ruddy. "So what am I supposed to tell Belen Verales?" His growing frustration broke into his voice.

"Back it up now, honey," she said, tapping a sculpted fingernail on the glass-topped desk. "Just tell her we're working on it."

"Are we?"

"Most definitely." She took another sip of tea and pushed it aside. "But rather than rely on the federales, I prefer to use a couple of Mexican nationals I know, discreet men who owe me a favor. They can go to Hotel Las Palomitas, do some sniffing around, maybe apply a little pressure on this El Corcho.

"You mean like physical intimidation?"

"We're not exactly talking water-boarding here, Stokey. I'm thinking more like offering an incentive."

"A bribe?"

"I was thinking more along the lines of a negative incentive."

"Is that legal?"

"Is that a concern?"

"Well, yes."

"Then get unconcerned. We're talking babies here, Stokey. How old did you say?"

"The boy's 9. His sister is 12."

"Think about it a minute. Put your son and daughter's face on it." She waited a beat. "Still concerned?"

He had already done that, and could see her point.

She had been doing the Dickerson's account when she got the call from Lucy. Her car was being serviced, but if Wiona could pick her up at the clinic, Lucy would like to take her out to lunch.

Now she was standing in front of the bathroom mirror, once again trying to decide what to do with her hair. She tried a bun, too matronly, tried a ponytail, too youthful. The braid was too Wiona, and she wanted something to make her different. She combed it out again. It fell about her face in thick waves of brown complicated by strands of red and gold, and more recently, silver. She caught up the sides with two fake tortoise shell combs, and considered the effect. It would do.

In the living room Emma was snoring softly in her recliner as some televangelist in a white suit and silver pompadour urged his viewers to meditate on Father God. "Love the things God loves," he was saying. "Hate the things God hates." For a moment Wiona considered what things God might hate. She could name at least three things she had done that the guy in the silver pompadour would hate. She wasn't certain how God would feel about them.

"Mother?" Wiona said softly.

Emma snored on, her chest barely rising and falling.

"Mother." She touched Emma's cool hand. The woman snorted, but did not rouse.

Wiona studied Emma's pale face. Were her lips a little blue? "Mother!" She shook her by the shoulder. "Wake up!"

Emma started. "What are you yelling about?"

Wiona jerked back. "I was afraid … well, I couldn't wake you up!"

"Well, God bless you, I'm awake now!"

Hand at her throat, Wiona took another step back. "Sorry, Mother. I just wanted to tell you I'm going into town to pick up a few things. Gaby will be here this afternoon. And Belen's here."

"Belen?"

"Gaby's sister. Will you be all right?"

Emma craned her neck. "I've been all right for all these years; don't know why you'd even ask." She took a hard look at her daughter. "What did you do to your hair?"

"Just combed it out for a change."

"Looks pretty."

Suddenly self-conscious, Wiona pushed her hair off her shoulders. "Well, thanks." She started for the door, stopped and considered the woman in the chair. She turned then and kissed Emma's puffy cheek. "Take care, Mother."

Emma reached for her daughter's hand. Gave it a squeeze and turned her attention back to the television.

They were sitting in a booth at the Shady Grove Cafe, which always struck Wiona as a funny name for a restaurant surrounded by asphalt. A single velvet red rose dotted with plastic dewdrops stuck in an empty chipotle sauce bottle nestled between a ceramic sombrero that held toothpicks and the salt and pepper. She'd finished updating Lucy on the health and welfare of Belen and Jesús, and now an awkward silence spread over the table. She'd never been adept at small talk. Now she was searching for a question to ask, an interesting detail to relate. Wiona smoothed out a wrinkle in the clear plastic protecting a cross-stitch tablecloth, then took a small bite of her enchiladas, trying to make it look like it was easy to swallow. When she first came in, she'd been hungry, but when the huge oval plate with its sides of rice and refried beans arrived she found herself unable to enjoy the food.

Lucy had ordered only a cup of chicken and rice soup, which she'd already finished, and had nothing to do but watch Wiona eat. "I guess you've heard the rumor that I've joined the Samaritans."

"I don't pay much attention to rumors."

"Except this one's true."

Wiona took a drink of water so she could swallow. "Are you sure you wouldn't like some of this? It's way too much for me."

Lucy shook her head. "If I ate like that, I'd weigh 200 pounds." She looked around the restaurant. When she caught the waitress's eye, she mouthed *coffee*. She turned back to Wiona, smiled. "So what do you think?"

"About what? The Samaritans?" Wiona shrugged. She wasn't sure what she thought and didn't much want to discuss it. "What is it you actually do with the Samaritans?"

"We go out into areas known for migrant traffic in teams of three, one person with medical expertise – that would be me – one person who speaks Spanish – me also – and one person who's there chiefly as a witness."

"Witness to what?"

"To any brutality on the part of the Border Patrol."

Wiona took another long drink of water. Until recently, she had never had feelings good or bad about the Border Patrol. They simply were. When she passed their white and green trucks on Highway 80, she raised her hand off the steering wheel in greeting as she did any truck on the road. But since the murder of Fletcher, her view of the B.P. had firmly shifted toward the positive. "Brutality? You see much of that on the part of the Border Patrol?" She made no attempt to hide the skepticism in her voice.

"Not me personally, but I've heard stories," Lucy said.

"You know, I feel like I owe you an explanation or an apology or maybe both."

These words heightened Wiona's discomfort. Mouth full, she

could only lift her brows.

"When I left Douglas," Lucy began. "Did you wonder why I never wrote or called? I wanted to explain."

Wiona held up her hand, chewed, took a sip of ice tea, swallowed. "It's OK. It was a long time ago," she said, then regretted it. She did want an explanation, felt she deserved one. "I mean …" She took another sip of tea. "I didn't mean to interrupt."

"It was … well part of it had to do with Frankie. I probably shouldn't tell you this. Shouldn't speak ill of the dead, isn't that the saying?"

"Please. I want to know."

"It was after he caught us skinny dipping that one time; he cornered me at school, said some pretty awful things."

Wiona leaned forward, felt the damp against her back where she had sweat though her shirt. "God. What did he say?" Suddenly chilled, Wiona leaned back again, rubbing her arms.

"I can't remember anymore exactly. Anyway it wasn't so much his choice of words, some of which were wetback, whore and dyke, but the hatred he felt for Mexicans in general and me in particular was palpable." Lucy sighed. Smiled. "Cold?"

"It's chilly in here, isn't it?"

"Maybe we should go."

Wiona nodded but neither of them moved.

Lucy ran her fingers through her hair. She was wearing cotton scrubs printed with pastel puppies. Despite the white hairs spiking the black, she looked like a child.

"So at first," Lucy continued. "I didn't contact you because of Frankie. I kept thinking if I called, he might answer the phone, or if I wrote, he might, I don't know, see the letter. I didn't want him to think … or rather, you still had to live with him. And there was school. I was busy. No excuse. Then I didn't write because I was embarrassed that I hadn't written." She made a noise in her throat that might have been a strangled little laugh. "And then … well, I fell in love. And you know how that is."

Actually, Wiona didn't know how that was. She didn't count Stokey. That had been a calculated act of desperation, not love.

The waitress arrived with a mug of coffee. Wiona waited until she was out of earshot. "I'm sorry about Frankie. I don't know what to say."

"Like you said, it was a long time ago. And really, it had nothing to do with you."

Wiona shook her head. She figured Lucy was wrong about that, but wasn't about to say so.

"Anyway, you're probably wondering why I even brought it up."

Wiona hadn't gotten that far ahead of the conversation, so she remained silent and waited.

"Anyway, I finally really fell in love. We were together for almost 10 years."

"What happened?"

"Motorcycle accident. My partner and I were running a clinic in Chiapas at the time."

Partner. Thinking business, Wiona was a bit confused.

"That's why I came home, actually. I couldn't stand to be there without her."

"Her?"

Lucy laughed then. "Of course her. I thought you knew that I was gay."

Wiona's hand flew up to her burning cheek. "I … well. I guess I wasn't thinking. I mean, I …"

"It's OK. I just figured you'd somehow heard by now." Lucy drank some coffee, blotted her lips with finality. "Her name was Leanna, by the way."

"I'm sorry." Wiona hoped she didn't sound mechanical, but at the moment she was more startled than sorry. How could she be so dense?

"Thanks. My heart is still broken. I think it's going to stay that way, maybe, for a long time." She looked down at her plate. "But I want to say that I don't know anyone here anymore except for you and the people at the clinic. I want us to be friends again."

Wiona extended her hand across the table as she might at Methodist fellowship, and smiled.

Lucy took her hand, eyes steady on Wiona's. "Boy you have a strong hand." She turned it over to examine it palm up and down. "I bet a person could trust this hand."

The compliment struck Wiona like a stomach punch. She struggled to maintain eye contact.

After a moment, Lucy began searching for the waitress again.

Wiona pulled a $10 dollar bill from her wallet.

"I've got it." Lucy said. "Why don't you go ahead. My car's probably ready by now. I'll just walk over and get it."

"Sure?" Feeling at once dismissed and relieved, Wiona got up from the table, then smacked her forehead with the palm of her hand. "Lord, I almost forgot. Monday morning I'm taking Belen to the port of entry. Stokey's meeting us there at 9. You've already done so much I hate to ask, but I think it would mean a lot to her."

"If I can get away, I'll be there."

Wiona smiled, nodded. "Thanks." She pulled her jacket from the back of the chair and started to leave.

"Wiona?"

She paused.

Lucy shook her head. "Never mind."

"What?"

"It's nothing. I'll probably see you Monday. Take care."

"You too." As Wiona walked out, she felt a spot warming between her shoulder blades and wondered if Lucy was watching her go. She turned, but Lucy was standing at the cash register, her back to the door.

James was standing at the bedroom door, smiling. "Rise and shine, beautiful. Doc's here."

"What time is it?"

"High noon, padna," he said, in his jokey drawl. "Get up now. He's awaitin'."

She closed her eyes and didn't move.

"Dawn?" James came in and sat on the edge of the bed. He put his hand firmly on her shoulder. "Get up."

"I don't want to."

"What do you mean you don't want to? You've done this a dozen times."

"I just don't want to." She rolled over, her back to him.

"Come on, baby. Old Doc doesn't hurt you, does he?"

She was silent.

"Hey, we're partners, remember? You know I won't let anybody hurt you." He was rubbing her shoulders now, stroking her back. "No one's ever hurt you here, not really. "

And he was right. No one here had ever crammed a beer bottle up inside her, no one here had pounded her head on the concrete or pressed her cheek against shattered glass. No one here had ever punched her in the chest for biting down. She'd learned not to bite long before she'd ever met James.

"Dawny? Look at me. Doc's got to examine you. This baby could be ready anytime now."

"He's not even a real doctor."

"Of course he's a real doctor."

"Then why are you taping us?"

"Because that's my job. You know that. It's what I do. It's what pays the bills." He made a gesture around the room. "It paid for this furniture. It paid for little Romeo over there and the cage he's sitting in."

"He doesn't seem like a real doctor."

"Well he is, and he's such a good doctor that when the time comes, you won't feel a thing, no pain. With other doctors there'd be a lot of pain; you know that. And after it's all over, we'll go on the biggest shopping spree ever. I'm going to dress you up like a living doll. Won't that be fun?"

She wasn't so sure it was worth it, but James' hands were warm where he was rubbing her back. And it was true. He'd done a lot for her and she'd never been hurt, not really.

"Dawny? Won't that be fun?"

"I guess." She pulled back the blankets. "I'll be there in a minute. Got to pee, first."

"That's my girl." He kissed the top of her head. "Now make it snappy, padna. Everything's set up."

Dawn sat on the edge of her bed for a moment, waiting for the dread to settle. Even if he were a real doctor, she hated Doc. He was old, older than James, and his breath smelled like liver. She didn't like his poke, poke, poking fingers. And his hands, when they slid over her belly and pinched her tits were clammy, like something squishy from the bottom of a lake. Everything about him was squishy. Even his shoes squished.

They were waiting for her on the set: James with the video camera, Doc, dressed in a crisp white jacket, standing by the examination table, which could be collapsed, folded and carried away like an ordinary suitcase. But Doc never took the table with him when he left. James just put it in the closet with the other the props.

"Good morning, Dawn," Doc said when she opened the door. His teeth were too white and when he smiled, he looked like the Cheshire cat from "Alice in Wonderland." He patted the examination table. "Up you go now." He took her by the arm.

She pulled her arm away. "I can do it."

Dawn could hear Pancho Villa screaming in the living room. She took a deep breath and climbed onto the table. She was wearing nothing but a hospital gown, loosely tied in front, and the thinly padded table was cold against her back and butt.

Like always, he began by running his squishy fingers up the inside of her thighs. "How did you get this scratch on your thigh?"

"Scratch? It's nothing. I don't even remember," she said, gazing up at the ceiling. Dawn figured this room must have been a real bedroom once. It probably had belonged to a baby or a little girl, because somebody had papered the ceiling with clouds. One by one she located the familiar shapes. There was the baby with puffy cheeks, the princess with hair flowing over her pillow, the dog, the goat and if she squinted, the rabbit. Once she had found each cloud picture, she closed her eyes, tried not to breathe, tried not to hear or feel his squish, squish.

Before long she was in the bright place, and there was the voice, low and warm, "Hop, hop, hop, quick like a bunny," he whispered.

And she hopped once, twice, three hops into his lap. Like always, the light was in her eyes and she couldn't see his face, but she reached out and felt it with her little hands, ran her fingers over his smile, twined them through the long hair that fell on either side of his face. He nuzzled her cheek with his nose, rocking her back and forth, back and forth. "Hitch my old horse to the rack," he was singing. "Buckle my banjo on his back."

His voice was clear, quavery, nice, but not too loud because he was singing just for her.

Day 7

Stokey took his morning coffee into the garden. It was still chilly, and the bright sun felt good across his shoulders. He pushed his sweatshirt back from his wrists and bent to pluck several blades of Bermuda grass tucked tightly against a flagstone. "Little fuckers," he whispered. He could never understand how Bermuda could come up overnight, grow two inches in two days, while the arugula he planted for Becka because she thought it was fancy, still hadn't sprouted. The seed packet promised it'd be up in six weeks. Hell, it had been at least eight. He'd thought she would be home by the time it came up. Planned to surprise her.

Since Becka had left, he found weekends provided time to kill rather than time to spend. He made a mental list of the things that needed to be done. There was grocery shopping, laundry, ironing. He thought of Katie. He would clean not only his bathroom but the kids' as well. That would take care of the rest of the morning, maybe take him into the afternoon, but then tomorrow was wide open. Maybe he'd save the ironing and the bathrooms for Sunday.

He took a sip of coffee. It had gone lukewarm and he tossed it over the chicken wire fence that kept out the rabbits and rock squirrels, but not Mrs. Pack Rat. He knelt to examine his rows for the least tip of green that was not Bermuda, and wondered if the pack rat was eating the sprouts as soon as they surfaced. Maybe he should go to the hardware store and buy a live trap. If he trapped the mom, the babies would die a slow death. Stokey felt more than a bit chagrined that he should care about the demise of baby pack rats. Maybe there was something worth doing at the station. Had Rosy dispatched her goons yet and, if so, what may have come out of that? Whatever, it would have to wait until Monday. He had no intention of calling Rosamond Beauxchamps on the weekend. He wouldn't dare. Still, if he dropped by the office, she might have left an email.

Inside the house the kids and dog were still sleeping. Stokey slid two pieces of bread into the toaster and set the burner on medium high. Deftly, he broke three eggs into a bowl, broke each yolk, then dropped a dab of butter into the frying pan. He swirled it around until it sizzled then scraped the eggs into the hot pan. When the toast popped, he flipped the eggs, buttered his toast and poured himself another cup of coffee.

At the breakfast table he opened the Phoenix Republic. He scanned the front page. It was dominated by the latest suicide bombings in Afghanistan. There had been three. He put it aside and took up the sports section. After his third deployment, Stokey found that news from anywhere in the Middle East quite simply ruined his day.

Down at the station Stokey checked the coffeemaker. In Florence's absence, no one had bothered to make a pot. He tossed yesterday's grounds, added fresh, filled the top with water, then wandered down the hall to see who might be in. He stopped at the door of Rudy Garza's office. Rudy looked up at Stokey from over the top of the newspaper, reading glasses set low on his nose.

"I put the coffee on," Stokey said.

"Thanks, honey."

"Anything for you, sweetheart."

Rudy smacked the paper. "Now that the Big Unit is back, maybe the D-backs'll have a shot at the series."

Stokey shrugged. Since the Diamondbacks got rid of Luis Gonzalez, he'd sort of lost interest in the team. The Gonzo was younger than he was, for Christ's sake. It rankled that he would be put out to pasture. It also rankled, but not as much, that he'd been passed over for the position that Rudy, at least five years his junior, had gotten. Well, he had Afghanistan to blame for that one.

"In case you haven't noticed, it's Saturday. Don't you have a life?"

"At the present time, not much."

Rudy put the paper aside. "Yeah, well. That's a shitty deal, but she'll probably come around."

Stokey nodded, shrugged. "I just thought I'd get that sexual harassment stuff taken care of."

"Andele, pues, amigo. Once you finish we'll be in 100 percent compliance."

"That must be very gratifying." Stokey didn't wait for Garza's response. He figured Garza probably did find shit like 100 percent compliance gratifying, and maybe *that's* why he was made agent in charge.

Stokey got himself a cup of coffee and began scanning quickly though his emails. He opened the one from Rosy. "Call me."

While he waited for Rosy to pick up, Stokey swiped at the dust with the terry cloth rag, straightened the stacks of paper and sipped his coffee. Just as he was about to give up, there was the lush drawl. "Rosamond Beauxchamps."

"Ah, Rosy. Stokey here."

"How you doing, Stokey?"

"OK, thanks."

"And the family?"

"Great, everybody's great." Sometimes he wished Rosy wasn't so damn polite. "How are things going your way?"

"Just fine, Stokey."

"So what you got?"

"I wanted to let you know that the business we discussed is underway. So you need to be alert just in case the pigeon tries to fly north to escape the heat."

Stokey considered this. If Corcho were to cross the border, there'd be no interference from the federales. He could apply leverage directly, maybe get the guy to name names. "Got an ID?"

"Take your pick. There's Oscar Guerrero de Soto, Oscar Soto, Oscar Guerrero, Oscar Rigoberto Soto, Corcho Soto. You get the picture."

He jotted down the names. "Thanks for the heads-up, Rosy."

"You're entirely welcome, Stokey. Keep us posted."

"You bet." He hung up. Took a sip of coffee, then punched in the number of the port of entry.

"Stokey Stokelund here."

"How ya hanging, Stokey?" Arla inquired sweetly.

"In there, Arla." Since Becka had left, old Arla had been keeping a pretty keen eye on him, so he always kept their encounters as brief as professionally possible.

"Listen, Arla," Stokey continued. "A guy might be crossing today or maybe in the next few days from Agua Prieta." He ran down the list of names for her. "He must use one of those on his passport." He repeated the names. "Got that?"

"Got it."

"If he comes through, I want him pulled over to secondary and I want to be called immediately. Here's my cell number in case I'm not on duty." He recited the number. "Pass the word, please."

"You betcha. Anything else I can do for you, Stokey?"

"Nothing I can think of, Arla. Thanks." He hung up the phone.

He figured he'd stick around the station until noon, just in case. He turned his attention to the policy memos and field intelligence bulletins, still neatly stacked and unread. He could go through those, but he really should take that sexual harassment training, or at least the test, since that's what he told Garza he'd come in to do. He opened the program, looked it over.

In this day and age, to Stokey's mind, if some jerk actually needed that kind of training he/she should be summarily fired, and though he had plenty of time to kill, he didn't have time to waste. He closed the program.

Despite Rosy's lack of enthusiasm, Stokey figured it wouldn't hurt to put out an intelligence report on the kidnapping with a description of the car and the perp. Wouldn't hurt to get local law enforcement agencies on the lookout for the Chrysler 300 and the green-eyed guy with the flashy boots who might still be driving it. Then he might give Fattyboy Farris a call, see what his take is on the weapon that killed Fletcher Hart.

As he approached the border crossing, Corcho felt a sense of relief. After a few months spent with his woman in Phoenix – this woman plump and young enough to be his daughter, as opposed to his woman in Hermosillo, the mother of his children – it would be safe to return to Mexico. Two months or so would give the American authorities enough time to lose interest in the missing children. After all, he was thinking, what concern could they possible have for two negrito indios? When the gringos lost interest in the kids, they would lose interest in him as well and la gente in Mexico City would have no reason to suspect his loyalty.

Agua Prieta was quiet these days, he noted with regret. The little restaurants that used to line the dusty streets were gone, and stores that once sold liquor and curios were now mostly farmacias. These days gringos crossed the border only to buy cheap drugs for their high blood pressure and limp dicks.

He smiled as his thoughts turned to his Phoenix woman, who was neither Mexican nor American, but Serbian – every hair on her body blond. Marlena spoke no Spanish and little English, and he felt totally safe in her ignorance. He was looking forward to making a baby with her to keep the little cabrona busy when he needed to be elsewhere.

Double rows of six-foot-high steel fencing funneled his car, a late model, cobalt blue Chevy Impala, toward the low-slung, dung-colored port of entry. As he waited in line, he readied his border crossing card and passport.

"Good morning," he said to the agent, a big healthy woman whose chest strained the buttons on her uniform. He handed her his documents with a smile.

"Good morning, sir." As she accepted the documents, she returned his smile. After a quick glance around his car, she looked directly into his face.

Always suspicious, la Migra, he thought.

After checking his papers, she said, "Sir, you need to pull your vehicle into the parking bay to the left and wait."

Again he smiled. "Is there some problem, miss?"

"Just pull your car over to the left, sir." She did not return his smile this time.

I'm fucked, he thought. "OK." He smiled once again, putting the car in gear. But instead of pulling off to the left, he sped forward down the main street of Douglas toward Highway 80. If they took him into custody, he'd be a dead man anyway, so what did he have to lose?

Stokey pushed the grocery cart slowly down the aisle as he scanned the hundreds of cereal boxes for the raisin bran. Earlier he'd talked to Farris. The fact that the murder weapon was a shotgun rather than a semiautomatic hadn't altered Fattyboy's deep-seated conviction that the killer was running drugs. Stokey was not surprised, but he was irritated as hell. And he hadn't even touched on the subject of motive or the lack thereof. Right off the top of his head, Stokey could think of two men who had a better reason to kill Fletcher Hart than some lone drug mule in an old pair of running shoes. Carter was against that conservation easement thing his brother was about to sign, and, as a developer, wouldn't Weldon probably be opposed as well? How opposed?

Of course, as Garza so eloquently pointed out, it was no longer "our fucking fiesta," except that it did concern Stokey that somebody walking around, possibly in expensive work boots, was getting away with murder.

As he reached for the raisin bran his cell phone rang.

"He made a run for it Stokey, but we're on him," Arla said. "He's headed north on 80."

"He'll probably try to head back into Mexico. Tell 'em to put up a road-block on the road to Naco. Roll out the spikes. I'm on my way."

Stokey abandoned his cart in the middle of aisle 12 and headed for his truck.

Corcho's mind raced to form a plan. His best chance was to get rid of the car and cross back over the line on foot. He had a friend in Naco who had a big garage, and this friend owed him a favor. When he was safely back in Agua Prieta he would make arrangements for the car to be dismantled and sold for parts. He looked in his rearview mirror, nothing yet. He was smiling until he rounded the bend and saw the flashing lights ahead. Quickly he executed a U-turn through the desert, burr sage and creosote whipping the Impala's undercarriage. His passage into Mexico blocked, he headed back through his own dust out to 80.

Halfway up the Mule Mountains, Stokey saw the flashing lights. The dust hadn't settled when he pulled in behind the three Border Patrol cars already parked on the side of the highway.

He flung open the door. "Christ," he muttered, as he peered down the embankment where Corcho's car had come to rest against a gnarly old mesquite tree. Stokey slid down the rocky bank.

The vehicle itself looked to be in pretty good shape, just a mangled front end. Stokey was hopeful until he saw the tree limb sticking through the windshield. That, and the fact that the other officers were not rendering immediate assistance, didn't bode well.

A kid who'd recently been transferred to the Douglas station stepped out of the louvered shade of an ocotillo. "Sorry, Stokey. He was flying. Must have been doing 110 at the bend."

He caught the scent of blood before he saw it. A mesquite limb had impaled Corcho's chest. Blood was soaking his shirt and pants, pooling on the seat between his sprawled legs. As he stood there, the man's face paled from the brown of tanned leather to gray.

Stokey asked for latex gloves.

"He's a dead man, Stokey," Arnie Johnson, a Border Patrol veteran of 13 years, advised as he handed over a pair of flesh-toned gloves.

"Looks like it," he agreed.

Entering the car on the passenger side, Stokey did a hasty search through Corcho's pockets. He tugged a wallet from his back pocket, poked through the contents, extracting slips of papers, business cards. When he was finished he stuffed the wallet back into the dead man's pocket, then turned his attention to the glove compartment. By the time the ambulance and sheriff arrived, he'd sifted through every bit of paper trash lying about and stuffed his blood-smudged gleanings into a plastic evidence bag.

"Must have died instantly," old Arnie observed, as the EMTs began to load up the body.

"Must have," Stokey replied flatly. He figured it was an easier death than the bastard deserved. He hauled himself into his truck then wound slowly back down through limestone hills studded with thousands of spindly ocotillo tines stabbing the hard blue sky.

Stokey's search had yielded fewer than a dozen meaningless sobriquets, El Camaleón, Dutch, El Gigante, Rojo, El Pendejo among them. Next to each name was a phone number. Four of the numbers had Tucson or Phoenix prefixes. The rest were from the Mexican states of Chihuahua, Sonora and Sinaloa.

Now Stokey entered the names and numbers in the smuggling database, hoping for matches. There were none. He updated Rosy with an email, including the list of names and numbers, his intel report and BOLO for the guy in the Chrysler, although he suspected that she was already way head of him.

He looked at his watch. He still had a good chunk of the afternoon left. Deflated, he got up from his desk. There was nothing more to do but go home. On the way, he'd stop by the grocery store. Maybe his cart would still be in aisle 12.

Though each day the sun cut another notch north, a prolonged chill accompanied the drought and Wiona still needed her jacket in the deep shade of the oaks and junipers where she had spent the morning raking dead grass and leaves into a great pile. Later, if it ever rained enough to make it safe, she'd burn it.

The commencement of the summer monsoon, with its lightning and God's raspberry, as her father had called the ragged vales of rain that tantalized but barely reached the ground, posed a threat of wildfire. People just held their breath until the driving rains of July and August arrived. But those storms were still three months away. All she could do for now was cut down on the amount of tinder that accumulated against the house and outbuildings, and hope for a rare spring rain before the wind undid all her work.

Now she looked at her watch. If she stayed chore-minded, she could finish the Dickerson's account and still have time to clean tack. On her way to her office, Wiona stopped by the shed to put up the rake. Link whinnied a welcome, but old Thunder merely farted.

The moment she stepped inside the shed, she smelled the fusty stink of mouse. It occurred to her then that she hadn't seen Punkin, who did a pretty good job of keeping the mouse population down to zero in all the outbuildings, since ... well she really couldn't say how long it'd been, she'd been so out of her routine the past week, at least a day or two. A bad sign. Of course, what with owls, coyotes and bobcats, barn cats came and went, but she had broken the rule and named this one, and in the naming made the cat her own. She checked Punkin's food bowl. The kibble she'd dished out yesterday was gone, but that didn't mean much, given the mouse stink.

"Punkin," she began to call without the least hope of hearing a responding meow. "Punkin?" She pursed her lips and made that squeaky, rodent-in-distress sound that always drew Punkin's attention. No cat.

The air was muzzy with hay dust, and the smell of dry grass, mouse and manure was all about her, that and some other scent layered beneath, rank and damp like leaf mold. Something about that combined smell clicked in her brain, then pooled like acid in the bottom of her stomach. She had to sit where she was amid the hay and mouse droppings, or fall there, so strong her body's response to the smell, familiar and nameless at once. Sweating now, she pulled off her gloves and jacket.

It didn't happen often, mostly she didn't think about it, but now it was upon her – he was upon her, pinning her against the wall as he'd done so many times when they were kids.

"Stop kicking at me, Wiona."

"Let me go."

"Not until we've had a little talk about what I saw you doing at the second tank."

"We were cooling off."

"You were holding hands."

"So? What were you doing spying on us anyway?"

"I don't want you to hang out with that wetback anymore."

"Wetback? You're crazy. One, she was born here. Two, she's my best friend."

His sweating face was inches from her own as he pressed against her with his pelvis. "Well, your best friend's a dyke."

"That's a lie."

"Well, it's what the guys are saying and if you keep on hanging out with her, they'll say the same about you."

"You and your stupid friends are so full of BS."

He let go of her arms then, and stepped back. "Maybe you are a dyke."

He yielded when she pushed past him, but when she started to walk away, he tackled her to the ground. Pushing her face into the rotten hay, he fumbled beneath her shirt. Though she was nearly as tall as Frankie, he was denser, broader at every point save the hips and she could barely move beneath his weight.

She jabbed him with her elbows. "Get off me. I can't breathe." She jabbed him again, and he relented but only enough for her to turn beneath him. Now she was pinned by his chest and his grinding pelvis.

"Get off me!" She yelled into his face.

"I saw what you two were doing out at the tank, so don't act like you don't want it. You must want it real bad to get it from a girl." He was tugging at her clothes, his hands everywhere at once.

"What are you talking about? You're crazy." Her face was wet with sweat and tears of exertion. "Get off me!" She began to claw at his face.

He punched her in the jaw. The shock and pain of the blow caused her to stop struggling for a moment. He continued to tug at her jeans with one hand, while the other kneaded her breast. Gathering all her strength, she tried to buck him off, almost succeeded, too. That's when he punched her in the gut.

Afterwards, they'd pulled their clothes back together without looking at each other. "I didn't take anything that you hadn't already given away, so you better not say one damn word about it."

She pulled a bridle off its hook and flung it at him.

He picked it up and hung it back on the hook. "Hell, Wiona. You just got what you've been asking for all along." He lifted his chin. "And you better take my advice. I don't want to see you with that wetback again, at the tank or anyplace else. You're my little sister," he said, pushing a swath of damp, black hair off his forehead. "It's my business to take care of you."

That's what he had told her. Well he'd taken care of her all right. Later, after she had showered and changed, her mother asked her how she'd gotten the bruise on her face.

"Ran into one of dad's horseshoes," she'd said. It never once crossed her mind to tell her mother the truth.

Now she looked around the stall. The same old bridle still hung on the same hook. Had she asked for it? Whenever she relived that first time, she could never remember what had brought her out to the shed that afternoon – the same afternoon he'd caught her with Lucy at the second tank. She'd known he'd be waiting for her, hadn't she? It was this fact that grieved her most. She'd known, some part of her had. Some part of her had been expecting him to come after her.

Wiona leaned back against a bale of hay, felt its prickly surface and a strand of bailing wire cool and hard against her back.

Her shirt was damp and now she shivered, tired to the bone of this spring that seemed never to quicken. After a few minutes, she roused. Putting her hand on top of the bale, she hoisted herself up, dusting the chaff from her bottom with her gloves. Link craned his neck in her direction. She went over and leaned into his warm neck, nuzzled his velvet lips with her palm.

For a long time she'd believed Frankie, believed that she'd been asking for it. Just about the time she'd figured out how he'd been pushing her most of her life toward that outcome, he was killed. What do you call love turned inside out? Not hate, but something else, bitter, unseizable. Add to the mix shame, guilt and grief. Where does somebody put all that?

She went into her office, turned on the ancient Mac. In so many words, it told her she'd been a bad girl and refused to open the Dickerson's account.

"You are so full of shit," she said to the computer, running through all the punitive little steps it took to open the file.

Rubbing her eyes, she leaned back in her chair. When she tried to reconcile the things she'd done, the things Frankie had done to her – things she'd allowed – when she tried to reconcile these with what was supposed to be Christian, right and moral, she never could, of course. Still, part of her believed there'd been some kind of mixed-up love behind it all. Everybody on earth mostly wanted the same thing, she supposed, to be loved and to be safe in that love. It sounded like it should be sweet and simple.

Stokey put the groceries away, leaving a package of frozen hamburger out on the counter to thaw. If the kids were going to be home for dinner, which he doubted, he'd barbecue some burgers and make a salad, if not, he'd just fry up one for himself. He'd bought a six-pack and planned to spend the rest of the afternoon drinking the better part of it in front of the television. The housework, he'd save for tomorrow.

Just as he was about to open his first beer, Katie came in the back door. He stuck the beer back into the refrigerator.

"Where have you been?" She asked, her arms full of books. She slammed the door with her foot. "Mom's called three times."

"And what did she want so bad that she called three times?"

"She needs help setting up her computer."

"Computer! She bought a computer?"

"Just a rebuilt Mac. I don't think it cost her much."

"What does she need a computer for?"

"Dad. Everybody needs a computer."

"I've got laundry and ironing to do, toilets to clean. Your mother must think I'm made of time."

"Well, I'd go, but I promised Darin I'd help him with a paper he has to write for English."

"Darin? Is this *the* Darin, or some other Darin."

"*The* Darin." She set the books down on the kitchen table.

"So let me get this straight. You're spending Saturday night helping *the* Darin write a paper? You must be in love."

"In like. Seriously in like is the way I'd put it."

His daughter, Stokey was thinking, how did she get to be so squared away?

"Are you going to help Mom set up the computer or what?"

"I've got hamburger defrosting. What am I supposed to do with that?"

"Take it with you. Or better yet, put it back in the freezer and take Mom out to dinner."

Dinner? This was beginning to sound like a mother/daughter plot. Hope sent a soft blow to his chest.

Frances Stillman and Pogo, a Cairn terrier the exact color of a Triscuit, were finishing their daily three-mile walk. From late autumn to early spring they went out in the afternoon. In the summer, they had to get started well before sunrise. She did this for Pogo's health as well as for her own. Use it or lose it. That was their motto. It was Frances' hope that Pogo's heart would outlast hers, or better yet, that they'd go together, for she would never get over this little dog, so dear, such good company, better company than Raymond had ever been if truth be told. For 52 years, her husband's virulent allergies had precluded any notion of pets. Acquiring Pogo was practically her first act as a widow.

Pogo paused to sniff some message deposited at the base of a palm tree, the only thing living in that sea of white quartz that passed for landscaping in her neighbor's front yard. While she waited, Frances enjoyed the fine afternoon. Warm and sunny, it was marred only by haze, the dingy yellow of an old toenail, butting against the Superstition Mountains.

Just as she was about to give Pogo's leash a little jerk to hurry him along, she heard the cry. Awful, begging. The words were indistinct, but it was definitely a child's voice screaming for mercy, it seemed to Frances, making goose flesh rise on her arms. And it was coming from that house. That house, with its blinding quartz and shutters at every widow always tightly closed even on the nicest days!

Terrified, poor Pogo was pawing at her leg. Frances Stillman knew something terrible was going on there, knew it in her bones. Once in a while she would see a man, an older man with white hair and mustache and a young girl pull in or out of the drive in a maroon car, what kind? A Nexus or a Neon, something like that. Sometimes a different car would pull up and a man would go into the house, always a man, never any little friends for the girl. She hadn't see the girl in months, but the white-haired man came and went – and his friends, stealthy looking men, up to no good kind of men. And now those cries.

She tugged at the leash, but Pogo was reluctant. "Come on, Pogo." She gave the leash a yank and the two hustled – didn't even stop to pick up the mail – across their lawn and into their house.

The doorbell rang. James looked at his watch. He wasn't expecting anyone. The boys were in their bedroom watching TV. He motioned to Dawn, who was sitting on the living room couch painting her stubby fingernails navy blue. "Get the girl and take her in with the boys. Leave the TV on, but keep everybody quiet. Stay in there with them unless I come and get you." He winked, then hurried to the door, confident that Dawn would hold up her end.

Officer Reynaldo Montoya rang the doorbell again, then ran long fingers through his hair, mostly still blue-black and thick. Trim and long legged, he played trumpet and sang in a mariachi band. They played for weddings, birthday parties, anniversaries, usually for friends or friends of friends.

Humming a few bars from "Volver Volver," he noted the shuttered windows, the quartz, the single palm tree crackling in the slight breeze. Still humming, he rang a third time. The place, with its vacant, low-maintenance appearance, looked like a stash house more than anything. The guy who finally answered the door, however, looked like somebody's grandfather, with his thick white hair and mustache, and crinkly, blue eyes. He opened the door wide. To Montoya, this translated as *nothing to hide here*, which could mean either that the guy had nothing to hide or that he wanted to give that impression.

"Well, hello, officer ..." The guy squinted as he read the name on his chest. "Officer Montoya. To what do I owe the honor?"

"Wellness check, sir. A neighbor reported hearing screams coming from this house. Thought somebody might need help."

"My, my." The guy offered his hand. "James Trillig." He smiled, stepped aside. "Would you like to come in?"

"If it's convenient, Mr. Trillig," he said, stepping into the foyer. "Do you live here alone?"

Trillig led the way into the dimly lit living room. "I live here with my daughter," he said glancing at the baseball game on the television that dominated the living room. He pressed the mute on the remote.

"And what is it you do for a living, if I may ask, sir?"

"You may. I'm a videographer, mostly commercial stuff, ads for realtors, local politicians and the like. Not very exciting, but it's a living. Google me. It's all there."

"And your daughter, how old is she?"

"Fifteen."

"Is she in school?"

"It's Saturday, officer. But no, she's not currently enrolled in school. She's due to have a baby any day now, at least that's what the doctor says. Hard to believe. When my ex was pregnant, she was huge all over, like a house. But Dawn, that's my daughter, looks more like she's trying to hide a soccer ball under her shirt. The rest of her is just like before, skinny. Poor kid. When she got in trouble, my former wife flat kicked her out, if you can imagine that. So the ex gets the house – I lease this one – and now I've got Dawn."

Suddenly there was screaming. "Fuck the fucking fucker."

Startled, Officer Montoya swiveled toward the source, then

chuckled when he saw the parrot. "Nice language."

"Charming woman, my ex-wife. She also gave me the bird, literally and figuratively, as if were."

"I see. Is Dawn home now?"

"As a matter of fact; shall I call her?"

"Yes, sir, if that's possible."

"Dawn," Trillig yelled. "Come out here a sec." When there was no response, he yelled again. "Dawny?" After a few moments, he shrugged his shoulders. "Why don't you have a seat, Officer Montoya. I'll go get her."

Montoya took the opportunity to look around the living room. The furniture was the kind you get by the roomful, cheap. It was sagging and battered. Maybe it had come with the house.

In its cage, the parrot was ripping at the feathers on his chest. The poor bird had already plucked all the feathers from one leg. While the parrot screamed, he shuffled through the stacks of videos on the coffee table – mostly Disney, he noted. Would a 15-year-old pregnant girl watch *The Little Mermaid, The Lion King*? Possibly, if there was nothing else to do. And the guy, he seemed kind of old to be the father of a 15-year-old. But that's just how it works out sometimes. He should know, he was about to turn 50. At age 6, his son, Reynaldo Junior, was only a year older than his granddaughter.

"Dawn," he heard the guy say. "Could you kindly get your butt in gear, if it's not too much to ask?"

When Trillig returned to the living room he slumped onto a chair. "I'm getting too old for this," he said. "Do you have any teenage daughters, officer?"

"Only one right now."

"You have my condolences. Dawn?" he yelled above the screaming parrot.

Finally, the girl sauntered into the living room then slumped on an arm of a chair. She was wearing a cropped black T-shirt. Tight as a second skin, it exposed her hard white belly with its knobby belly button. It was a popular look among pregnant girls these days, but for the life of him, Montoya couldn't understand why. The girl sighed, dug at her fingernails a bit, then stared in his direction as if she'd been reading his mind.

Montoya was familiar with the expression on the girl's face, could read it like a sign: Beware, Surly Teenager. His oldest daughter had been like that for a while. But last year she'd graduated from State and now, in a couple of weeks, she was getting married.

"Your name is Dawn?" He asked.

"Yeah."

"And your last name?"

Montoya noted an odd little beat of hesitation.

"Johnson," the girl said, then quickly added. "My mother's maiden name."

"And how old are you?"

"Sixteen."

"Not until next month," Trillig corrected, looking up at the ceiling.

She didn't look anywhere near 16. With the crap scrubbed off her face, Montoya would put her at 13, 14 at most. He nodded toward the girl's belly

"And the father's age?"

"Of my baby? Seventeen."

"Sixteen," Trillig corrected once again. "Both are just a couple of kids. Babies making babies." He shook his head, sadly.

"And what are your plans after the baby arrives; going back to school?" Thinking of his own daughter, Montoya had to ask.

She shrugged. "I'll be taking care of the baby," the girl said firmly.

"That's still up for debate," Trillig said.

She glared into midspace. "I'm keeping it!"

"OK, OK. Let's not get into that again right now."

This all sounded too familiar. He looked at his watch. He had wanted to wear his black mariachi suit for the wedding, but his daughter was insisting on a tuxedo. In an hour, he was due to meet his wife for the fitting. If he were late, she would give him hell.

"May I be excused now?" The girl was not really asking.

Trillig deferred to him. "Officer?"

"Sure. Thanks, for your cooperation, young lady. Good luck with the delivery."

For the first time she smiled. Maybe she'd get to keep it. Montoya was on her side of that debate.

Trillig walked him to the door. "As for the screaming ..." He directed his chin toward the parrot. "I imagine it was old Poncho Villa the neighbor heard. Clearly, we're not 'Father Knows Best' here, Officer Montoya, but I am trying, and I've never given my daughter occasion to scream, though sometimes she screams at me anyway."

Montoya nodded. It wasn't always easy to be a father, he understood that, understood screaming daughters. And though he hadn't been happy with the news of his daughter's pregnancy, he was happy to be a granddad, couldn't imagine life without his Camotita. His little sweet potato, that's what he called her.

As he got into the patrol car, something nagged at him. He couldn't quite determine what it was, but something didn't settle right in his gut. What, for instance, would make a parrot crazy like that, screaming and plucking out his feathers? And the kid's hesitation when he asked for her last name. He wondered if maybe there was a custody thing going on here. Wondered if the ex even knew where her daughter was.

Once the cop was out of the door, James began to chuckle. That Dawn. What a character! When he first picked her up from the streets, she was a wormy little kid with pinkeye, for God's sake. Now she was the best. But he had to be careful how he handled her. Dawn liked to be the one in control. He'd figured that out early on. He never said *I love you*, not to Dawn, even though some part of him did. No. Better with Dawn to praise, emphasize their partnership, the reciprocal deal.

With every kid you had to find a key. Dante was the just the opposite of Dawn. He wanted limits, wanted to be controlled, needed a firm father figure. And there was poor little Honey who didn't seem to need much more than peanut butter sandwiches and hugs. He was having trouble figuring out the new ones. They didn't speak English, and both of them were still very resistant, not that resistance was such a bad thing. On the contrary, resistance sold well. Still, for management's sake, he preferred complacency.

Well, he'd be rid of them soon. There was no hurry, though. He could wait. Bids were just starting to come in.

Dawn stormed back into the living room. "So why can't I keep the baby?" She demanded.

Pretending that he didn't hear what she'd just said, he opened his arms wide, giving her two thumbs up. "Congratulations. That was quite a performance! You're the best, Dawn."

"Answer my question."

He smiled, brows raised in friendly curiosity. "What question was that?"

"Why can't I keep the baby?"

"The show's over. This is reality now, Dawn."

Hand on hip, she was glaring at him. "Why can't I keep the baby? It's your baby, too."

"Hold on there, kiddo. At my age, I'm probably shooting blanks. But as far as keeping the baby goes, you need to keep your mind on the prize here. At this stage in your life, do you really need a baby? Think about it. A baby would put your entire career on indefinite hold."

He sat down beside her on the couch and flung his arm around her companionably. "You were really terrific with that cop. The best. Oscar material, I swear."

"Yeah, except I almost screwed up when the cop asked me my last name."

"You handled it beautifully. That maiden name thing, a genius detail. Acting is all in the detail, Dawn. All in the detail."

"So what is your last name?"

"Nobody has a last name in this business, Dawn, not even you. But pretty soon you're going to be at the point where you'll need one. Then you can take your pick, but whatever name you choose, it's going to be on everybody's lips. That's for sure."

Back at the station, Montoya put on the reading glasses he'd recently purchased at Walgreens. He filled out a hasty report and then dialed the neighbor. "Mrs. Stillman? Officer Montoya, here."

"Yes, officer. Well?"

"It turns out they have a parrot."

"A parrot? I don't understand what that has to do …"

"A screaming parrot."

"Officer Montoya, for 34 years I taught fifth grade, and I can assure you that I know the difference between a screaming child and a screaming parrot."

"Well there is a child living there too, a teenage girl. I think you mentioned seeing her?"

"Yes, but I haven't seen her recently."

"Well, I have, and she looked … she didn't show any signs of abuse, Mrs. Stillman, though I imagine, the two of them, the girl and her father, might have had a few shouting matches."

"This wasn't shouting, Officer Montoya. This was screaming, a child screaming for mercy. I know what I heard. They say it takes a village …"

"Yes, and I appreciate that, but I'm pretty certain what you heard was a parrot. For now it seems everything is OK over there. And I do thank you for your concern."

"You're welcome," she said stiffly.

"Ah, Mrs. Stillman?"

"Yes, officer."

"You just never know. Keep your eyes and ears open. If you have any other concerns about this girl's welfare, her name is Dawn by the way, please let me know."

Montoya gave her his extension number and hung up the phone. He frowned. That girl. Something sure didn't sit right. "Almost 16." He shook his head. "Like hell."

He looked at his watch. He was as good as late already. How long would it take to google the guy. He typed in James Trillig, scrolled through the listings. As promised, it was all there and pretty humdrum. O'Mally's Chevrolet, Fit and Flexible Yoga Center, a few political spots, mostly state Legislature. There were dozens of entries, verifying that Trillig was indeed a videographer, and one who probably wasn't trying to hide from his ex.

He turned the computer off and hurried to meet his wife. Most likely, she'd have Junior and Camotita in tow. Cute kids, adorable actually. As ring bearer and flower girl, he imagined they'd steal the show.

Stokey leaned back against the pillow and sighed the contented sigh of a man freshly laid after a long hiatus. After installing the computer, they'd gone out to a nearby steak house and drunk a bottle of Cabernet – and now she lay beside him, round breasts crushed against his side, fingers trailing through the hair on his chest.

"Man. Did I need that." And as he said it, it occurred to him that possibly she had made love to him so that need wouldn't send him into someone else's bed. If that was her motivation, he was happy at this moment to be the beneficiary of her insecurity. He let his hand play over the crepe of her belly, the result of her second pregnancy. She hated it, but he loved its velvet warmth, loved to nuzzle her there, before inching down into the soft red bush, then rolling his tongue into the cleft and over the clitoris, round and hard as a marble.

From beneath the sheet, emanated the sweet, ripe aroma of their sex, and his penis began a recovery. On the dresser he noticed a family picture. It was the same one he had on his desk at the station. He considered their conversation of a week ago, wanted to say something that would make her feel guilty. She had certainly put a guilt trip on him. Mostly he wanted to say something that would convince her to come back home so she would be next to him in bed every night.

"This last time in Iraq, I think I would have shot myself in the head if I hadn't had you to come home to."

She sat up abruptly, swaying breasts soft and white as Wonder Bread. "God, I hope that's not true."

He had to think about it for a moment. No, it was not true. He wasn't the type to shoot himself, but what was he supposed to say now? "Some guys did, you know. They'd get a Dear John and shoot themselves in the head. It happens."

"But you'd never do such a thing!"

"Hard to say. Iraq's a different world. Hard to say what a person could be driven to do." There. He'd leave it at that.

Becka rolled out of bed. She'd put on a little weight recently and it looked good on her. Stokey admired her round bottom, jiggling prettily as she made her way into the bathroom. Her legs, a bit heavy on top, tapered down to trim knees, nicely rounded calves and ankles so slim he could encircle them with thumb and forefinger. And her feet, somehow he'd forgotten about those feet and their beautiful, sensitive, high arches. His erection was now tenting the sheets. "Come back to bed for a minute, can't you?"

"It's getting late."

Still rummy from sex and wanting more, he didn't get it at first. "So?"

"So you better get going."

"Jesus! It's a two-hour drive back to Douglas." He heard her turn on the shower. "Becka?"

She poked her head out of the bathroom. "Sorry. Maybe you

should get a motel."

"I can't believe this." He threw back the sheet, his erection collapsing, and stormed into the bathroom. "Why can't I stay here with you?"

"Because if I let you stay, I might get used to it." She turned off the shower now, tucked a towel around her.

He stood there naked, arms folded across his chest. "What's wrong with that?"

"They're sending more troops to Afghanistan. What happens when you're redeployed, say, for another 18 months?"

"What was I when you married me?"

She grabbed a pack of cigarettes off the nightstand, thought better of it, and tossed the pack onto the bed. "A Marine."

"I still am."

"Good. Be all that you can be."

"That's Army."

The red freckles across her chest and shoulders deepened in hue. "Right. Semper Fi. Ever faithful, how could I forget?"

He wiped his hand over his head. "God. Here we go again. I thought we'd gotten beyond that."

"I guess *we* were wrong." She poured herself a glass of water, took several deep swallows. "You know, if it had happened in Iraq, I think maybe I could accept it. But you were home. Hadn't been back a month before you started fucking … what was her name? Something Mexican ending in an 'a.' Rosa? Flora? Maria? How do you think that made me feel?"

He had no answer for that. "I've told you a hundred times I'm sorry."

"Yes, but you never told me why? Why Stokey?"

He had no good answer for that either, just knew that it felt good to be with someone who hadn't known him from before, someone who had no expectations. "This is going to sound lame, but … when I got back, I knew you wanted to get pregnant, and, I don't know, I just couldn't handle it right then."

"That sounds beyond lame. You couldn't just tell me? You couldn't trust me to get it?"

He shook his head. "I didn't want you to get it. All that shit. I didn't want to … infect you, change you with it … to change what you thought of me."

"You went out and fucked another woman so I wouldn't change what I thought of you? Interesting explanation."

"What can I do to make it up to you?"

"Even if I knew, why would I tell you? So we could begin another cycle? You go off to war, suffer, come back, reward yourself with an affair, expect me to forgive you because you've been off to war? You chose that!" She rubbed a spot between her breasts. "I don't know what you can to do make *this* better, Stokey."

"But we were doing good, things were getting better. Then you just got up and left. Why is it that all of a sudden you didn't even want to try anymore?" He sat on the bed, felt the cigarette pack beneath his butt, got up and tossed the pack on the nightstand. "Is there someone else?"

"There's no one else. I wish there were. And it certainly was not all of a sudden." She paused, took another drink of water. "For how many months were we lying next to each other in bed. You're not asleep. I'm not asleep, but we're both pretending to be asleep. I'm not willing to pretend anymore. It never was only about Maria or whatever her name was. You have no idea what it's like, Stokey. You go to one of those places – Kuwait, Iraq, Afghanistan – they're all the same to me. And I'm trying not to think, not to feel. I'm walking around, cleaning, cooking, checking people out at Albertsons. I'm smiling, but at the core of me, there's this sucking hole. I'm afraid of the evening news, a knock on the front door fills me with dread. Who do I share all this with? Not you, not the kids. There's no one. Then you come back and expect everything to be the same as when you left. Pretty soon, very quietly, inch by inch you take over my life and then you're gone again? That's no life, or at least no life that I want to live. On top of that you go out and fuck some other woman? Who the hell do you think you are?"

He tried to put his arm around her but she shrugged it away.

"And who the hell do you think I am? Listen. I need to have something, be something. That's what I'm trying to do here, Stokey. I want to get a job that's more than an extra paycheck. And when I have a conversation, I want to be able to talk about books, politics, I don't know … quilting."

"You want to take up quilting?"

"No!"

"Then what is it you want, Becka?"

"I'm telling you; I've been telling you, but you just don't want to get it. Who the hell am I, Stokey? After 20 years, you tell me. And don't you dare say my wife or the mother of my kids."

"You're the one woman I've always loved," he said quietly.

"Very pretty. It used to be enough to be the little planet spinning around you and the kids, then you knocked me right out of orbit. Maybe that's a good thing. I want you to leave now, Stokey. I need a chance to breathe and I can't do it with you in my space."

He shook his head, and went to find his clothes. He thought he remembered leaving his shirt and pants in the living room. He didn't know where the hell his Jockeys were.

She followed him out into the living room. "I don't want to keep taking money from you. I'm looking for a better paying job, put in a dozen applications around town. You have no idea how hard I'm trying."

"Can you tell me very specifically, Becka, what it is you've been trying to do, day to day, for almost three months now?" he said, pulling up his pants over his bare ass.

"Like I said." She wiped a tear away with her thumb. "I'm just trying to breathe."

"Well, keep at it. Practice makes perfect." He took his jacket off the back of a kitchen chair, and headed for the door.

"Don't forget these," she said, flinging the undershorts at him.

Stuffing them in his jacket pocket, he charged for his truck.

"Shit! Goddamn! Fuck! He banged his palm into the dash. "Fuck!" He rested his forehead on the steering wheel a moment to let his fury subside, the smell of her still all over him, inescapable. The next time she needed something she could whistle down a goddamn well. He started the engine, took a deep breath, then pulled away from the curb, slowly, like a man in control.

Part 4

Awaiting Deliverance

Day 8

Wiona had gotten up once again determined to finish the Dickerson account. Warmed by a thermos of coffee and a fire in the little stove, she began the chore she'd been dreading for the past week. As she updated the books, Osa's head was pillowed companionably on her boot. In less time than it took her to finish the thermos she was done and wondered, as she often did, why she felt so burdened by bookkeeping.

Now she poured the last of her coffee and sat back to appreciate the spicy fragrance of burning juniper and morning calm, though the canyon was never quiet. The curve-bill thrasher had started up while it was still dark. At dawn the white-winged doves and the canyon wren joined in. One lone ground squirrel was piping from the woodpile.

Over the years, she'd come to think of the little office as her own private place. She had never felt that way about her bedroom. Both Emma and Frankie would burst in on her without so much as a knock on the door.

While her father was alive, the office was his sanctuary – no one would enter uninvited. Now it was hers.

The sun had crested the canyon wall but the barn was still dark and cold. She figured she'd clean the tack outside where it would be a little warmer. Quickly, she gathered up a small scrub brush, an old plastic garbage can, terry rags, saddle soap, Neatsfoot oil and Woolite – she liked to have everything at hand so she wouldn't have to interrupt herself once she got started.

In the shed she pulled the bridle and cinch off the horseshoe hooks attached to a post. One of the challenges of ranching was to find a way to use all the old horseshoes, a challenge her father had risen to. Every post had its horseshoe hook, every wall held shelves bracketed with horseshoes, the back of her office door had several on which to hang hats and jackets, in the old garden there was a rusting trellis made of rebar and horseshoes, and above every outside doorway, one was nailed for luck.

She hefted the saddle with its pad and blanket from the sawhorse where they'd been gathering dust all week, and took them outside. Wiona ran the hose into the garbage can, added Woolite to that, then put the saddle blanket, pad and cinch in to soak. While the can filled, she separated the headstall and reins from the bit. With a fingernail, she scraped a little of the greasy dirt away. One part dust, one part sweat, it combined into corrosive mud, which caked in the nooks and crannies where the leather looped over itself or the bit and buckles. These places she inspected closely, rubbing saddle soap into the leather with a terry rag. The bridle's throatlatch needed a few stitches, she noticed.

The sun was hitting her neck and back, loosening the tension that gathered there whenever she was at the computer. She rolled her shoulders; inhaled the soothing aroma of saddle soap and leather. Cleaning tack was one of those chores that took just the right amount of attention. A person's mind couldn't wonder too far.

This was the way she spent her life. So caught up with the day to day, she often didn't know how she felt about something until after it had long passed. Had no idea if this was a good thing or a bad thing.

She'd just laid the headstall aside and was about to start on the reins when Belen raced out the back door, the ends of her rebozo trailing behind like two blue wings.

"Esta su madre, Wiona," she yelled. "Se cayó! Ven! Apurase!"

She understood only the words mother and come, but Belen's tone was clear. Something bad had happened to Emma. She dropped the tack and ran for the kitchen.

Emma was lying on the linoleum, eyes closed. Dead? Was Emma dead? "Mother?" She knelt by her side. "Mother?"

Emma's eyes fluttered upon. "Dear girl, what have I wrought?"

Wiona noted the overturned stepladder, the old percolator on the floor. "Looks like you wrought a bad fall."

"What have I wrought?"

"Mother. You didn't wrought this. It was an accident. Tell me. Where do you hurt?"

Emma's faded blue eyes darted around the cardinal points of her body as if taking stock. "Everywhere, but nowhere in particular."

"Did you hit your head?"

"I don't think so."

Gently, Wiona ran her fingers over the grizzled head. No blood or knots that she could discern. "Wiggle your toes."

Emma complied.

"Now your fingers."

Emma wiggled her fingers, her hands, then flapped her arms a couple of times. "I'm going to die soon, Wiona. Can you ever forgive me? Maybe you can't forgive me, but can you understand what it was like?"

"What what was like?"

"Can you forgive me? Do you understand?"

Wiona understood nothing except that Emma was asking her forgiveness. She didn't know why or for which offense. There had been many. "It was an accident, Mother. You didn't mean to," she said, simply because it was too late for specifics. "Now, do you think you can get up?"

"Not right now, Wiona. Just fetch me the afghan and a pillow."

As Wiona got up from the floor, she realized that Belen was still standing in the doorway, rebozo covering her mouth. "Ella esta OK, yo pienso. Necesita …" Wiona couldn't think of the word for *rest*. "Ella esta OK," she repeated, and went to fetch the afghan and pillow.

Wiona cleaned the refrigerator while Emma dozed on the linoleum. Periodically, she paused to watch Emma's chest rise and fall. Part of her would be relieved to see the chest fall, never to rise again. She looked so peaceful lying there; surely it would be an easy passing. "Descansa," she whispered. The Spanish word for *rest* belatedly popping into her head. "Rest in peace."

It wasn't that she didn't care for Emma or wanted her to die. In some ways they were closer now then they'd ever been. But it was clear that her condition – she tried not to even think the word Alzheimer's – was growing steadily worse. They had no health insurance, and Emma wasn't eligible for Medicare until next year. What if she had to take her into emergency?

After the better part of an hour, she shook Emma's shoulder. "Time to get up now."

Emma opened her eyes. "Look under the table, Belva. Frankie's playing there with the baby."

"I'm Wiona, your daughter."

Emma squinted her eyes into focus. "You look so much like Belva."

Wiona should have felt flattered. Belva was Emma's older sister and favorite person in the world. But she'd died more than 10 years ago from pancreatic cancer. "Let's get you up now."

Emma sighed. "Not right this minute." She looked around the room. "I was having such a nice dream, something about you and Frankie."

"Come on. Get up now." She tugged at Emma's elbow.

"Bless your heart," she said, slapping at Wiona's hand. "Can't you just leave me be for once?"

"No. It's too cold there on the floor, Mother. Let's get you into the living room where it's warm and cozy. I'll get Belen in here and we'll help you to your feet."

"I don't need any help." Grunting, she rolled over and up onto all fours. Leaning hard on a kitchen chair, she got to her feet. Wiona offered an arm. Emma batted it away, eyes narrowed to lance points. "I told you; I don't need your goddamn help."

"Now, Mother …"

"Now, Mother, nothing." She headed, slow but steady, for the living room, Wiona following at a safe distance.

Once she settled herself on the recliner, Emma fell back into a deep slumber.

"Está bien?" Belen asked. Jesús, hidden beneath her rebozo, was at her breast.

"No sé, Belen. No sé." And she didn't know. She didn't know what to think or do. Should she take Emma to the emergency room? She would never go peaceably. She imagined the scene in the hospital, imagined Emma screaming *goddamn it, Wiona, bless your heart!*

Wiona reached out and brushed Emma's cool cheek with her fingertips. She didn't stir. Good Lord, she thought, covering her face with her hands. I don't dare bother Lucy again. She looked again at Emma, slack-mouthed now and snoring gently. Seeing her like this, helpless, made it much easier to love her.

As Wiona tucked the old afghan around her mother, her hand brushed against something wedged in the corner or the recliner, her mother's coin purse. She took the purse into the kitchen and counted the bills folded inside – $58, the remains of the emergency fund. She stuffed the fives and tens into her jeans pocket, but put all the ones, there were 13 of them, neatly folded back in the purse.

In the living room, she wedged the purse back into the corner of the recliner, figuring everyone, even her batty old mother, deserved to have a little stash of ready cash.

Stokey awoke to the smell of bacon. He looked at the clock. It was past 9. When he was home, Sunday was his day to make pancakes, a tradition that dated back to Jackson's birth. He pulled on sweats over his shorts and padded out to the kitchen barefoot.

Katie stood over a pan of bacon that was just beginning to crisp, while Jacks studied the back of the Bisquick box.

"Dad!" Katie said. "You're home. I thought maybe …"

"Nope," he said, cutting her off. "Just got in late; I guess I overslept." He patted Jackson on the shoulder as he walked by. "Morning, son."

"Morning, Dad." Jackson opened the refrigerator and pulled out a carton of eggs and a half-gallon jug of milk. "Don't you do something to the milk?"

"Squeeze a lemon in about a cup and a half of milk, when it curdles, mix it into the Bisquick, then add some of that bacon grease to it."

"How much bacon grease?"

"I don't know, tablespoon or so. Want me to do it?"

"I've got it."

Feeling displaced, Stokey looked around the kitchen for something to do. "Hmm. It looks like everything's under control in here. I guess I'll just set the table."

"So how was Mom?" Katie asked.

He didn't want to talk about Mom. "You put the plates in the oven to warm, Sissy?"

"Yup. So how was Mom?"

"Got the computer set up."

"Good. So what's Mom been up to?" She was determined, apparently, to find out how the evening had progressed and just why he didn't stay overnight.

"Been practicing her breathing." To preclude any more questions, he added. "I don't see the paper. Did anybody bring it in yet? No? Then I'll just go fetch it."

He took his time, pausing in the front yard to look at the sports page. Though he couldn't quite focus on the words, he did look at the pictures. Other than the D-backs, he didn't follow baseball much, and college basketball, which he did follow, had been a disappointment – the U of A losing again in the Final Four. The pros didn't interest him much. Just a bunch of way overpaid druggies and prima donnas, was the way he saw it.

He felt himself getting angry at Becka all over again. Should just give up on her, but 20 years. He rubbed his knuckles across his head. What he did was wrong, way wrong, but all those years he'd never strayed before, not once. He didn't even remember anymore what the burning attraction was, except that he wanted … Shit what was it he had wanted from her? Oblivion? Maybe. Maybe just a few hours of oblivion.

Stokey's feet were getting cold, but he was reluctant to go back inside and face Katie the inquisitor. He glanced at the front page. A mistake. More car bombs in Baghdad. Baghdad! When he'd left, Baghdad had been pretty secure.

Disgusted, he scanned the remaining headlines. His attention was caught by one in the bottom, left-hand corner of the paper. *Girl Snatched Walking to School Bus.* He read the first dozen lines. The kid was only 6. With all the creeps and crazies running around, you'd have to be nuts to let your 6-year-old walk to the school bus stop alone.

His thoughts turned to Belen's children. What were their names? Edgar was the boy. He couldn't remember the girl's name and that troubled him.

It had been a week since the kidnapping. If the kids were being held for ransom, the father would have heard something by now. That left him with the other sick possibilities. He didn't want to think of those now, but it was too late. He'd already lost his appetite for pancakes.

Sunday. It flowed before him like a river of molasses. He started back up the drive. When he passed his truck he noticed the juniper posts he'd loaded back there last week. Should have delivered those to Wiona yesterday, he thought, and the day seemed a little shorter.

Back in the house, he snatched a couple pieces of the bacon

from the plate warming in the oven and watched his son flip over the first batch of pancakes – not a pretty sight. "So Jackson? What's on your agenda?"

The boy shrugged, flipped another splat of batter.

"OK. Sounds good. How about you, Sissy?"

"Maybe drive into Tucson with Darin. Maybe go to the mall or see a movie. Oh yeah, before I forget. Grandma just called to remind you of Grandpa's colonoscopy Wednesday."

"Got it covered."

"So what're you doing today?"

"Thought I'd take those juniper posts over to the Rutherford's place, been putting it off. Maybe help repair her corral." He sat at the table, reached beneath and patted Shorty's rump.

"Wiona Rutherford?" She put three plates on the table. Set out knives and forks, paper napkins, butter, a small pitcher of warm maple syrup. "I'm pretty sure she's got the hots for Dr. Lucy."

"Lucy Altamirano? Hmm." He munched the bacon with studied indifference. "What makes you think so?"

Katie held her father's gaze for a moment before speaking. "Wiona was in the clinic this past week with some Mexican woman and a baby. I don't know what the deal is there, maybe it's her housekeeper or something. Anyway, when she sees Dr. Lucy, well, her face gets all red and she can't quite meet her eyes, but if Dr. Lucy's not watching, Wiona looks at her with – I don't know – this intensity. I can't quite say what all, but a woman can just tell these things, Dad."

Stokey considered this information. To his mind, Katie was still more girl than woman, so he didn't know how much faith to have in her intuition.

Though it was after noon, Dawn was still in her pajamas – plaid flannel bottoms and a T-shirt stretched tight over her belly. IPod in place, she was searching the new Weekly James had brought her from the grocery store for pictures to add to her fashion album. She had decided to reorganize the pages into categories. She had one section for swimwear, one for sporty, one for evening wear and one for accessories. Once she got to Hollywood, she'd know exactly what she needed to wear for any occasion. She found a good one of Gwen Stefani wearing white knit shorts and sweater for the sporty category. Carefully she began to cut it out, singing along with Pink, head bobbing.

There was a knock at the door. "Come in," she called, knowing it could only be James.

He stuck his head in the door, smiling. "Guess what?"

She hated it when James said that, like something really cool was about to happen. Nothing cool ever happened around here. She ignored him.

"Dawn? Take out the iPod, a sec."

She removed the earplugs, but didn't look at him. She was still mad about the baby and wanted him to know it.

"Doc says it's time. Isn't that great? Pretty soon you'll be your old self."

How could it be time? Aren't you supposed to have like cramps or something when the baby's ready to be born?

"I know what you're thinking, but Doc's going to give you something to make the baby come. That way there won't be any midnight emergencies. Right? And he's going to give you something so there won't be any pain."

She put her scissors down. "Like what?"

"Just a little shot."

"I don't want a shot."

"Just a little one so you won't feel any pain. Come on now, Dawn. We've gone over this before. Doc's going to deliver the baby at his clinic. It's going to go to a good home, plenty of money and love. The best possible place. Then in a week or so, we'll go on that shopping spree. A whole new wardrobe, inside to out, once the baby's gone."

She slipped the photo into a plastic sleeve, then turned another page of the Weekly. There was a photo of Jessica Simpson in a pair of red high-heel boots that came up to her thighs. She picked up the scissors and began cutting. From the corner of her eye, she saw him standing beside James, heard his squish, squish as he crossed the room.

She didn't resist when he took her arm. Didn't resist when he pinched her skin. Didn't flinch when she felt the quick, stinging jab of the needle. Didn't even blink.

Frances Stillman just happened to be looking out the window when she saw him pull out of the garage. There was another man in the passenger seat. One of those up-to-no-good fellows she was almost certain she had seen more than once before.

As soon as the car was out of sight, she decided to take the opportunity to have a look around for herself. After all, Officer Montoya had asked her to keep her eyes and ears open. She couldn't do that very well from inside her own home, now could she?

"Pogo? Come on Pogo." The little dog came trotting in, tail wagging with great enthusiasm. "We're going for a walk." She attached the red leash to the red collar.

When she got to the man's front yard, she looked around to see who might be watching, then bent over as if to tie her shoe. Instead, she unclipped Pogo's leash. When she stood up, the dog trotted across the white quartz, pausing here and there to savor the aroma of a particular spot.

"Oh, my, Pogo! Come back here." She hurried after the dog as it sniffed its way around the side of the house. There were two windows on this side. Both were shuttered in the same manner as those in the front. A six-foot high fence enclosed the back yard, its wood planks weathered and silvery. She peered though the crack between the fence and the gate, but couldn't see much. She tried the latch. To her amazement, the gate was unlocked. Heart beating wildly, she pushed the gate open intending only to take a peek. Pogo bolted through, leaving her no choice but to follow.

The back yard was worse than the front, just dirt and tall dried weeds. There was a swimming pool, but it looked as though it hadn't held water in years. There were cracks in the bottom and more weeds grew from these. Turning towards the back of the house, she noticed that the windows and a sliding door were draped rather than shuttered. Something struck her as odd about those drapes. She studied them for some moments until she finally realized what was wrong. "Strange," she whispered, drawing nearer. The pattern, a faded floral, was facing out rather than in. In fact, they weren't drapes at all, but appeared to be fabric or perhaps it was wallpaper pasted on the window, but no. It wasn't pasted on the pane itself, but on something else, plywood perhaps, pressed against the sliding glass door and the same on the windows.

"Very strange." Why would he seal off these windows, she wondered. Wouldn't that constitute a hazard if there were a fire? There was definitely something going on here, something peculiar and, she knew this in her viscera, very wicked.

Though it was a warmish afternoon, suddenly she felt chilled, vulnerable. "Pogo," she called. The dog came happily. Snapping the leash back on his collar she hurried back through the gate, careful to close it behind her.

Osa was barking in the yard. Wiona looked out the window. "Stokey." What in the world, she thought, then remembered the juniper posts. "Damn."

She strode out to the corral where he had parked his truck. "Morning, Stokey. I'm afraid we're in a terrible mess here right now."

"How's that?"

"Mother took a fall this morning. I think she's OK, but …"

"Well, you just go on about your business, Wiona. I'll take care of this."

She shook her head. Those calves needed bringing in and the corral needed fixing, and Emma needed watching. "Thanks, Stokey. I got to admit, I could really use the help. Can I bring you some coffee, at least?"

"No thanks." He started unloading a half dozen stout posts. "And you're welcome. Should have done it yesterday but I got busy. How's Belen and the baby?"

"The baby's doing good, and Belen's feeling stronger." She shook her head. "But I can't imagine."

Stokey nodded. Neither could he.

Montoya looked at his watch and was startled to see that the better part of Sunday morning was spent. He'd intended to work only an hour or so to catch up on paperwork then meet the family for the 12 o'clock Mass.

He rose from his desk, tucking his glasses into his shirt pocket. Just then the phone rang. He ignored it. If he left right now, he'd still make it. The phone rang again. Why would anybody call him on a Sunday? He picked up the receiver, determined to make it quick.

"Officer Montoya? Thank God. It's me, Frances Stillman."

She sounded a little breathless. Montoya glanced at his watch again. "Yes, Mrs. Stillman," he said, trying to hurry her to the point.

"I'm so glad I caught you in; didn't think you'd be working on Sunday, but I took a chance. I need to tell you what happened just now on our walk. Pogo and I take a walk every day and well, I'm not sure how it happened exactly, but he got away from me right in front of the next-door neighbor's house, the one with the parrot. The little dickens ran down the side of the house and, wouldn't you know it, into the back yard. I called and I called, but Pogo wouldn't come. Well what could I do? I followed Pogo back there and …"

As she spoke, Montoya was getting a mental image that didn't quite jibe with Mrs. Stillman's account. "Excuse me, Mrs. Stillman, but I seem to remember a fence."

"Oh yes, there is a fence, but it has a gate and ... well, I suppose someone must have left it open. Anyway, as I was saying, I followed Pogo into the back yard and while I was getting him back on his leash I noticed something peculiar, something very peculiar." She paused now, as if waiting for encouragement.

"And what was that?"

When he finally hung up the phone Mass was not quite underway, but he had to agree with Mrs. Stillman. Something very peculiar was going on in that house, though feelings of the "viscera" were not the kind of evidence that would produce a search warrant.

He sat for a moment staring at the photograph he'd received last Father's Day sitting prominently on his desk. In it, Camotita and Junior sat smiling amid his wife and daughters. His was a beautiful family. Junior and his girls, lean and dark, took after him, but Camotita had her grandmother's beautiful lips, plump round face and light brown hair.

Then there was James Trillig and Dawn – father and daughter, yet there was no resemblance between them and none of the flashing intensity that he experienced with his own children in times of anger. Every family was different, he supposed.

He needed more to go on. He'd tried to impress upon Mrs. Stillman that trespass was going beyond keeping her eyes and ears open, and might even put her in harm's way. Nothing more, he hoped, would be coming from Mrs. Stillman's investigation.

It occurred to him then that the mariachi band's bass player was a manager for the department of sanitation. Sunday, he should be home. Montoya picked up the phone and dialed his number. When he heard his friend's voice he greeted him, "Hola Compa. Qué onda?"

The setting sun hung a fist width above the canyon rim. Wiona stood at the front window, one ear cocked for Emma, as Stokey replaced the last of the posts along the alley leading to the squeeze chute. The day had gotten away from her. She hadn't even offered him lunch, her neck felt hot with embarrassment. Except for the five minutes it had taken Emma to eat a piece of toast with peanut butter and make a trip to the bathroom, she had spent the morning and a good chunk of the afternoon sleeping in her chair. Well, either Emma would snap out of it or she'd quietly sleep away what was left of her life. How bad could that be?

Belen came in with a tray. "Sopa de arroz con pollo," she announced.

There were two steaming bowls of chicken and rice soup and some tortillas wrapped in a dishcloth to keep them warm. Wiona inhaled the aroma of cilantro and suddenly she realized that she hadn't eaten lunch either. "Muchas gracias, Belen." She took the tray and set it on the coffee table.

"Wake up now, Mother." She took Emma's hand and gave it a little shake. "Belen's made us some nice chicken soup for supper."

Emma opened one eye. "Belen?"

"Gaby's sister."

"Oh. Well, I'm not hungry." She shut her eyes as if for emphasis.

Not hungry? Wiona sat on an ottoman spooning soup into her mouth while she considered the woman lying in the recliner, pudgy arms resting on the soft mound of her stomach. Emma might have lost her mind, but she'd never in her life lost her appetite.

"Mmm. This is really good soup, Mother. Lots of chicken. And oh look, Belen made fresh corn tortillas." Wiona sat back and took a bite of tortilla. "Still warm."

Emma popped the recliner into sitting position. "Well, maybe I could eat a bite."

Wiona set the tray on Emma's lap, watched her roll the tortilla so she could use it as a scoop, watched her face close down in concentration as she chewed.

"Is there more?" She asked before she had even finished the first bowl, and Wiona knew that Emma would recover, though recover was probably not the right word to use in this case.

Wiona poured what remained of her own soup into Emma's bowl. "I'll be out by the corral if you need me." She grabbed the cord jacket from the hall tree. In the kitchen she slipped two juice glasses into her pocket, and stepped out the back door.

"Hey Stokey," she called, striding toward the corral. "I can't invite you in for a beer. Mother won't allow it in the house, but there's chicken soup and fresh corn tortillas."

"Thanks, but I probably should get going."

Wiona held the Powder River panels steady while he bolted them in place. She noticed that he'd replaced the pulley ropes on the squeeze shoot. "Thanks, Stokey. I've been meaning to get that. Hey, I've got some Jose Cuervo out in my office. How about that?"

"Hmm." Squinting into the setting sun, he pulled off his gloves. "I'll take you up on that offer, but I need a little wash-up first."

"Meet you out there."

She set the glasses on her desk and began rolling a few pages of old newspaper into doughnuts. These she put in the stove, topped them with twigs of mesquite. Stokey had become a good, decent man, she was thinking. As she balanced two pieces of split juniper on top of the twigs she wondered why his wife had left him.

By the time Stokey arrived, she had the fire going and two fingers of tequila poured for each of them. She handed him a glass. He sank down on the cot, legs nearly touching the opposite wall. She raised her glass to him. "I really appreciate what you've done for me today. With all that's been going on, I don't know when I'd have gotten to it."

"My pleasure." He touched his glass to hers, took a sip. "I oiled all the pins on the squeeze chute, so you should be ready for branding. When's roundup?"

"Hell or high water, next Saturday."

"Who's going to help you?"

"Gaby and Beto."

"That enough?"

Wiona took a sip of tequila, held it in her mouth until her tongue burned, then swallowed. "Lucy Altamirano said she'd help."

"Dr. Lucy?"

"The same."

"Will four people be enough?"

"It's going to have to be."

"Well, Saturday, if I'm not working, I'll lend a hand. Used to be pretty good with a brand."

"After what you've already done? I couldn't ask."

Stokey knocked back his tequila. "I'm offering."

Belen glanced around the beautiful kitchen. She especially loved the pantry with its shelves lined with neat rows of canned tuna, beans, corn, peas, tomatoes. There were jars of pickles, relish, jams, sacks of rice, potatoes and onions, a box of apples, a stack of toilet paper and another of paper towels, a big box of laundry soap. So much abundance, yet Wiona seemed so unhappy.

Belen ladled another bowl of soup for la vieja. The old woman had the mind of a child, it seemed, but the appetite of a grown man. Her own grandmother was like that toward the end, but sweeter than this one, and not so hungry. And what a temper, though she directed it mostly at the daughter. Too bad. Wiona was kind, a good, hard worker. She deserved a happy life, a husband and children. It wasn't too late.

Through the kitchen window she watched the sun sink below the canyon rim, leaving behind a slender ribbon of crimson. The man from la Migra, she didn't remember his name, had been working all afternoon. Perhaps this man and Wiona were more then friends. Belen hoped so. Life was difficult enough. Sometimes it pressed down so hard on your heart, you wanted to die just to escape the pain of it. No one should have to go through life alone.

Jesús, fist at his mouth, was making little mewing sounds from his plastic cradle. Yes, her pain was great, but gracias a Dios, she was not alone. She had this sweet one to ease her heart and tonight Jacabo would call. Together they would pray.

Wiona poured more tequila into Stokey's glass. He'd been telling her tales of the good old days, with Frankie.

"Frankie was just a natural," he was saying. "Good at everything he took a hand at, quarterback in the fall, pitcher in spring. Fact is, Frankie and I were as much rivals as friends, always going after the same things. If I liked a girl, next thing I knew, Frankie was going after her. If he hadn't been your brother, I figure he'd have been the one dating you instead of me."

Considering this, Wiona sucked in her bottom lip then dribbled a bit more tequila into her glass. "I think you underrate yourself, Stokey. And you definitely overrate my brother." Suddenly sweat was pearling on her forehead and upper lip. She took off her jacket. Unbuttoned the cuffs of her faded blue work shirt and rolled up the sleeves. Beneath the shirt she wore an old waffled, long-sleeved undershirt. It had belonged to her father and had holes in the armpits. She unbuttoned the front of her shirt, would have flung it off but for those holes and the fact that she wasn't wearing a bra, not that she had much on top to worry about. She opened the shirt, flapped it like a bird flaps its wings. "That stove's really cranking out heat."

"It's the tequila," Stokey offered. The fire in the stove cast a glow on Wiona's cheeks. Suddenly he was conscious of her tired beauty, her long legs, sprawled and strong from all that riding around chasing cows. He rearranged his legs. Sometimes it scared him how the little head could take over the controls while the big head was in default mode. What the hell, he thought. Might as well ask and get it over with.

"I know this is none of my business, but blame my nosiness on the tequila, too. You're an attractive, competent woman, why is it that you've never married?"

"I guess I've never … Hell I don't know."

Katie tells me you're in love with Dr. Lucy."

Caught off guard, Wiona let out a strangled little giggle.

"I wouldn't hold it against you. One of my best soldiers was a dyke, I mean a lesbian, or gay I guess is the politically correct term these days. So are you, I mean, gay?"

Wiona grabbed hold of her braid and brushed the tip of it across her damp brow. "Gay? Well, I'm not particularly unhappy, all things considered and put into perspective, but gay?"

"Come on, you know what I mean."

She shrugged. "I guess I've never given it any thought. But then, I'm finding out, there're lots of things I've never given any thought."

"Hmm. Well, you don't have to answer. As I said, it's none of my business anyway."

"It's OK." Wiona tossed the braid back over her shoulder. "There's only one thing I know for sure, except for Mother, who's losing it one button at a time, God bless her, and an illegal alien in my spare bedroom, I am alone. I haven't had sex with anyone, man or woman, in over 20 years." She paused a moment. "In fact, now that you bring it up, you were the last."

Stokey jerked to attention. "Remarkable!"

"Yeah, well. I suppose that's one way to look at it."

"Whatever, it makes no difference to me. You're a fine woman."

"Thanks, Stokey."

"I admire the hell out of you."

"Well, thanks, Stokey."

"Don't mention …" He belched into his fist. "It." He was quiet for a moment. "Wiona, I've been wanting to say this for a long time, sort of clear my mind of it once and for all."

"Clear away."

"I feel I owe you an apology for what happened back then. I think I took something you hadn't really offered."

"You're talking about the time a million years ago we screwed in the bed of your truck?"

Stokey was a little abashed that she'd put it so baldly. "Well, yes. I want to say I'm sorry, is all."

"Well don't be." She watched the flames, orange shot with oxidized blue, tongue the juniper logs like a coyote might a bone. The tequila made her feel reckless, made her want to do a little clearing away of her own. "Stokey?"

"What is it, honey."

"Since we're blaming everything on tequila ..." She hesitated, not knowing exactly how to begin. "Can I tell you something, just you, not Becka or Katie or your friends at work or anybody else?"

"Certainly."

She leaned forward, elbows resting on her knees. "That night in the back of the truck? I was already pregnant."

"How can that be? It was the first, the only time we ever did it." He paused a moment to reflect. "Hmm ... OK. So can I ask who?"

"Your old friend and rival. In fact, it was Frankie that put me up to it. Said if I had sex with you, everybody, including you, would naturally figure the baby was yours."

"Wait. You're going too fast. I can't ..."

"Can't what? Imagine your friend and rival and me? Frankie'd been at me in some way or another since I was little, but I didn't understand it and he didn't actually ... the first time was the summer before you guys joined the Marines."

"So you and Frankie ... I don't know what to say."

"You don't have to say anything."

"So what happened to the baby?"

"When I couldn't follow through with the scheme to make you the father of Frankie's child, I snuck up to Tucson and had an abortion. Funny thing is, Frankie never seemed to notice. Never asked a thing about it. I guess he figured ... well I don't know what he figured."

"Wow." He shook his head. "Back when we were going together, if I'd realize I was in competition with your brother, I'd have tried harder."

"It wasn't like that, Stokey."

"No? What was it like?"

Wiona's mouth went dry. "It was like rape." There, she'd said it.

"Pardon me for being skeptical, Wiona, but I know what it takes to get a big strong girl out of her jeans. It takes cooperation. As I recall, you had no problems fending me off."

"That's because you lacked determination, Stokey. You didn't sock me in the jaw or punch me in the gut."

He ducked his head. "God, Wiona. Frankie?"

Wiona shrugged.

Stokey took out a handkerchief and swabbed the perspiration from his head. "I'm sorry. Sometimes I'm such an asshole."

"It's OK, Stokey. I guess you can't help yourself."

His face collapsed. She must have hit a nerve. Well good. She held up a hand to keep him from talking. "To my mother, Frankie was God's greatest gift. He was the football hero, the war hero, everybody's hero, mine too, in a way. Anyway, so now you know." She sat back then, feeling relieved. No it wasn't relief, exactly. But what was it? She drained the last of her tequila. Satisfied that she'd burst the Frankie bubble, she allowed herself a little smile.

She poured more tequila. "Now it's your turn."

"To spill by guts? Not much to spill, I'm afraid. My wife moved out."

"So I've heard. Do you miss her?"

He nodded.

"Is there another man?"

"I don't think so. It has more to do with … how did she put it? Breathing and space and finding out who she is. That kind of bullshit."

"So you think maybe she still loves you?"

"I'm not sure. My guess would be no."

"So why are you guessing? Why don't you just ask her?"

"Hmm." Frowning, he shook his head. "Don't know. Maybe I'm not ready to hear the answer."

Stokey looked so sad then, Wiona reached over and patted his knee. "For whatever it's worth, I think your wife's a damn fool."

He hung his head for a moment, then met her eyes. "I cheated on her, is one reason why she left. Apparently there's a long list of other reasons, too."

"I'm sorry to hear that. I figured you for better."

"Yeah, well … the biggest mistake of my life. I'd have saved myself a world of hurt if I'd just shot myself in the head."

"Stokey?"

"Yeah?"

"You're still a pretty good guy."

"Thanks, honey. Nice to know somebody thinks so."

After coffee and a couple bowls of chicken soup, Stokey was almost fit to drive. As he pulled onto Highway 80 he considered Wiona's revelation. Sure, he'd seen a rough side of Frankie, they'd all been kind of rough in those days, especially before shipping out, but rape. In boot camp, Frankie had been accused of using too much persuasion with one pretty little Marine, but nobody had called it rape. Still, he believed Wiona. What she said rang true. He remembered Frankie saying, "Once you've worked the girl's panties off and everything is in place, you're supposed to back off just because she suddenly has second thoughts?" Stokey was ashamed to admit it, but at the time, he'd probably agreed.

Day 9

Head muzzy and dully throbbing, Wiona awoke to a man in a lavender suit and shiny purple tie shouting, "Good morning, Jesus!" His *Jesus* had three syllables in it.

Last night, after Stokey left, Emma had refused to get out of the recliner. Still a bit drunk and too tired to fight, Wiona made a bed for herself on the couch in case she was needed in the night. Now the man in lavender threw up his arms. "I want to hear you all say, 'Good morning, Jesus!'"

"Good morning, Jesus!" Emma obeyed.

Wiona noted that Emma's *Jesus* had only two syllables, which was probably because hers was a Methodist Jesus.

She recalled last night's conversation with Stokey. Even sober, she didn't regret a word she'd uttered, but if his daughter Katie thought she was a lesbian, who else held the same opinion? Did it matter? She felt a twinge of mortification to go with the headache.

And so the new day began.

Wiona unfolded herself from the couch, stretched out the kinks and headed for the kitchen to make coffee. Belen was already there. The coffee was hot and she was bathing the baby in the plastic crib that was now a bathtub.

"Good morning, Jesús!" Wiona said using the three-syllable version and wiggling the baby's tiny toe.

"Buenos dias," Belen called over her shoulder. She was wearing another one of Emma's housecoats, this one printed with daisies, and an old gray cardigan.

"Buenos dias." Wiona poured a cup of coffee and stood for a moment transfixed as Belen deftly washed the baby. Jesús, slick as a little trout, kicked his legs in spasmodic response to the warm water Belen trickled over his head. When Belen finished washing the folds around his neck, she wrapped him tightly in a towel that had been warming in front of the oven and offered him to Wiona, so she could dry the plastic tub and turn it back into a crib.

Wiona set her coffee cup down and accepted the warm bundle, examined the round face, the unfocused eyes that were still a slaty blue rather than the coffee they would become.

As she watched Jesús, she felt that blue, fist-sized muscle knock against her sternum. I would have made a good mother, she thought, running a finger over the perfect head with its feathery black hair. If she had kept her baby, life would have been totally different, she knew, but would it have been better? After a moment's consideration, she concluded that it would have been harder probably, but sweeter. At the time it had seemed impossible. Emma, such a stern, conventional Christian, would have been outraged and shamed. It would have been hard enough to face her, but the one she had really feared was her father, feared his disappointment. And what would she have told him when he demanded to know the name of the father?

Belen reclaimed her child then unbuttoned the front of her housecoat. For a moment Wiona watched the baby tug at the nipple, hands groping then settling on the warm breast marbled with pale blue veins.

So little, but with such an intense need, she thought. No one would ever need her that way. She sighed, took another sip of coffee, then set the cup aside.

Bad head or not, the saddle blanket, pads and cinch were still lying out by the barn. They needed to be rinsed and hung out to dry.

Before heading out to the barn she went to check on Emma who was again dozing, hand gripping the remote. Wiona became aware of a warm, yeasty odor rising from the recliner, noted Emma's hair, weighed down with oil.

"Mother, wake up."

"What? I'm not sleeping."

"You need to take a bath before breakfast."

"I took one yesterday."

"Not yesterday. Remember, yesterday you fell down so you didn't get around to it."

"Then it was the day before."

"Not then either, not even the day before that. You need to take a bath and put on clean clothes before breakfast." Wiona was in no mood to argue or negotiate. As an afterthought she added, "Do you want help?"

"Well, bless your heart. I should know whether or not I took a bath."

Wiona considered this for a heartbeat. "Forgive me for saying this, Mother, but you stink."

Emma looked as if she'd been slapped. "Wiona, I don't like being treated like a child."

"Then stop acting like one. You stink, your clothes stink and you need a bath!"

"God damn it, all right! I'll do it after my program."

"Before breakfast. Now do you need help?"

"I said I'll do it. Just go away."

Wiona nodded, unconvinced. How do you say, *don't feed my mother breakfast until after she's taken a bath* in Spanish? On her way back to the kitchen, she practiced the words she would use to explain the situation to Belen.

When Dawn awoke she was aware only of the need to pee. She started to get out of bed, but pain ripped through her belly, hammering her back down. Without even daring to turn her head, she tried to figure out what was wrong. Her hand made a tentative exploration of her stomach, fingers tracing over the seam of bandages covering the incision. They had cut her open and taken the baby.

Suddenly she was overtaken by her aloneness. Tears slid down her cheeks and into her ears. This was not the way it was supposed to be. James had broken his promise, had lied, and she was alone.

Adriana, who'd been dozing beside her, sat up. "It's OK. It's OK," she whispered. She put a pill between Dawn's lips, then helped her take a sip of water.

After a few minutes, Dawn was pulled back into her drugged sleep.

It was one of those perfect spring mornings, just breezy enough to blow the smog out of the valley. The sky was once again the vivid blue of his childhood and every facet of the Superstitions, towering to the east, was in rare, sharp focus. Overhead a contrail swelled, deepening the blue by contrast.

Unfortunately, Montoya didn't know the guy driving the garbage truck well enough to express how such a morning was like church to him, made him feel pure and full of purpose. Better for his soul than confession, he thought.

The garbage truck rolled to a stop in front of Trillig's place. As Montoya pulled down his sunglasses – the only disguise a Mexican in this neighborhood needed – he couldn't suppress his smile. Easy pickings, he thought. No warrant required and perfectly legal as long as the trash was at the curb.

Casually he hopped down from the truck. Apparently, James wasn't into recycling. That bin was empty. But the garbage can, one of those big green plastic jobs, was near to overflowing and he needed the driver to help him empty it into the sturdy, black bag he'd brought for that purpose. They threw the bag into the back then trundled off in the clean light of early morning.

When Stokey got to his office, there was a memo from Garza taped to his computer screen reminding him that he hadn't completed the sexual harassment training. There was nothing else he felt pressed to do, so he figured he might as well get it over with. While he waited for the program to load, he ran the terry rag around his desk, over the telephone and the picture of his family, took a sip of coffee, neatened a pile of folders, took another sip then turned his attention to the computer screen. It occurred to him then that it might be a good idea to see what Wikipedia had to say about pack rats.

He discovered that what he had in his garden was actually a white-throated woodrat. Woodrats, it clearly stated, eat desert plants, cacti and insects. No mention of arugula. Most surprising was that the babies, there were usually two or three, aren't weaned until they're over 2 months old. That would mean momma would be snacking in his garden until June. "Hmm." He sat back to consider the problem.

Just then Florence knocked on the wall of his cubicle.

"Stokey, there are a couple of guys who want to talk to you," she whispered, eyebrows raised in warning. "Men in suits."

"Suits?"

"Two. They're waiting for you in Rudy's office."

He turned off his computer. Usually *men in suits* was not a good thing, but this morning he welcomed any diversion.

Wiona took off her muddy boots before entering the kitchen. As she stepped through the door, she saw Emma sitting at the table, still unbathed, working on a pile of scrambled eggs, bacon and toast.

She looked at Belen with exasperation, but Belen only smiled and shrugged her shoulders. Without speaking Wiona went to the bathroom for aspirin. She couldn't possibly deal with this while somebody was poking at her eyeballs from the inside out.

Back in the kitchen she made herself a piece of toast and poured a second cup of coffee. Leaning against the counter, she ate the toast, sipped the coffee and considered her next move. "I thought you were going to take a bath before breakfast," she said at last.

"I took a bath yesterday."

The clock on the wall said five to 7, but Wiona figured it must be close to 9. "Would you like to go shopping with me today?"

"That would be nice."

"After you take a bath, we'll go."

"I just took a bath yesterday."

"Not yesterday." This opposition to bathing was something new and she'd have to find a way around it. "So Mother, why is it you don't want to take a bath. It would feel nice to be all clean, wouldn't it?"

"It's all just vanity. If people bathed less and prayed more then maybe …"

She waited for Emma to finish the thought. When Wiona determined that Emma had lost the end of her sentence, she said. "I think they're having a sale on pork roasts at Safeway. And we can stop by Walgreens and get a new kitchen clock."

Emma looked up at the clock on the wall. "What's wrong with the old one."

"It's broken."

"Doesn't look broken to me."

"Well it is."

"Well, bless your heart. If you say so."

"So we'll go right after your bath?"

"If you say so."

Wiona filled the tub herself, making sure the water was just hot enough, the shampoo and cream rinse handy. She opened the bathroom door and called down the hall. "Mother? I've got your bath all ready." When there was no response, she marched down the hall to the living room where Emma was once again asleep in the recliner.

"Come on now, up you go," Wiona urged.

"What? Go where?"

"To take a bath." Wiona flipped the recliner to upright and used this momentum to pull Emma to her feet. "There now."

Once in the bathroom, she helped Emma with her robe. A stink was rising from Emma's various cracks and crannies as she eased the nightgown up. It was all so simple, she was thinking.

"What are you doing?" Emma said, tugging her gown back down. "I'm not going to take a bath and you can't make me!"

"Mother!"

"I said no!" She picked up the scrub brush from the side of the tub and threw it. Osa was at her heels as Wiona stormed out to the horse shed, hand covering her mouth. Her bloody upper lip was already puffing up like a fritter in hot grease and if she didn't find some place to put her anger, she'd … well she didn't know what harm she might be capable of.

Link nickered as Wiona passed the corral. She grabbed his mane and slung a leg over his warm back. He stood patiently while she lay there, arms draped loosely down his sides, her head against his warm neck. Wiona considered her options. She could flat run away. She could strangle Emma in her sleep. She could put Emma in a home. The last was an option she could not afford.

Too injured and tired to think, she closed her eyes and allowed herself to be still. She must have dozed a bit. Slowly she became aware of Osa whining and snuffling though the hay. Wiona dismounted, careful not to jog her lip.

"What ya got, little girl? A mouse?" With the toe of her boot, she scraped away some hay. Not a mouse. Her breathing stopped as she knelt by the small mound of black and orange. Tentatively, she reached to stroke her blood-matted fur. She drew back her hand. "Oh God, still alive."

Quickly, she lined a wooden crate with an old saddle blanket and placed the limp body inside. Punkin opened her eyes, then, mewed, though it was more a rasp. "Poor baby." Wiona picked up the crate and carried it gently into the house.

Defeated, she dialed the clinic. "Is Dr. Altamirano there? This is Wiona Rutherford."

"Can you hold, please?"

"Yes, I mean no," she said, but it was too late, John Denver was already crooning "Rocky Mountain High."

"Damn." She drew a lungful of air deep into her chest, breathed out, took another deep breath. For a few moments Punkin just stared up at her, then her head fell back down and she closed her eyes.

"Wiona?" Lucy was there at last "What's up?"

Until she heard Lucy's voice, Wiona hadn't felt the need to cry.

Stokey turned on the computer screen once again, determined to channel his anger into something productive, though the sexual harassment shit didn't quite meet his criterion for productive.

The suits were from Homeland Security. They claimed that somehow, they declined to say how, his investigation of the kidnapping was jeopardizing the nation's security. Demanded he turn over to them whatever he had retrieved from Corcho's car, and "desist" from further investigation. Desist!

"What bullshit!" To date, he'd made zero progress on his so-called investigation. What interest would Homeland Security have in a zit like Corcho? Certainly not the kidnap of a couple of Mexican kids. Corcho must have been into some other action, or maybe it wasn't Corcho at all, but Grumpy, Dopey and Sleezy … What were the names of the other guys? He took a small notebook he'd withheld from the suits out of his breast pocket, thumbed through a few pages. El Camaleón, Dutch, El Gigante, Rojo, El Pendejo he'd written, each name followed by a phone number.

He picked up the phone, dialed, then punched in numbers, as the recording directed, until he got a human. "Is Detective Rosamond Beauxchamps available? No?

This is Stokey Stokelund. Would you have her call me as soon as possible? Ask her to use my cell. She knows the number. Thanks."

Montoya spilled the contents of the garbage bag onto the asphalt alongside his patrol car and studied them. Trillig, it seemed, had a taste for expensive vodka. There were two fifths of Absolut among the debris. Neither he nor Dawn appeared to care for fruits and vegetables. Other than a few of orange rinds and a scattering of sunflower seeds, there was not a single apple core, banana peel or wilted leaf of iceberg lettuce among the debris. What was conspicuous was the number of boxes of macaroni and cheese, sugary cereals, Pop-Tarts. The bread of choice was Wonder and there were 10 jars of Peter Pan peanut butter, extra crunchy. He smoothed out a cellophane wrapper – Top Ramen – a dozen or more of those. At least Dawn was getting plenty of calcium: There were four plastic half-gallon jugs of milk, 2 percent.

One bundle of trash was contained in a plastic grocery bag, handles tied in a knot. Montoya pulled a pair of latex gloves from the box in his patrol car. He tugged them on before breaking open the bag. Amid the wads of tissue and toilet paper was a nest of hair, the gleanings from a hairbrush, he supposed. He pulled loose a strand. It was long, dark, coarse. Could be the hair of an Asian, Native American or Latino.

From the pile of tissues he plucked a small cellophane bag. "Saladitos, Hecho en Mexico," the label revealed. Saladitos – he remembered eating them by the bag when he was a kid. Strange item to find amid a gringo's household trash. After all, it was something of an acquired taste. Even his own children turned up their noses when offered a saladito.

"OK," he said aloud. It seemed that Dawn and Trillig were not the only ones living in the house. It also appeared that those others had a yen for the comfort foods of childhood. And at least one of them was a Mexican. The questions marks popped up in quick succession. Why would Trillig hide the fact that other children lived there? Why would Dawn play along with it? How many children were there – from the number of milk jugs, Montoya would guess at least two others. Who were they and why were they living with Trillig?

Reluctantly, he turned his attention to the tissues. Some were soiled with blood, some with fecal matter, some with both. Certainly Trillig could be gay, but why tissues wadded and thrown into the trash and not flushed? Montoya could think of only one explanation.

Recalling the screaming, self-mutilating parrot, he got a sick, urgent feeling. What had Mrs. Stillman called it? Visceral.

He took out his digital camera and snapped several photos of the trash. Next he gathered up the tissues and the hair and stuffed them into Ziploc bags, which he would drop off at the forensics lab. Once he got the report, he'd still have to figure out a way to get a search warrant.

"Those Homeland Security guys," Rosy was saying. "They think they're all that plus a bag of chips."

Stokey, holding his cell phone, glanced out the door of his cubical to see if anyone was within earshot. "I don't know about the bag of chips, but apparently, they are all that. Garza told me to drop the investigation."

"Just means you're on to something."

He sat back down at his desk. "Must have been one of the phone numbers I put in the database."

"Probably. My guess would be your kidnapper is diversified. If Homeland Security is involved, he's probably into arms smuggling, something of that nature. Lots of illegal munitions going into Mexico from Arizona and Texas these days. So what are you going to do?"

"What can I do? I guess arms smuggling trumps kid snatching."

"You just keep on doing what you're doing, Stokey. That's my advice. There is a higher authority, you know. Ultimately, it's Him you gotta serve. Anyway, we'll keep working it from this end. Hang on a minute, will you? Somebody's on my other line."

Serving a higher authority was all well and good, but it was a lower authority that authorized his paycheck. Besides, he was out of his element, didn't know how to proceed even if he were so inclined. He had some phone numbers. One of them belonged to the kidnapper, maybe. One of them, possibly the same guy, was into arms smuggling, maybe. Pressing forward with this investigation could get him fired, definitely.

"Still there, Stokey?"

"Right here where you left me."

"Guess who that was."

"Somebody from Homeland Security."

"You got it."

"So where do we go from here?"

"Back to those phone numbers. There are ways and there are ways. I'll stay in touch."

Stokey dropped his cell phone into his breast pocket. While Homeland Security didn't have to worry about little details like search warrants, he'd need one to get any kind of information about who those numbers belonged to and that was simply not going to happen.

Lucy met her at the back door of the clinic.

"Ouch!" she said, when she saw Wiona's swollen lip. "What happened to you?"

"It's nothing."

"Doesn't look like nothing." Lucy peered into the box. "Poor thing." Bring her on in and I'll see what I can do."

"Katie?" Lucy called, as she passed by the office. "Bring a little bag of ice, would you? We'll be in room 4."

Seeing Katie made the blood rush to her face, which made her lip start to throb anew, which brought tears to her eyes deepening her mortification. She followed Lucy into an examination room.

"First I need to … what's your kitty's name?"

"Punkin. Her name is Punkin."

"I need to anesthetize her and then we'll start her on some fluids. In Mexico, sometimes I treated animals, cows mostly, dogs, once a monkey. I've never worked on a cat, though." She placed the crate on the scale. Gently, she lifted the cat onto the examination table, then noted the weigh of the crate. "Punkin weighs about eight pounds."

Katie came to the door with the ice. "Here you go."

Wiona accepted the ice and tried to smile. "Thanks, Katie." She thought to offer an explanation, but what would she say? That Emma hit her in the mouth with a scrub brush, her cat had been shot and she couldn't afford a vet? That would be a fine story to tell Stokey at the dinner table. Gingerly, she placed the ice against her lip. Tears sprang to her eyes once again. She was grateful that Katie had already turned to leave and Lucy was too busy to notice.

Once Punkin was asleep, Lucy shaved her fur. Working quickly and efficiently, she located each pellet, probed it out, then took two or three deft stitches to close the wound. "Luckily these are all pretty superficial," Lucy said. When she finished sewing up the final hole, she added a shot of antibiotics to the IV bag. "There, the worst is over."

"Is she going to be OK?"

"I think, as long as the wounds don't get infected." Pulling off her gloves, Lucy turned her attention hard on Wiona. "So tell me. What happened to your lip?"

Wiona inhaled, held her breath. She owed Lucy so much, the least of which was an honest explanation. Exhaling, she said, "My mother …"

"Your mother hit you?"

"Yes … well, no, not exactly. I was trying to get her to take a bath. I don't think she meant to hurt me. Look, do you really have time to hear all this?"

Lucy sat down on a stool. "Go ahead. I'm listening."

Oh no, Wiona thought. I'm going to start crying again. She clamped her teeth down against the tears. The ice in the plastic bag had melted, but she pressed the bubble of water hard against her lip. If she had to talk, she needed the distraction.

By the time Wiona pulled into the yard, the day was nearly spent. She was surprised to see Gaby's Honda parked in the yard, especially so late in the day. When she opened the door of the truck, Osa scrabbled out from her place under the porch, performing her happy dance, tailless butt wriggling.

"Hey, sweet girl."

Wiona toted the crate with the groggy Punkin directly to her bedroom, setting it gently on the floor of the closet. Suddenly, she became aware of how quiet the house was. No one was in the kitchen and the television was off in the living room.

It occurred to her that hours ago she'd left Emma standing in the bathroom in her nightgown, had rushed out with hardly a word to Belen, didn't know if the woman had even understood where she was going or why, and now Gaby was here, somewhere. God's knows what might have happened while I was gone, she was thinking, when she heard muffled laughter. Out in the hall, she determined that it was coming from the bathroom. "What on earth?"

Wiona opened the bathroom door and a rush of warm, humid air hit her face. Belen was perched on the toilet, the angelic Jesús tucked within her rebozo. Emma and Susana were in the tub, heads covered with so many soapsuds they looked like they'd been dipped in whipped cream. Hands over her face, Emma squealed happily as Gaby poured water from a saucepan over her head.

"Qué limpia, qué linda," Belen crooned.

"Qué linda," Susana seconded, laughing and clapping her chubby little hands.

Emma seemed to agree. "Qué linda, linda, linda," she cried,

oblivious, but happy to join in.

When Wiona stepped into the room, all of them looked up at her and smiled.

"Ah, Wiona," Belen said. "Buenas tardes."

"Close the goddamn door," Emma shouted. "You're letting all the warm air out."

Wiona closed the door. "Buenas tardes, you guys." She pointed to Emma. "Como?"

Gaby poured another pan full of water over Emma's head. "Dr. Lucy called and said you could use a little help.

"Su madre es como una niña hoy, necesita tratarla como niña, pues, entiende?" Belen added.

Wiona nodded. Yes she understood. So that was the secret. Emma was the child now, though a blasphemous one, and needed to be treated as such. Dish-soap bubbles, maybe next a rubber ducky? The fact was that Wiona felt embarrassed, even a bit jealous that Gaby had been able to gain Emma's cooperation. She and her mother had lived together for nearly 40 years and yet Wiona could not lift the woman's nightgown over her head and persuade her step into the tub. Even Belen, a stranger who didn't speak English, seemed on intimate terms with her mother. Whereas she had not shared a moment of intimacy with Emma since ... well since she'd been big enough to climb on her pony and spend the better part of the day outside the reach of her mother's voice.

As she watched Susana and Emma in the tub, Wiona almost laughed, for now apparently she would become a mother after all. Never too late, she supposed and promised herself to try to be a better one than her own. She leaned over the tub and kissed the top of Emma's head. "Don't you look pretty in all those bubbles."

Emma smiled then craned her neck to look up at Wiona. "What happened to your mouth?"

"Don't you remember? You threw the scrub brush at me."

"Well, bless your heart, Wiona. You must be losing your mind."

Wiona considered the promise she'd just made to herself.

"Maybe I am, Mother." Certainly there were times lately, when it seemed that way.

Earlier Lucy had been full of suggestions. Wiona could put Emma in a group home; said she knew of a pretty good one. Of course there was no money for that. Lucy suggested Access. Didn't realize that ranchers, as property owners, didn't qualify. And even if she could afford a nursing home … well, Emma was Emma. The woman had loved her as much as she was able, fed her, provided for her. Wiona would do the same for her as long as she was able.

Wiona watched as Susana and Emma, warm, happy and blessedly clean, blew soapsuds at each other. Touching her swollen lip with her tongue, she thought, the problem is this big baby of mine will never grow up.

Adriana shifted her weight, careful not to disturb her friend. It was best Dawn sleep through the pain. The room smelled bad. Earlier Adriana had tried to tuck a towel beneath her friend to sop up the blood and urine, but there was only so much she could do without hurting her. Maybe tomorrow Dawn would be able to sit in a chair. She'd help her into a nightgown then, there were many to choose from in the dresser with its big mirror. For now she would have to remain as she was – naked except for the large bandage covering the place from which they took the baby. She imagined the wound, wide and red as the mouth of a clown.

Tomorrow she would put clean sheets on the bed. There were many of those, too – beautiful sheets, some trimmed in lace, others made of red or pink or even black satin. Adriana wondered how it would feel to lie between sheets of satin. El viejo must have given her all those sheets and nightgowns. The thought of him made her chest hurt. He had come in the room only twice since he'd brought her to watch over Dawn: once to give her the pills for Dawn's pain, once to simply stand at the side of the bed. When he finally left, she had not heard the bolt slide into place. Perhaps he was worried;

perhaps he'd just forgotten.

Her thoughts turned to Edgar. Earlier she'd been dreaming that he'd stepped on a nail. He howled as she tried to pull it out of his bare foot. When she awoke, her heart banging nearly out of her chest, the big green parrot was screaming.

She'd seen Edgar only twice since they had arrived in this place. Was he still safe? "Señora de los Angeles, protegelo," she prayed.

Lying there so still was becoming almost painful. She eased back the covers. Romeo sat on his perch, head nestled beneath one green wing. He looked sad. Adriana opened the door to his cage, offered him a sunflower seed, but he didn't rouse.

She closed the door and looked around for something to do. Already she had paged through the magazines strewn across the floor. The room was like something out of a movie. There was a closet full of clothes and shoes just like in a movie. And there were stuffed animals everywhere. She picked one up, a large white bear, held it against her chest to ease the sudden pressure there. As if she had accidentally swallowed a piece of hard candy, she could not take a full breath.

How long had it been since she'd left her mother? Two weeks? Three? What about her father? She repeated his phone number, testing her memory. If she could find a telephone, she would call him and he'd come for them. Since she had been moved into Dawn's room, she'd ventured out to go to the bathroom several times and once to the kitchen for food, but she hadn't seen a telephone.

Still holding the bear to her chest, she opened the door and stepped out into the hall. The house was quiet except for the sound of a television in one of the back rooms. She imagined Edgar in there watching cartoons. Edgar loved cartoons. She thought to go to that room and knock, but was afraid the other boys might tell the old man.

In the living room, the big green parrot dozed in a cage. Beyond was the front door. As she made her way through the foyer, her heart was pounding so hard she was afraid she'd wake the bird. She tried the doorknob. It was locked from the inside. Next to the door was a nicho where one might place a statue of la virgencita. Instead there was a pile of mail. She looked beneath the pile thinking the key to the front door might be hidden there, but found nothing. It occurred to her then, that if she got a chance to call her father, she'd have to be able to tell him where she was. She picked up a piece of mail and slipped it into the waistband of her shorts.

Once again she scanned the living room and kitchen for a phone. If she could call her father he'd come and break down that door. He'd take them all, Dawn included, to his house where her mother would be waiting with the new baby. But there was no phone.

Day 10

Montoya stood in the front yard of a smoldering duplex in an old, mostly Hispanic neighborhood. The fire had started in the early morning hours, and the firefighters were still mopping up. The cause was not immediately apparent, though several neighbors on the block had reported hearing a series of explosions. Fortunately, the building was unoccupied at the time. Maybe the absentee landlord – he looked at his notebook – one Francisco Ochoa, was trying to bilk his insurance company. Well, the arson team would probably make short work of it. Right now, the debris was still too hot to work on.

He walked around to the side of the house. Parked in back was a somewhat sooty, but otherwise undamaged, white Chrysler 300. Kind of a classy car for such a dump, he thought. On the trunk of the car was one of those magnetic yellow ribbons – "God Bless Our Troops." He tried the door. Locked. He jotted down the license plate number in his notebook.

Dawn awoke to the aroma of Top Ramen. A bowl of it was on her nightstand. She looked around the room and there was Adriana sitting at her dresser, flipping through the fashion album, several magazines fanned out at her feet.
"What day is it?"

Adriana looked up, smiled, shrugged.

"How long?"

Adriana placed the album carefully on the dresser. "Two days, three?"

Dawn tried to sit up, winced, collapsed against her pillow.

"I you help."

With Adriana supporting her, Dawn struggled to a sitting position. Slowly she brought her legs over the side of the bed, then waited motionless for the dizzy-sick feeling to pass. Adriana handed her the bowl of Ramen. It felt warm in her hands, and suddenly she was hungry and very, very thirsty. "Water first."

Adriana exchanged the bowl for a glass of water and shook out a pill from the small bottle on the table. "Pain?"

Dawn opened her mouth. Adriana placed the pill on her tongue then guided the glass to her lips. She managed only a few sips before the nausea returned. Adriana offered the bowl of Ramen, but Dawn waved it away.

"I wet the bed," she said, a tear slipping from each eye. For a long moment, she sat there contemplating the enormous task of getting up and walking to the bathroom. "I stink."

"It's OK, amiga. I you help."

After a few minutes the pain in her belly, though still searing along the edges, had become less raw, less personal. She took Adriana's outstretched hand and stood, a bit shaky, then walked ever so slowly toward the door.

Dawn had eased the dressing off the incision in the shower. Now, propped up against two pillows, she pulled down the waistband of her sweatpants so they could examine it. It was only three or four inches long and she wondered how they'd pulled the baby through such a small opening. Running just below her bikini line, the incision looked like an evil little railway track to nowhere. Once again the tears started.

"It's OK. Not bad." Adriana swabbed the incision with peroxide and the two girls watched it fizz. She patted it with a cotton ball then gently affixed six overlapping Band-Aids crosswise over the wound. She sat back. "Hungry?"

Dawn shook her head, then sank back against the pillows, too tired and empty to speak.

Stokey stopped by Garza's office before checking out for the day. His boss was on the phone, listening rather than talking for once. He pointed to a chair. Stokey sat, curious to learn the nature of the one-sided conversation.

"OK ... OK ... OK," Garza was saying. "Gotcha." He hung up the phone.

"Damn! Damn it to hell! I knew it. I told them; we all told them. Hell, it was just a matter of time."

"What's that?"

"Minutemen, two of them, were whacked down towards Sasabe."

"When'd this happen?"

"Sometime between midnight and 4 a.m. I knew it! They were like goddamn sitting ducks out there, with their green tents plunked down in the wide open. Extra eyes and ears my ass. Poor dumb dicks were probably sleeping, probably never even knew what hit 'em. Well, the shit's gonna fly like a hippo spinning its tail."

Stokey nodded. He wouldn't go so far as to say it served them right, but nobody had asked them to place themselves in harm's way. Even so, it was best to keep his thoughts on the matter to himself. It wouldn't serve to get Garza going any harder than he already was on the subject. He liked Garza. Didn't want to see him bust an artery. He shook his head. "Umm."

"Another goddamn boondaster, is what it is. You can bet somebody, somewhere will make big political hay off of this."

Stokey nodded again. "Umm."

"Is that all you've got to say?"

"That's about it."

"Then get the hell out of here."

"See you tomorrow."

"Yeah." Garza picked up the telephone and started to dial, determined, apparently, to find somebody to fuel his righteous indignation.

It wasn't that the death of the two guys failed to move Stokey, or that stupidity, incompetence and the machinations of the politicos failed to anger him, but after tours in the Middle East, Stokey simply wasn't going to go all ape shit over it. Besides, it had suddenly turned warmish and he wanted to get home in time to see what effect that might have had on the arugula, if in fact there was any arugula.

Wiona had long been the ranch barber. Earlier she'd cut her mother's hair. Now the two women stood shoulder to shoulder before the mirror on Wiona's dresser.
"What do you think?" Wiona asked.

Emma looked suspiciously at their reflection. "About them? Who the hell are they?"

Uncertain if she was joking, Wiona smiled. "That's us, Mother."

Emma looked at Wiona and then back at their reflection. Her cheeks reddened. "I don't know what's wrong with me." She ran her hand over her face. "I'm getting old, aren't I. We're both getting old and what in heaven's name did you do to your lip?"

Wiona put her arm around Emma's shoulder. "Bumped it."

"Must hurt." For a moment Emma leaned into Wiona, then stiffened. "Why are we standing in front of the mirror like a couple of ninnies?"

Wiona let her arm drop to her side. "We're looking at your new haircut. How do you like it?"

Emma turned her head from side to side. "It'll do, I guess," she said and hurried from the room.

Wiona figured that was as much gratitude as she was going to get. Even at her best, Emma had always been long on demand and short on appreciation. Still, the hair was cut, the body clean. Progress, if something of such a temporary nature could be called progress, had been made.

Punkin was still recuperating in her closet. Wiona peered in, then plucked the cat out of her box and set her gently on the rug. Quickly she balled up the soiled bath towel and lined the crate with a clean one. "Come on, baby." She put the cat back in the crate along with water and a bit of cat food laced with an antibiotic she'd crushed over the surface.

As she caressed the cat's head, she could only think of one person mean enough to shoot a cat. Suddenly full of determination, she strode to the kitchen. His number was in the address book. She punched it into the phone.

"Burl, this is Wiona Rutherford." She said after the beep. "You've got three cows up at my second tank. You need to get them off my property as of yesterday!"

There, that felt better.

The arugula, in fact, was poking out of the soil and a few of the poppies had bloomed, though by the time he got home, they were already closed. After pulling up the Bermuda grass and checking for pack rat damage, Stokey had a solitary dinner, scrambled eggs, half-pound of bacon and a few cherry tomatoes for roughage. When he dined alone, he didn't feel compelled to set an example.

When Jackson's car pulled into the drive, he was watching a rerun of "Cheers," his fifth beer of the evening a quarter gone. He checked his watch. It was 10:30 and a school night.

"Come on in, son," he called when he heard the front door close.

Jackson's lips were puffy and red and his hair looked like he'd been held prisoner by a mama cat and licked up one side and down the other. It wasn't a bad look, actually, and might have brought a smile except for the fact that Stokey in no way wanted to be perceived as complicit. He pressed the mute on the remote. "Rough night at the library?"

Jackson smoothed the front of his T-shirt. "Drove Sara home after we'd finished studying for the test."

"I see. Well, I hope when she went in her house she looked a bit more presentable than you. So?"

"So?"

They sat in silence while the predictable action played out on screen. The boy was nearly 18, after all. Too big to scold. Still, as long as he was living under this roof ... No! Too big to scold, threaten or boss. He'd been doing that for years. Either it had taken by now or it hadn't, and more of the same would not bring about the desired results, which would be to turn the clock back about eight years. Oh well. "What's new at school, son?"

"The Marine recruiter was there again today."

"Oh yeah? Have a seat, why don't you?"

Jackson sighed, dropped his backpack to the floor and collapsed onto the couch in the boneless manner Stokey recognized as impatience to be elsewhere. Ignoring the body language, he asked, "So did you talk to him?"

"We had a few words."

I bet you did, Stokey was thinking. He remembered his recruiter, big black dude, thick bull neck and you could file your fingernails on his head, it was so close-shaved, impressive. At the time, Stokey thought his recruiter offered the ways and means to liberate him from dusty little Douglas where all growth was horizontal. But Jacks had other opportunities, both his kids did; he'd made sure of that. The money was just sitting in the bank waiting for them to use it for something that would offer them a future.

"Well?"

"So what's it like over there?"

"Sandy."

"No. Really."

"Really. There's sand in your eyes, ears, mouth, of course, but also in your chest hairs ..." The fact that his son did not as yet have chest hairs had not escaped him. "Sand in your armpits, in every pore and crack, sand grinding under your balls. There's two basic seasons over there: hell and hotter than hell, unless it's freezing ass cold. And then there's the boredom. You think algebra is boring? You haven't been bored until you've enlisted in the Marines, because it's all about waiting. When you're not running your butt into the sand, humping 80 pounds of gear in your rucksack, and that's not counting your Kevlar helmet and vest, your rifle and bayonet, pistol, ammo and canteen, you're waiting. You can't even imagine the things you have to wait for. You even have to wait to take a shit."

"So why did you go?"

"Didn't have a choice. Once you sign that contract, the Marines own you."

"I mean enlist, why did you?"

"Because I was young and stupid – not in the sense of stupid, stupid, but in the clueless sense of the word, plus I had no imagination." Stokey looked at his son to see if he was truly listening. He was gratified to see that the boy was. He took a sip of beer.

"So now that you know what you know ..."

"Would I do it again? Good question. Let me ask you a question."

"Go ahead."

"Why do you think they call recruits grunts?"

"Because they carry heavy packs?"

"Well there's that. But it's also the sound a person makes when they take a shit! So to answer your question, knowing what I know now, would I enlist again? I would hope not. As I said, it's something you have to be young and stupid to buy into."

"What about combat?"

"A waste, mostly." And that's about as far as Stokey was willing to go on the nature of war in general and the Middle East in particular. He'd long made a habit of keeping all that shit stuffed in a little box, and he didn't want it to come spilling over into what he tried to think of as his real life. And it was not just about the wars in Iraq and Afghanistan. It was about the Marines, all the hours spent talking trash and acting hard. He would not mention the addiction of the adrenalin rush or the passion, sometimes love, sometimes hate, he felt for his brothers, or the mental comfort one can take when there are no choices to make, the brutal, beautiful simplicity of the life. It was too complicated, or maybe just plain unexamined, for him to begin to explain. Like sand, it's a life that fills every pore, maybe even enters your semen. How else to explain the generational nature of the Marines – grandfathers, fathers, sons and now daughters, all proud Marines.

"I will say this with all honesty," Stokey continued. "It's a hell of a life, a kind of an addiction, and I truly hope you will not enlist."

"But …"

Stokey held up his hand, palm out. "Sure there's something to be gained from the Marines, if you survive the experience, that is. And I'm not just talking physical survival – I know plenty of guys, good buddies of mine who went to war who are seriously fucked up because of the life. So yes, there are things to be gained, but there's a lot to lose. I think in the long haul the scale tips towards the losses."

"You survived."

"Sure I survived," he said, but wondered what that was worth. Recently there were times he thought it was worth about as much as a bucket of warm spit. "But you?" he continued. "You have other opportunities. There's college, for one, or any kind of school or training you want to take up. And what about this girl? This Sara? What does she have to say about you joining up with the Marines?"

He shrugged. "She's OK with it."

"OK with it? Hmm … Well, give it some hard thought, son." He tipped back the last of his beer. "Those losses creep up on a person.

Fifteen, 20 years down the road, boom! Your wife can't stand you anymore." Now that was more than he'd intended to say.

Part 5

Abiding

Day 11

Stokey held his mother's arm as they made their way toward the outpatient entrance of the VA hospital. Vision limited to the peripheral, she kept her head tilted to the left so she could see where she was going with her right eye.

They'd had to leave Douglas at 5:30 that morning to make the 8 o'clock appointment, his father talking the whole way. Stokey had refrained from interrupting the monologues, which ranged from property taxes and the environmentalists, to the 2,000-mile border fence and why we needed it. Now that he'd moved onto Afghanistan, it was harder to simply let the words blow over him like so much hot air.

"You mark my words," he was saying. "By summer, all those cowards will be backstroking as fast as they can."

By cowards, Stokey guessed his father meant the folks who supported troop withdrawal in Afghanistan. Stokey didn't bother to point out that maintaining the troops might mean his third deployment. He knew guys who had been redeployed two months before their term of service was to end.

"Where am I supposed to go for my colonASScopy?"

"Just over there." Stokey pointed with his chin. "Well, if Bush had finished the job in Afghanistan …"

"What? And let that terrorist Saddam get the jump on us with his WMDs!"

"No such weapons were ever found, Dad, and as for Saddam …"

"Aw, don't be a jackass."

His mother's head tilted up toward Stokey. She had that pleading look he knew too well. What was the point anyway? All his father seemed to remember these days were old sound bites. He supposed that if you hear a lie often enough, even when the truth comes out, you continue to believe the lie. His father thought Saddam Hussein was behind 9/11, and nothing could shake that belief. Now that both Hussein and Osama bin Laden were dead, Stokey wondered who the next bogeyman would be? Besides, his father, who'd frozen his ass on the edge of the DMZ just after the Korean war, considered himself an expert on all things military.

Stokey guided his mother through the door and to a chair. He started to accompany his father to the front desk, but the man waved him away.

When he sat down, his mother patted his arm. "Don't let him get to you, dear. He can be an old fart, but he loves you."

Stokey had to laugh. His mother might be losing her vision, but she was holding her own in terms of wisdom and grace. And it was true. Though he and his father rarely agreed on what was basically just politics, anyway, the old man loved him, even respected him. Sure, it would be nice to hear the words, but his father would choke first. Stokey tried to remember when he last said those words to his own son. He couldn't and made a mental note to change that as soon as he got home.

"Your hair looks nice, Mom."

Smiling, she patted the stiff, forever-blond poof. "Just had it done yesterday. So tell me. What do you hear from Becka?"

"She's still trying to find herself."

"Can't be looking too hard."

He allowed himself a little snorting laugh. "Yeah, well." Time to change the subject again. "While I'm here, I thought I'd run a couple of errands, maybe stop in at the Tucson sector. See what's up. You have my cell phone number so you can call me when he's ready to go home?"

His mother fumbled in her purse for a moment, then handed him a slip of paper. "Is this it?"

"Yup. I guess you're all set then." He leaned over to kiss her cheek.

"Oh, and Teddy?"

Only his mother still called him Teddy. "Yes, Mom."

"Before you go, be sure to tell your father you love him." She looked at him from the corner of her eye, raised one brow. "You never know."

Jesus. That was one thing he hated. Since he was a kid, she'd always insisted he declare his love before going out the door, because "you never know." Well, what could you do? Fact was, you never did know. "OK, Mom. Love you."

"Love you too, dear."

As he approached the front desk, Stokey noted that his father did look … well, insubstantial was the word. His shoulders were now narrower than his hips. His hair was thin and brittle around the edges and only a few white wisps remained on top.

Stokey patted the old man on the back. "Got to go now, Dad."

"You're not going to wait with your mother?"

"I've got some errands to run. I'll be back by the time you're ready to go."

"Well, OK, son."

"Take care, Dad."

Looking embarrassed, his father patted the hand that still rested on his shoulder. "You too, son."

In the foyer, Stokey checked his watch. It would only take a minute. Before taking the elevator to the second floor, he went into the canteen and purchased three Hershey's chocolate bars with almonds.

At the nurses' station a woman with sandy-blond hair spilling out of a lopsided bun gazed at a computer screen.

"Excuse me," he said. "Is Lance Corporal Nathan Henderson still here?"

"Nate? Still here, unfortunately. We can't seem to get rid of him."

"How's he doing?"

"He's doing. He's a great kid, a real sweetheart."

Stokey nodded. "Yeah. It's tough to …" He shook his head. "What room's he in this time?"

"Room 237, down the corridor and to the left."

The boy lay propped against a couple of pillows, an IV in his left arm. His right leg was suspended from a complicated trapeze apparatus "Hey Nate. I heard they had you back in this dump. How's it going?"

"Hey, Sarge." The boy smiled out of what was left of his mouth. He'd been badly burned when his helicopter was blown out of the sky. Shrapnel had taken most of his right arm directly and the doctors were in the process of carving off his right leg, one inch at a time, it seemed. The current hope was to save the knee. This was the boy's 10th surgery to date.

Stokey set the candy bars on the tray table next to a framed picture of Nate's children, a girl of 5 or 6, a boy maybe a year or so younger. He must have started young, because this Marine, if he recalled correctly, was only 24.

The television was turned to some talking heads yammering on about the latest oil spill. He unwrapped a bar and set it on the boy's chest. "Hershey's with almonds, right?"

The boy placed a piece of chocolate on his tongue and closed his eyes.

Stokey looked around the room, then out the window. He was never any good at chitchat. "There's two more for later."

"Thanks, Sarge."

"So how long you in for?"

"I've got another infection in the bone." He nodded toward the

IV. "They're trying a new antibiotic. After they get this thing squared away, they're going to start on my face."

"Hmm," Stokey nodded, studied the newscasters for a moment. "So how's the family?"

"Good. Everybody's good. How about you?"

"Good. We're all good." There was no point in sharing the truth with this boy. The point was to cheer him up. "So."

Nate nodded toward the television. "Think you're going to get redeployed?"

"Maybe this time they'll pass on me. I'm out for good July 16."

"You're not going to re-up?"

Stokey shook his head. "Kuwait, Bosnia, Iraq, Iraq, Afghanistan. I've done my bit over the years."

"I'd go back in a heartbeat if I could."

Stokey picked up the picture of Nate's wife and kids. "Looks like you've got a job to do here."

"Yeah, well ... I've got me a little jock there, that's for sure. Just before I landed back here, I was working on my pitch. You know getting used to throwing left-handed. Lizette there will be starting T-ball this summer."

"Well then, you better work at getting the hell out of here."

"That's what I'm trying to do. I hate this place. Can't sleep. You have any trouble sleeping, Sarge?"

"Me?" He thought of all the hours spent in front of the TV while everyone else in the house was asleep. "Some. I guess it goes with the territory."

Stokey patted Nate on his good shoulder. "Well, I'm out of here. Got some errands to run. You take good care now, son."

Stokey stood in front of Becka's apartment. The front window was open and he could smell fresh cigarette smoke. He glanced into the window box. There were several more butts mashed into the dirt than the last time. He could picture Becka sitting on the couch reading a paperback or maybe filing her fingernails. She had nice nails, pretty, slender, white fingers.

Suddenly abashed, Stokey hesitated. What excuse did he have for being there? Nothing came to mind. Jesus Christ! He thought. I'm her husband. I don't need excuses. He pressed the bell. Waited. Pressed again.

"It's me. Open up."

There was no response, yet the unmistakable smell of smoke still wafted though the open widows.

"Becka?" He rang again.

"Open up, Becka!" She was sitting right there. He knew it. Why wouldn't she fucking open up?

After taking another Percocet, Dawn managed the distance between her room and James' in baby steps. Now she hesitated, trying to gather courage from her anger. The door was ajar. After a few moments, she nudged it open.

James looked up from the computer, smiled. "Howdy, padna. Feeling better?"

"No," she said, glaring.

"No? Well, it takes a little time."

"It looks like I've got a railroad track down there."

"When you get the stitches out, it will look like a little smile."

"You promised it wouldn't hurt."

"There were complications."

"What complications?"

"You were too small to deliver a baby. Doc thought the cesarean would be safer for both of you so …"

"I want my baby back."

"Dawn, I'm trying to work here."

She stepped farther into the room, hands balled into fists at her side. "I want my baby back."

"We've gone over this and over this. You agreed …"

"I didn't agree to being cut open."

"Doc had no choice, Dawny. Now it's time to put all this behind you. Keep your eye on the prize."

"What's the prize?"

"You're the prize, babe. You're the best, and pretty soon the whole world will know it. Trust me. You're going to be fine."

Dawn didn't think she'd ever be fine again. The corners of her mouth turned down as she fought off tears. "I'll have this big old ugly scar."

"Not to worry. When it heals, it won't be more than a faint scratch, which I could make disappear with a couple of keystrokes. Really Dawn, I've got to get back to work here."

"What about the baby?"

"The baby's great, a healthy little boy as a matter of fact. The parents are delighted, thrilled to death."

"How much did he weigh?"

James took a deep breath. Dawn could see he was losing his patience, but she didn't give a damn. "How much did he weigh, James? Did Doc even bother to weigh him?"

"He weighed 7 pounds 2 ounces and he was 20 inches long. OK?"

"What color was his hair?"

"Brown."

"Eyes?"

"Blue, Dawny." His expression softened. "His eyes were blue just like yours, big blue eyes. Come here, padna." He reached out to her.

Dawn stepped up to the desk, allowed him to take her hand.

"I know this hasn't been easy, Dawny. I know you're hurting. If I could take away your pain, if I could take it as my own, I would in a heartbeat."

His eyes swam behind his glasses and Dawn thought he might start to cry.

"But in a week, 10 days max," he continued. "You'll see.

Everything will look different, we'll take that shopping trip."

Dawn shook her head.

"Ah come on, baby. Give me a little smile."

She shook her head again.

"Look, I'm not supposed to do this but …" He paused a moment, then wrote something down on a small notepad, then held it out to Dawn. "The names of the folks who adopted the baby."

Dawn reached for it, but he pulled his hand back. "First, you've got to promise me that under no circumstances will you try to contact your son until he's at least 18."

She hesitated. How old would she be in 18 years? She added 10 to 13 then used her fingers for the additional eight. Thirty-one!

"You've got to promise, Dawny. Think about it. I know it sounds like a long way off, but in 18 years, you'll be at the height of your career. Dawny?"

"OK, I promise," she said. He handed her the notepad; a little smile seemed to tickle the corners of his mouth.

Lips moving, she read the names. Fred and Ethel Mertz. Fred and Ethel Mertz? The names didn't sound rich.

Another clear, blue-sky day warming into spring. Wiona used the fence line as an excuse to take advantage of it. Link was tied under a juniper and Osa was sacked out nearby. Wiona, stripped down to her undervest, had been splicing barbed wire where it'd been cut. Now she cranked the handle on the come-along, keeping a close eye on the old post, then drew the wire as tight as she dared. In the distance, she could hear the wheeze of the windmill turning in the mild breeze, the shaft pumping up and down and beneath that, the distant rumble of a truck. She pulled the free end of the strand around the post, took three tight turns, and stepped back. "Guess that'll do."

Wiona pulled off her leather gloves. Wiping her sweaty palms on the sides of her jeans, she started for the top of the rise, Osa, now on alert, snuffling a few yards ahead. From the summit, she could see the road. Within a few minutes, Burl's nearly new Dodge Ram, its red dulled by dust to the color of chili paste, came into view. Stock trailer in tow, he was coming up the road to the second tank to pick up his cows and the calf.

"About time!" Tapping her cheeks to release the tension in her jaws, she made a mental note to stop clenching her teeth then headed back down to retrieve Link.

She stood in the shade sipping tepid tea from her dented canteen and contemplated the grass. A waste of time, she concluded since there wasn't a damn thing she could do about it. She emptied the canteen and slung it over the saddle horn.

Before going back to the ranch, Wiona figured she'd make a detour to the second tank. The roundup was slated for Saturday, and she wanted to make sure nobody had wandered off. She'd be shorthanded, no doubt. Beto and Gaby she could count on. She had no idea if Lucy would remember her offer of help and Wiona wasn't about to remind her. That left Stokey. Well, she wasn't going to remind him either. They'd just have to make do with three, if it came down to that.

She heard the cow's bawling before she saw it. It was the brindle, but her pretty little black calf was nowhere to be seen. It didn't take a genius to figure out what had taken place.

The old brindle was staring right at her. Wiona looked at her, then at the sky. The sun was already directly overhead. "Sorry mama, no time to take care of it today," she said, but those big shiny eyes did bore right through to her soul. The cow released another mournful bellow.

"OK, OK. I'll go get the truck. Damn that son of a bitch!"

Montoya took a sip of coffee as he scrolled through the intelligence bulletins. Routinely he did this on Mondays, but he'd been out of the office most of the day, collecting garbage among other things.

Tuesday there'd been that fire in the morning. He'd spent the afternoon in court. In between, there'd been the reports from forensics and the arson team. The forensic report merely confirmed what he'd figured, feces, semen, K-Y jelly, blood. The surprise was the report from the arson team. Mortar shells and half a dozen launchers were found in a deep, metal-lined safe dug under the kitchen floor.

He scanned each bulletin. One stayed his attention and he put his coffee aside. Two illegals, one a boy age 9, the other a 12-year-old girl, had been kidnapped. Most situations like this involved an estranged husband who'd snatched the kids and taken off back to Mexico. But this was more like a load-jack, except that only the kids had been nabbed. As yet no ransom had been demanded.

The kidnappers had been driving a late model, white Chrysler 300 with a yellow "God Bless Our Troops" ribbon on the back. Both perpetrators were described as Hispanic males; one was slender and light-complected, the other portly, dark-complected, with either green or blue eyes. The latter was wearing white ostrich-skin boots.

For a moment, Montoya considered the contents of Trillig's garbage can: the little nest of long black hair, the saladito wrapper. Mexican kids? Definitely. Was the Chrysler at the scene of the fire the same one the kidnappers had driven? If so, what was the connection to Trillig? Suppliers? Probably. It wasn't unusual for human traffickers to also smuggle drugs and munitions.

He took out his notebook and wrote down the particulars, noted the source, a Border Patrol agent out of Douglas by the name of Stokelund.

Montoya picked up the phone, dialed. "This is Officer Reynaldo Montoya of the Phoenix police. Is Agent Theodore Stokelund available?"

"Who?"

"Theodore Stokelund."

"Oh, of course. Stokey Stokelund," a lilting female voice

responded. "He's out of the office right now."

"This is kind of urgent. I'm going to give you my cell phone number. If you could have him call me as soon as he comes in."

"Yes, sir. I will certainly do just that."

"And your name?" He wrote it down in his notebook. "Thank you, Florence."

He typed the name Francisco Ochoa, the owner of the duplex, into the DMV data base. The Chrysler 300 was not registered under that name. Next he typed in the license plate number. It was registered to a Graciela Rubio-Mejia, who lived in Chandler.

He looked at his watch. It was still early. He jotted down the address.

Montoya, pulled up to the house, a rambling adobe with additions tacked on here and there. It was probably an old farmhouse that had once been surrounded by fields of cotton. Now it squatted in the shade of a huge tamarisk on an acre or so among dozens upon dozens of sleeker tract homes. An oleander hedge full of magenta blooms separated the street from the yard.

He jumped down from his personal vehicle, a Chevy Tahoe, sporting full-bore mariachi: short black jacket, red bow at the collar of a white starched shirt, silver buttons down the sides of tight black pants. Adjusting his great swooping sombrero, Montoya knocked on the screen. After a few moments, a young woman appeared, a child of perhaps 2 peeking out from behind her legs. "Yes?" She looked him up and down, smiling uncertainly.

"Buenos tardes, señora. Busco para Graciela Mejia. Ella esta aquí?"

"I don't speak much Spanish."

"Are you Graciela Mejia?"

"She's my grandmother."

"Is she in? I'm collecting donations to help some of our less fortunate young women participate in the Mariposa Cotillion." And this was true. He did solicit donations under the auspices of the

Brothers of Aztlan so the daughters of Hispanic police officers killed or disabled in action could participate in the cotillion – sort of a communal debut for 15-year-old girls. "Are you familiar with it?"

She shook her head.

"No? It's like a big quinceañera, but for lots of girls instead of just one. I believe your grandmother has helped out in the past. I'd like to speak with her if I may."

"Come in." She pushed the screen door open and stood aside. "She's in her bedroom. Nana? Someone's here to see you."

The original house was built shot-gun fashion, with rooms opening off a central hallway. From one of the back rooms, he heard the television blaring in a familiar, emotionally heightened Spanish. His bad luck.

"There she is." The young woman indicated a birdlike, ancient creature propped up in bed by pillows and swathed in crochet. "Nana?"

"Shush," Señora Mejia admonished, without taking her eyes from the television screen.

Quietly, Montoya took a seat. He knew better than to interrupt a grandmother's afternoon telenovelas. While he waited for a commercial, he looked around the room.

Every surface was covered with mementos of a long life. On the corner altar, a seven-day candle burned, setting the image of Santo Niño de Atoche glowing amid family photos. A single red rose, its head drooping, sat in a bud vase next to a plaster statue of the Virgin of Guadalupe. On the dresser were more photos, among them a large picture of a man – dark complected, with green eyes and substantial jowls. Montoya could imagine him sporting fancy, white ostrich-skin boots. In the picture he was standing with his arm around a slightly younger version of the viejita who lay on the bed mesmerized by the drama unfolding on the television.

Montoya placed his sombrero carefully on the back seat of his car then glanced at his watch. His wife had rescheduled his tux fitting for that afternoon, but if he hurried, there was still time to drop by the station and put out a BOLO for Francisco "Dutch" Ochoa de Mejia. He'd also need to set up surveillance at the home of the man's mother. As the viejita had explained, "Mi Butch es un muy buen hijo." And a good son would not let too much time pass before paying his ailing old mother a visit.

Too excited to wait, Osa sprang through the open window of the truck. As Wiona got out of the cab, the pup eyed her keenly, awaiting direction. Wiona blew her whistle. After a few minutes, she blew it again. Before long the cows came ambling in with their calves. Even the bereaved brindle, still bawling, filed in.

Normally, loading a cow into a trailer required two people on horseback, but for Wiona, normal didn't exist.

"Stay, Osa," she ordered. The dog licked her chops a couple of times as if considering, then sat as Wiona unloaded Link. Once mounted, Wiona shifted in the saddle, urging Link forward. When they were alongside the brindle, she dropped a houlihan over the cow's head then quickly tightened the loop.

"It's just me, mama. We're going to get your baby. Easy now."

She tossed the loose end of the rope around a trailer ball welded high up on the back end of the trailer, then dallied it around her saddle horn. She gave a low whistle and Osa, practically skipping, took her place at the heels of the cow. With the dog snapping encouragement from behind and Link pulling back on the rope, the brindle made her reluctant way up the ramp and into the trailer.

Surrounded by a mongrel assortment of cattle dogs, Burl came striding out of the house. A man concerned with his appearance, he wore a crisp, black Western-style shirt that contrasted handsomely with his thick white hair. In his hand, he carried an evil looking rifle, undoubtedly the one he'd used on Punkin, and it gave Wiona pause. She pulled her truck in front of a corral full-up with the Black

Angus steers he was bulking up for auction. A second, smaller corral held a couple dozen or more cows and calves.

"Afternoon, Wiona," he said pleasantly enough, pointing the gun toward the ground.

"Burl."

He craned his neck some to get a peek into the back of the trailer. "What's brings you out here on this fine afternoon?"

"Stay, Osa," she commanded as she hopped out of the truck. "I believe you rounded up one of my calves by mistake."

"Don't think so. You called me to come get my cows and their calves and I did."

"I've got a slick here."

"Sorry to hear that."

"I believe you've got her calf."

"I cut out my cows, all three Black Angus, and their calves, all three Black Angus, come with them." He nodded his head towards the back of the truck. "I see the cow you got there's brindle."

"Her calf was black. If I could just unload her, we could see if she'll let any of those calves you brought in today suckle."

"Don't go to the trouble. I'm satisfied I got my cows and the calves that belong to them."

Wiona knew a confrontation with Burl would be ugly, but she wasn't about to let this bastard take the brindle's calf. "Well, I suppose I could come back later with the cattle inspector."

"I suppose you could."

By the time she could get back out with the cattle inspector, they both knew her calf would be veal. "I'd like to get this sorted out now, Burl. I mean, since I'm here. My cow's pretty uncomfortable you see, and I bet her calf, if you took him by mistake, is pretty hungry by now."

As if on cue, the brindle let out a long, low bellow. From somewhere in the sea of black, came a pitiful bawling.

"Hear that, Burl? Maybe I don't even have to unload her."

"Well, I'll be damned, Wiona."

Already are, you old cattle thief, she said to herself. "Oh, and one other thing. You haven't seen a cat around here, by any chance, a homely little thing, black and orange with white on her chest."

He shook his head. "Why do you ask?"

"Mine got shot up, and I was wondering …"

"See this here?" He held out the rifle with both hands. "This here's a .223 caliber, military, semiautomatic assault rifle. If I'd fired this at your goddamn cat, there'd be nothing left but a few scraps of raven feed, believe me."

Wiona did. "Well then, if you'll just get my calf."

He nodded again. As he turned toward the corral, he muttered. "Goddamn old dyke."

Heat shot up her neck and fired her cheeks. She couldn't say which was worse, being called a dyke or being called old – she never thought of herself as either. Well, folks around here were hard up for any scrap of gossip. What the hell! She didn't give a damn what the likes of Burl Rollings thought anyway. With the money he'd socked away stealing other folk's calves, he'd have enough to buy all the coal he'd need to keep plenty warm in hell.

Old dyke. If that's what she was, it changed nothing. When she got home she still had to take care of her cow and calf, feed and water them as well as Link and Thunder, still had to work on the accounts and clean up after her mother. She was who she was and did what needed to be done as soon as she could get around to it. And each night she got into bed alone. Beyond that her mind would not go.

"By the way," he said, hand on the gate to the corral. "I hear you've got you a wetback working for you now. What does the Border Patrol have to say about that?"

"Actually, she doesn't work for me, she's a guest." She took a step forward, chin offering a challenge. "Why don't you just ring up the Border Patrol, Burl, and find out for yourself what they think about that." She offered him what she hoped was a winning smile then. "Now about my calf?"

Once in the truck, Wiona's hands began to shake. She hadn't noticed his footwear, but a fancy dresser like Burl might just have a fancy pair of boots; what had Stokey called them? And that rifle. What does a man need a rifle like that for? Although Burl wasn't exactly a cattle rustler, given the opportunity, he obviously wasn't above rounding up someone else's unbranded calves. What if Fletcher Hart had caught him at it? Burl might be capable of shooting a man, but a man like Fletcher and in the back? She didn't think so. Still, she'd run it by Stokey on Saturday if he showed up.

Day 12

Stokey sped east down the sandy drag toward the electronic sensor alert that had been activated. Within half a mile of the sensor he pulled off the drag and parked under a mesquite. Once out of the truck he glassed the area. Only the occasional yucca interrupted the gray-greens and browns of the prickly pear and rock-studded slopes. He put on his CamelBak and green ballistic vest, which provided only so-so protection, then considered the assault rifle cradled in its rack. He had his sidearm, and the less he carried the faster he'd be able to move. He pushed the lock button. Quietly he nudged the truck door closed, then jogged off down the drag. He figured to pick up the tracks as they headed north from the border.

When he was within spitting distance of the sensor he saw a fresh set. The guy was wearing cowboy boots, the kind with pointy toes. From the look of the track, either he was fat or carried a heavy load. Stokey figured a man wearing cowboy boots wasn't planning to walk very far. Quickly and quietly, he followed the tracks where they led up a draw. Edged by cat claw acacia, it would eventually connect with Doubtful Wash and an old jeep trail.

Man it was dry. He imagined a single flung match, a campfire in a rising wind, or the first bolt of cloud-to-ground lightning striking just about anything, an acacia snag or clump of bear grass. Could see the flames grow as they were sucked up the draw. With so much dry fuel on the ground, a fire could spread beyond control in a few hours and the Peloncillos would be up in smoke.

Up in smoke. He thought of Becka. It only took a drought and a malignant spark and there you go, up in smoke. He imagined her sitting in her tiny living room, silently fuming. So angry she was ready to toss a match on what was left of their marriage. Was there any way he could end the drought before that happened? Probably too late now. Should have done my watering a long time ago, he thought, glassing the draw. He could hear the clatter of displaced rocks, and picked up his pace.

It wasn't long before he saw the guy. He was fat *and* carried a backpack, though it was pretty small, more like a rucksack. Stokey put his hand on the butt of his gun. "Para!" he shouted.

The man stopped in his tracks and turned slowly. Stokey saw that his hands were empty and he had no visible weapon. Traveling alone and light, the man was probably just a commuter, although an illegal one, returning after a conjugal visit with his vieja.

"Ponga la mochila sobre la tierra!" Stokey directed.

The man dropped his rucksack to the ground. He took a swipe at his sweaty, round face and adjusted his straw cowboy hat. Smiling, he held both hands open before him, palms up.

Stokey acknowledged the man's open hands and sheepish smile of surrender with a nod. Over the years he'd seen the gesture hundreds of times and it never failed to make him feel a bit sympathetic. Bottom line: People need to eat, but they also like to fuck.

Stokey removed a pair of plastic handcuffs from his CamelBak. "Venga acá!" he demanded, though his heart wasn't really in it. Still smiling, the man stepped forward, wrists together obligingly. When he was so close Stokey could smell the chorizo on his breath, the fat man kicked him hard and swift in the groin. Stokey dropped to his knees.

When his vision cleared, he struggled to his feet, while his assailant, the unlikeliest mule Stokey'd ever seen, waddled back down the draw toward the border, leaving the rucksack resting on the sand. Good enough, Stokey thought, cradling his nuts. "Mission fucking accomplished."

Wiona was just slipping the stays into the last section of fence upslope from the wash when she heard the distinctive call, something between a croak and a bellow. A trogon was a rare bird in these parts and it was too early in the year to expect to see one. Improbable as it seemed, there was no doubt about it. Once you heard one, you could not mistake its croak for any other creature on earth.

As she searched the canopy for a flash of red or green, Osa started to pitch a fit. Startled, Wiona pressed her palm against the old Colt at her hip. When she spotted Wade Spalding scrambling up Doubtful Wash, her hand dropped to her side. He was dressed in crisp new camouflage, binoculars hung from a harness affair strapped over his narrow shoulders, and the pockets of his canvas vest and his cargo pants bulged with equipment she figured must be crucial to the pressing business of bird watching. He was holding some kind of small device aloft. Trogon mystery solved. Cheeks rosy from sun and embarrassment, she smiled.

"Hey, Wade," she said. "Fooled me again. I thought there was a trogon right here." She noticed that he was leaning on one of those ski pole-like walking sticks nobody but a birdwatcher would use. "Did you sprain your ankle, or something?"

"Just an old soccer injury acting up," he said, as he labored out of the wash.

"I'm trying out this new speaker here. See, it just plugs into my iPod." He held it out for her to admire. "It's smaller than a deck of cards – half the size of my other one with three times the broadcasting capacity."

"Imagine that." The only explanation was that this guy had too much money, she was thinking when she noticed the shotgun strapped to his backpack, double barrels skyward. She pointed at it with her chin then. "Kind of an odd piece of equipment for a birdwatcher."

"You mean the shotgun? It belonged to my grandfather. At close range, this old gal could stop a mountain lion, a jaguar even, not that I'd ever, but you know, since Fletcher ..."

"Yeah, I know what you mean." She patted the Colt. "The locals are offering a reward."

"Yeah, I hear it's up to $10,000 now."

He smiled then and Wiona figured that he'd made a hefty contribution.

Anyway, I started carrying this old gun when I go out birding. I'm not exactly a crack shot. I'm more likely to actually hit something with a shotgun than a pistol like yours."

"Do you actually think you're in danger out here?"

"Just being cautious. Besides, I'm on the lookout for a feral cat that's been stalking birds at my feeder."

"Feral cat?"

"Yeah. I shot at it the other day, but I must have missed. At least I didn't find the remains."

"That feral cat was mine, Wade. And you didn't miss."

"Oops."

"Oops? You shoot my cat and that's all you've got to say?"

"It was on my property, Wiona. And it was eating my birds."

"Your birds?" She felt the heat shift from her cheeks to the top of her head. "I didn't know you claimed personal ownership."

"Be reasonable, Wiona. How was I supposed to know it was your cat? Looked feral to me."

"So if it had been a bobcat, you would have shot it?"

"Of course not. A bobcat is a native species. House cat is not a native species, Wiona."

"Neither are you, Wade, but I wouldn't shoot you." She closed her eyes then so she wouldn't have to look at his gawky, stupid bird face and resumed her repairs.

"I'm sorry, Wiona, but ..."

She waved a hand to shut him up. Damn, she thought. Wiona

liked it better when there was only Burl to hate. Then she noticed his boots. The sight made the hair lift on her bare arms.

He dropped the pack on Garza's desk. "Roughly 30 pounds of heroin."

"Good job. Where's the mule?"

"Read my report," he said and limped out of the office.

As soon as he got to his cubicle, Florence was at his door. "An important message came for you yesterday when you were at the hospital with your dad." She looked at the memo. "Officer Montoya from the Phoenix police. He said it was kind of urgent, but I didn't see you come in this morning. Sorry, Stokey."

"No hay pedo."

"Ay, Stokey!" She laughed and handed him the memo.

"Gracias, señorita."

"De nada, Stokey," she said, but made no motion to leave.

Wanting privacy in case the call was related to the kidnapping that he was no longer investigating, he smiled. "Muchisimas gracias. Was there anything else?"

"Oh! Perdón." Looking offended, she dropped the memo on his desk. Stokey watched with appreciation as she departed. Mexican women, even old ones like Florence, did something with their hips that could communicate anything from degree of availability to profound disgruntlement.

He looked at the memo. Using his cell phone he punched in the number. "Officer Montoya? This is Agent Stokey Stokelund of the Border Patrol. You called?"

Stokey hung up and immediately dialed Rosy on his cell. While waiting for the real voice, he took out his wallet and clipped the slip of paper with the name of Francisco Ochoa de Mejia to the phone numbers he had collected from Corcho's pockets. Perhaps Rosy could manage a wiretap.

"Rosy?" he said before he realized it was her answering machine.

"It's Stokey. I've got a name for you. Francisco Ochoa de Mejia. Aka Dutch Ochoa."

As soon as she had settled the Brindle and her calf in the corral, Wiona had called Stokey, but he was not at the station and she didn't want to call him at home. Unlike Burl, it was hard to imagine Wade shooting anything, well anything other than a cat. What reason could he possibly have to kill Fletcher Hart? None that she could think of. The boots were probably just a coincidence. Well, she'd let Stokey sort it out. She'd left him a message to give her a call.

From the porch, she could see the brindle cow down in the corral placidly chewing her cud while the calf nursed. It was a pretty sight, and a satisfying one. Her father couldn't have handled Burl any better. At the thought of that man, her face got hot all over again. Dyke. Well, whatever she was, she couldn't help what folks thought about it. Besides, who would a person rather have as a neighbor, an old dyke or a cattle thief?

"Hello there," Emma sang through the screen. "I just made us some coffee."

"I'll be there in a minute."

"Stay right where you are. I'm bringing it out." Emma pushed the screen door open with her knee, and handed Wiona a mug. "Nice afternoon." She lowered herself onto the glider, then patted the spot next to her. "Let's sit and visit a minute."

Surprised, Wiona sat. She couldn't recall a single time she and Emma had a *visit*. For several minutes the women sipped their coffee, only the rhythmic protest of the glider interrupting the pleasant quiet of the afternoon.

"That brindle's got a nice looking calf," Emma observed.

"Yeah. For such an ugly old gal, she produces some pretty calves."

"Is it a little bull or a heifer?"

"Bull."

"Too bad."

"Maybe we'll keep him." Though she had developed a soft spot for the old cow and her calf, Wiona wasn't just being sentimental. The herd could use another bull. She'd have to give it some thought.

"Glider needs to be oiled."

Wiona nodded, determined to enjoy Emma's friendly chatter while it lasted. "Got a good do on this coffee."

Emma took Wiona's hand, smiled. "Just now, you sounded like my Frank."

"I did? Tell me a little about him, like when he was young. I don't even know how you met Dad."

"Met who?"

Wiona realized then that Emma must have thought she was entertaining a visitor, maybe some rancher-wife, now long gone. "Tell me about Frank."

"Well, he's always been a hard worker, you know. He abides in Christ, and he's good to my son, Frankie, always tried to treat him like his own."

"What do you mean, treat him like his own? He was his own."

"Why bless your heart, Belva, you know perfectly well that Arnold Volk was Frankie's father."

Emma had confused her with Aunt Belva again, she understood that now, but who was Arnold Volk? She'd never heard the name mentioned. "Arnold Volk?"

"Of course, Arnold Volk. The only boy I dated my entire senior year."

"So why didn't you marry him?"

"Belva!"

"Sorry. It's been so long. I've forgotten the details."

"By the time I finally figured out I was pregnant, the Army had sent Arnold off to Germany. You remember."

"Oh yes. They sent him to Germany."

"So he couldn't come running home to marry me. What was I supposed to do? Daddy would have killed me. You know that. And Frank had always liked me. He offered and that was that. I never dreamed we'd stay married, but by the time Arnold came home, I was already pregnant with Wiona. I told you all this, Belva. It was when you and Ford were living up in Wyoming."

"It's coming back to me."

"Frank never wanted him to know. Tried to treat them equal, Frankie and Wiona, but I think the boy always suspected."

"Is that why you always favored him over Wiona?"

"I didn't mean to favor him. It's just that from day one he was, oh you know. His father being my first love, my only love to tell the truth. Frank's a good, kind man, but you know how it was with Arnold and me. And Wiona, she was a good little girl, don't get me wrong, but she was always so independent, difficult that way. Maybe that's why she never married."

"So if you hadn't been pregnant with Wiona, you'd have left Frank and run off with Arnold when he came home?"

"After I got pregnant with Wiona, I never permitted the thought." Emma looked down at her hands, noticed the coffee cup and took a sip. "Now what was I saying?"

"Do you resent her?"

"Who?"

"Wiona."

"She's my daughter! It's just that Frankie was my first, and you must have noticed how he took after Arnold."

Arnold must have been a handsome man, Wiona concluded, unlike her own father whom she resembled. So her father was not Frankie's, her Methodist, teetotaler mother had sex out of wedlock, and she'd been an independent, difficult child, perhaps resented, perhaps not.

Wiona tried to determine how she should feel about these revelations and discovered that they all happened so long ago, they meant surprisingly little to her, less today than they might have even two weeks ago, given everything else that was going on. Thanks to Belen, Wiona was seeing her life a little differently these days. Besides, she sniffed, something about being called an old dyke makes a person less prone to judgment.

"You know, Frank always wanted more children. Me? I didn't have that need. One of each was plenty. Besides, if I'd had another boy, well, who'd get the ranch, Frankie or Frank's blood son? Isn't big enough to split up. But with Frankie overseas and my husband always out in the barn, it does get kind of lonely, doesn't it?"

"Yes, it does," Wiona agreed. "But we've got each other."

Emma looked at her now as if she'd only just sat down beside her. She patted her knee and smiled. "We certainly do."

Wiona gave a little push with her foot to set the glider once more in motion.

Stokey was out in the garden slipping little chicken-wire cages over his new tomato plants when he heard the phone ring. By the time he got to the kitchen the ringing had stopped. "Damn." He looked at the caller ID and recognized Becka's number. He had been suppressing the urge to call, but now quickly dialed. When he heard her voice, he hung up. Reconsidered, then dialed again.

"Becka?"

"Did you call just now?"

"Yeah, but something went wrong with the phone. Anyway ..."

"So how are you?"

"Fine. You?"

"Good, I think ..."

"You think?"

"Well, I've been needed to tell you this, I might as well get right to the point. I'm pregnant. Just finished the first trimester. I didn't want to tell you until ..."

"Pregnant? Is it mine?"

Without a word, Becka hung up on him. He did a quick mental

calculation and figured the baby certainly could be his. He dialed her number again, but she didn't pick up.

"Damn, stupid son of a bitch!" He hung up the phone just as Katie came in from the garage.

"What's got you so upset?" She set a plastic sack of groceries on the counter.

"Your mother just hung up on me."

"I take it she told you about the baby."

"So you already know about that."

She took several frozen dinners out of the sack and held them out to him. "You need to be more supportive."

He pointed to the frozen lasagna. "What do you mean? I've always supported her; I've always supported everybody around here."

"Emotionally supportive." She set a head of lettuce and two tomatoes in the sink.

"What the hell's that supposed to mean?"

"You need to figure it out, Dad."

"Is there anything your mother needs to figure out?"

"She's got plenty to figure out. Think about it. She's pretty old to be having a baby. Think about what that means to her. For once, think about what it's like being the woman."

"How the hell should I know what it's like being the woman?"

"See," she said, slamming the refrigerator door shut. "That's your problem, Dad. Lack of empathy."

Back in the garden he quietly sipped his second beer while readjusting the tomato cages. What was it like to be a woman? How was he supposed to know? He did know what it was like at the moment to be himself – shitty – but Becka? He knew she was unhappy, but what specifically made her that way? Part of it was him, and he was pretty clear about which part. But part of it was her, and that part eluded him. He took out his cell phone and punched in her number.

"Sorry I'm such an asshole. I guess I can't help myself."

"I should have told you sooner."

"Well, I guess you had to think about it."

"I did need time, Stokey. What am I doing? I'm too old to be having a baby."

"You're not old, honey. I think it's great."

"I think it's terrifying."

He adjusted a tomato cage, shimmying it into the ground another half inch until it was level with the one next to it. "Well, I can understand that," he said, trying for empathy. "But you know lots of women are … it seems that plenty of … and there's good doctors …"

"That's what I keep telling myself, but I'm still scared."

"You'll do fine. So when are you coming home?"

After a long silence, she answered, "I'm not."

"What? Hold on a sec." He took in a deep breath, fingers tracing a path from his throat and the base of his sternum to ease the tightness there. He blew out slowly. Swallowed a couple of times. "Sorry. I had to turn down the TV. Now what did you say?"

"I'm not coming home. I just got hired as a long-term substitute for a teacher's aide who was in a car wreck. I'll be at an elementary school not far from my apartment. It's a foot in the door."

"That's good for you, but if you expect me to move to Tucson..."

"I don't."

"So what does this mean? You want a divorce?"

"What do you want, Stokey?"

"I asked first."

"I want this baby. I want this job."

"But you don't want me."

There was another long pause.

"Get a lawyer, Becka. If the baby's mine, I'll pay child support."

"There's never been anybody else, Stokey."

Ignoring her, he continued a speech he'd already practiced in his head. "I can sell the house. The kids are essentially grown. You can have half of the money I get from the sale to use as a down payment on a place of your own and ..."

"Don't do this to me, Stokey."

"What the hell should I do, Becka?" He hung up the phone.

So she was dumping him. But the baby ... If Becka didn't snap out of it, whatever *it* was, he'd file for custody. He'd be damned if two, three, five years down the road he'd tolerate some other man raising a child of his. He started for the house; he turned back to the garden, then started for the house again as he dialed her number.

"It's me." His voice was flat. "So what did the doc say? Is everything all right?"

"So far. But I don't think I could take losing another baby."

"Now, honey, this baby's going to be just fine."

"You think?"

"I know."

"I quit smoking last week."

"That's good, honey." He didn't call her on the lie.

"Yeah, well. Stokey?"

"I'm listening."

"You have a right to be angry, but I'm not ready for all that other stuff. Can we just put it on hold?"

"Our marriage? It's been on hold for a while already."

"I know, but ..."

He tried to determine what he really wanted. At the moment, it didn't seem to make any difference whether they were married or divorced. He wasn't a happy man, but a divorce wasn't going to change that. "We'll put it off for now if that's what you want."

"OK, then."

"Yeah, well. Take care of yourself." Without waiting for a goodbye, he hung up the phone.

Suddenly redeployment seemed more appealing. He'd miss the kids, the garden. He considered his aching nuts. Obviously, he'd lost his edge – probably never survive another tour.

Holding his scrotum, he eased himself down to his knees beside the row. The earth was still warm. The arugula had finally come up.

There were dozens of tiny bright green sprouts. He pinched each one from the ground, now, figuring he'd put bell peppers in instead. When he finished he settled himself down beside the little pile of limp green, sipping his beer to keep the sob that had been building from rising to the surface.

Belen and her children were making their way along a narrow, winding trail, a shortcut that led to her grandmother's casita on the outskirts of San Pablito. To her right the yellow cliff rose so high it made her dizzy to look up to the rim where she knew her grandmother was waiting for them. A deep, blue ravine cut by a ribbon of dark water was to the left. Laughing, Adriana and Edgar raced around the next bend, eager to get to the top. When Belen rounded the bend, encumbered by a huge load of vegetables she carried in a sack on her back, the children were nowhere to be seen. She called to them, could hear her voice echo as it bounced off the yellow cliffs.

"Aquí estamos," Adriana cried, her voice a confusion of echoes. Belen peered into the ravine, and there they were standing next to the stream beckoning for her to follow, but how? She considered the depth of the ravine, the enormity of her burden, before stepping off the edge.

Belen awoke with a start. Her children had been so close. She closed her eyes, her heart knocking against her ribs.

Wiona and Emma had gone to bed hours ago, and her room was quiet and dark except for the moonlight shining across the bed. Belen had been sleeping so much during the day, she knew she would not go back to sleep now, even though she was exhausted. She threw back the covers.

Once out of bed, she wrapped her rebozo around her shoulders. Tucking Jesús in its folds, she went out to the porch. The chill air felt good against her warm face. She sat in the glider, rocking while the nearly full moon floated through the trees. Somewhere in the silver night, un tecolote called. She shivered involuntarily. Some thought the owl was an omen of death. But Belen did not subscribe to such superstitions. No. Her children were alive. She would know it in her heart if it were otherwise. She had prayed and prayed for their safe return. Surely the virgin would not deny her.

The screen door opened and la vieja came out on the porch. As she lowered herself onto the glider, she murmured something that Belen did not understand. Señora Emma continued, her voice low, kind, and when she put her arm around her, Belen allowed her head to fall onto the soft shoulder and her tears to fall. Half-mother, half-child, the old one did not understand the source of her grief, but offered comfort all the same.

Day 13

Wiona was braiding her hair when she heard the crash. "What now?" she said, letting the half-finished braid fall down her back.

Out in the kitchen Emma stood amid shattered glass looking shocked and bewildered. Seeing the expression on her mother's face, her annoyance abated. She willed calm into her voice. "What happened, Mother?"

"It just exploded."

Wiona recognized the black plastic lid of the coffeemaker, took in the red-hot burner on the stove, the glass and water splattered over the floor, and then Emma's bare feet. "Hold on, Mother. Don't move." She got out the broom and dustpan and started making a clean path to a kitchen chair. "There. Now go sit down."

"What was I thinking?" Emma asked, still looking bewildered.

"Take it easy, Mother. I'll have it cleaned up in no time."

"But what was I thinking?"

"You were probably thinking it was the old percolator."

"Where is that old percolator?" She asked, her voice now more peevish than confused. "It made the best coffee."

"We've still got it somewhere. I guess I better get it out."

"Well, bless your heart; I guess you better." She picked up her feet so Wiona could sweep beneath the table. "What a goddamn mess!"

Katie was already eating a bowl of cereal when he came into the kitchen.

"After such a late night, Sissy, you're up bright and early."

"Morning Dad. I told them I'd be in early to help with inventory. So did you ever get back to Mom yesterday?"

He poured himself a cup of coffee and sat down. "Yes I did."

"Did you talk her into coming home?"

"Nope."

"I was hoping …" She made a grimace. "How do you feel about that?"

"Hmm. Don't know." He added a teaspoon of sugar to his coffee, some milk. "Am I supposed to have feelings?"

"Ah, Daddy. I'm sorry. Sorry for both of you. I know Mom loves you."

"And how do you come by this knowledge?"

She shrugged.

He looked at his watch, then shot up from the table and yelled down the hallway. "Jackson? You up?" He sat back down. "So, how's old Alvin these days?"

"Darin."

"So how's old Darin?"

"A fling of the past."

"Pass the Cheerios, please. So why's that?"

"He wasn't enough like you."

Stokey considered this. He got up and opened the refrigerator for something to do while he tamped his emotions down a bit. He loved his daughter, thought the world of her, in fact. It was nice to think she felt somewhat likewise. He returned to the table with an unopened carton of milk. "I think that one's starting to turn." He picked up the open milk carton and poured it down the sink.

"Don't give up, Dad. It's a midlife crisis thing."

"I'm closer to midlife then she is."

"Yes, but you've actually had a life. She hasn't, or at least that's how she sees it."

"How do you see it?"

"I try not to have an opinion."

"You are a coward, Sissy. Well, midlife crisis or whatever, I wish she'd snap out of it."

She pointed her spoon at him. "There's your problem."

"My problem again? I thought we were discussing your mother's problem here."

"You dismiss the legitimacy of her feelings."

"I do? Hmm. I'll have to give that some consideration, Dr. Stokelund."

"You do that, Dad. In the meantime, I got to go. We'll talk about this some more later."

"Well, then."

She leaned over and kissed his cheek. "Love you, Dad."

He kissed the air. "Love you too, Sissy. Sorry about Erwin."

"Me too, Dad. But oh well."

Stokey glanced at the front page of the newspaper, then pushed it aside, wondering if 20 years ago, he'd been some sort of Darin to a less wise Becka. He looked at his watch again and figured he'd let Jackson sleep in for another five.

Romeo sat on Dawn's shoulder as she considered the contents of the drawer. She tossed Adriana a clean camisole. It had "Hot Baby" printed in rhinestones across the chest, but some of the rhinestones were missing and she didn't wear it anymore. From another drawer, she selected a pair of pink bikini underpants. "We need to get you some clothes of your own."

"What?"

"You need clothes. Shorts? T-shirts? Shoes?" She waved the bikinis in the air before tossing them to Adriana. "Hello? Underpants?"

Adriana nodded, but didn't seem very excited about the idea.

"James is going to take me shopping, maybe next week. You know shopping?"

"Yes, I know shopping," Adriana said, except the way she said it made it sound like they were going to go chopping.

"You can come, too." Adriana still didn't seem interested. Dawn didn't know whether she didn't get it, or just didn't care. Maybe it was some of each. She knew the girl was sad about being here, but she'd just have to get over it. Dawn smiled. "We'll make a list of the things we need. You'll see. It'll be fun."

Dawn was tired of being sick – not that she was actually sick, but she was tired of feeling like she was. It was boring, but by next week, she'd feel better. James had promised. A shopping trip would be fun and it would be a lot more fun with Adriana along. She'd go talk to James about it right now so they could start making their lists.

The boys were in the living room taking turns with a Game Boy. As she passed, she looked into Pancho Villa's cage. He needed fresh water and his food dish was empty.

James was working at his desk. Lately, he was always working at his desk. He looked up when she came in, smiled. "You're up early. What's the occasion?"

"No occasion. I'm just tired of sleeping."

"So you're feeling better."

She was some, but didn't want to say so. "It still hurts to walk, I can't turn over in bed, and every time I move, I have to go really, really slow. It's boring."

"You'll be back to yourself before you know it," he said and turned back to his computer. "Next week we'll go shopping."

"That's what I want to talk to you about." She waited a moment before continuing. "When we go shopping, we need to bring Adriana along. I'm tired of loaning her my clothes."

"Don't worry about it. I've got somebody who wants to adopt Adriana, and what's the boy's name?"

She took Romeo off her shoulder. He nibbled at her finger while she caressed his chest. "Edgar."

"Yeah, Edgar too. I've got a real nice home for both of them."

"When?"

"Today, tomorrow maybe, soon. I just have to work out the details."

"Will they both go to the same family?" She pressed her lips together. "I mean, Adriana would …"

"Of course they'll be in the same family. I wouldn't have it any other way. Now come here."

Slowly, she crossed the room, making sure he noticed each painful step. He took both hands and kissed the back of each. "You're the greatest, padna." He smiled. "The absolute greatest."

Before returning to her room, she put fresh water out for Pancho Villa, along with a slice of orange and a handful of sunflower seeds. The bird eyed her from the farthest corner of his cage. His bald spots were growing, she noticed. Pretty soon he'd be naked as a newborn baby. She thought of her own baby, then thought of Adriana's adoption. Dawn bit down hard on her tongue until she tasted blood. After a few minutes, she put a sunflower seed between her lips and offered it to Romeo. Gentle as a kiss, the lovebird plucked it from her.

Holding his cell phone to his ear, Stokey tried to keep his side of the conversation to a minimum.

Rosy was saying, "You know as well as I that Mejia is a prominent name in the Chihuahuan cartel. We're pretty certain Francisco Ochoa Mejia is one of theirs, probably has his fingers dipped in any number of pies, certainly human and narco-trafficking, but we haven't been able to catch him at it yet. Given Homeland Security's interest and the items found on his property, it's pretty clear that Mejia is involved in smuggling arms out of the U.S. as well. You still with me, Stokey?"

"I'm here."

"Everybody from the Mexican cartels to al Qaeda is armed with

U.S. weaponry, most of it is moving out of country across our southern borders. When they bring this guy in, have your friend call me. I have a few questions of my own I want to ask him."

"I'll keep in touch, Rosy. Thanks." Stomach churning acid, Stokey sat back in his chair now. Frustration and impatience were counterproductive in this business, but how could he feel otherwise? It had been almost two weeks since the kidnapping. Were the kids still in Arizona? They could be anywhere in the United States or even Canada by now, swallowed up and never to be seen again. If that were the case, what would happen to Belen? He'd allowed this case to become personal, a big mistake.

He turned to his computer and scrolled to the file labeled Sexual Harassment in the Workplace. Taking the training would be slightly more productive than sitting here eating his own liver.

Montoya smiled as he hung up the phone. Un muy buen hijo, he thought to himself. His officers had allowed Dutch Ochoa to have his little visit with the old lady before picking him up. He should be here within the hour.

First Montoya would address the question of the mortar launchers and shells stashed under the kitchen floor. Then he'd ask Ochoa about arms smuggling and his affiliation with the Mejia cartel. Those questions should rattle him enough that he might be willing to address the third question, the one that Montoya most wanted answered.

He picked up his phone, eager to let his new friend in the Border Patrol know of their progress.

Stokey looked at his watch – straight up noon and the sky was more white than blue. He got out of the car and pulled his sunglasses in place against the glare. Usually he hated Phoenix, but today he was happy to be there.

He'd made the trip from Douglas, flashers whirling, in less than

2½ hours, record time, and he was only a few minutes late for the meeting. By the time Stokey found the right office, Rosy was already deep in conversation with Montoya. The cop stood up when Stokey entered.

"Rey Montoya," he said, extending his hand over the desk.

"Stokey Stokelund. Glad to meet you in person."

Stokey turned to Rosy who was looking radiant in a suit of burgundy. Today, her head was covered with numerous, small braided pinwheels resembling snails. She smiled at him as serenely as Buddha himself.

"How you doin', Stokey?"

"Hanging in, Rosy. How about you?"

"I'm real good, thanks." She briefly examined her sculptured fingernails. They were the exact color of her suit. It struck Stokey that they'd make a fine weapon in an emergency.

"So this is what we know," Montoya said, getting right down to business. "Francisco Ochoa de Mejia, also known as Dutch Ochoa, is a member of the Mejia cartel. He's been involved in drug running, people smuggling, and now we believe he's taken up arms smuggling. He also matches the description of the load-jacker who kidnapped the two Mexican kids on the night of the ..." He looked down at his notebook.

"Monday, April 2, 12 days ago," Stokey said. By now, everyone present knew the facts of the case and he was anxious to move the process along.

"Right. And this is what we need to find out." Montoya looked back and forth between Rosy and Stokey. "I have reason to believe that he delivered the children to one James Trillig."

Stokey leaned forward. For the first time in over a week, he felt a small puff of optimism fill his chest.

Montoya continued. "What we need from this interview with Ochoa is enough evidence of this connection to obtain a search warrant of Trillig's residence. So. How to proceed?"

"We proceed by scaring the Holy Ghost out of him," Rosy said, tenting those elegant, dangerous fingertips as if in prayer. "And I'm just the person to do it."

Looking over at that gleaming, black mountain of a woman, Stokey imagined she could scare the Holy Ghost out of just about anyone.

Dutch sat on the opposite side of the table from the big negra. He crossed his leg at the knee, then took a handkerchief out of his pocket to wipe a bit of dust off the tip of his boot.

"Now that you know your options, what do you have to say?" she asked.

He refolded the handkerchief and stuffed it into his back pocket, thinking better to deal with the FBI than those cabrones from Homeland Security. At least he'd be allowed a lawyer. He also understood that if he did not cooperate this hija de diablo would let it be known through her informants that he had betrayed la familia.

"I don't have much time," she added, studying her nails.

It was clear he'd have to give up something. Clear as well that he'd be dead within the week, either in jail or out, if he gave up too much. Prison was probably unavoidable. Mitigation was the best he could hope for under the circumstances. In fact, it would give him a margin of satisfaction to offer Trillig in exchange for a bit of leniency. And he'd throw in El Pajaro as well. As a birder with his fancy binoculars and cameras and recording devices, he was a person of no interest to the authorities, and as such, could move around as if invisible, easily transporting small loads of heroin without interference. It would be hard to find a replacement, but he never really liked the man. Whenever they did business, his smile said, "You are simple and I am complex." Well, we are all simple. It's life that's complex. El Pajaro will soon understand this.

Rosy came back into the office, shutting the door behind her. Dropping a slip of paper on Montoya's desk, she asked, "Is that the correct address for this Mr. Trillig?"

Montoya affirmed that it was.

"Then I believe I can have that warrant on your desk by tomorrow, noon at the latest."

Part 6

Roundup

Day 14

Stokey sprinkled cleanser into the toilet bowl, scrubbed the inside. While he let that soak, he sprinkled more cleanser into the sink. What the hell, he had the whole morning, he might as well do the job right. He sprinkled cleanser on the floor as well, used a wet washcloth to wipe the floor around the toilet and sink then flung it into the laundry hamper.

After he finished both bathrooms, he turned to the hamper. Becka had always been fastidious about laundry and now he followed her example, separating colors from whites, knits and Katie's underwear from the towels and the rest. He considered all the little piles, now, shook his head. Suddenly he gathered them up into a lump. After tamping everything into the washer at once, he set the dial to wash and wear, a small, but satisfying act of revenge, though he doubted that Becka would care much about how their laundry was being done these days.

He pulled a clean but wrinkled Border Patrol shirt from a hanger. On a normal Saturday he'd iron all his clothes at once in front of the TV while drinking his evening beers, but this wasn't a normal Saturday. Today, he was going back up to Phoenix to get Belen's children, he was certain, and he'd awakened full of energy and purpose.

Stokey glanced at his watch. Still only 6:30. He wasn't due to meet Rey Montoya until midafternoon. If they got up before noon, there'd be plenty of time to fix the kids French toast for breakfast.

"Damn! Should've called Wiona." He looked at his watch again. Early, but not too early for a rancher.

Everyone sat around the kitchen table, plates piled with scrambled eggs, pork chops, potatoes, refried beans and tortillas. Ranch etiquette required the feeding of friends and neighbors who offered help with roundup, branding and castration. Wiona, the last to fill her plate, took a place at the table next to Susana who was happily dropping tiny pieces of egg on the floor. Wiona watched Emma spoon so much jam on her toast that it dripped off the edge and onto the front of her housedress as she drew it to her mouth. She didn't try to stop her. This morning she wanted no arguments.

According to the new electric clock on the wall, it was nearly 6:30. Lucy had yet to arrive and Stokey had never gotten back to her. Gaby would have to go out with them, which would leave Belen to manage Emma, Jesús and Susana all by herself. Wiona had spent a good deal of the previous night picturing one disaster after another. Now she was worn out before the day had begun, and a long day it would be.

Just then the telephone rang. Stokey or Lucy, she figured. In an instant, Emma was up and going for the phone. In a single stride, Wiona headed her off.

"Pretty sure it's for me, Mother," she said.

"Morning, Wiona. It's Stokey."

"Morning, Stokey."

"Don't mention it to Belen, but we got a lead on the possible whereabouts of the kids. Can't say much at the moment, but it means I won't be able to help with the roundup."

"That's OK. We can manage. Will you call later?"

"If I've got anything, I'll call. Oh, by the way. You know a guy by the name of Wade Spalding?"

"Funny you should ask. He's one of those birders. Sold him 20 acres a couple years ago. He's my neighbor now. Anyway, I ran into him day before yesterday, and he was wearing fancy boots like the ones you described."

"Ariat Packers?"

"I guess, like lace-up cowboy boots. That's why I called you. Then I got busy and didn't think it was all that important anyway. If you knew Wade … "

"By any chance, does this Wade have a kinda limp or something going on with his left leg?"

"Don't remember if it's his left leg, but yes, some sort of old injury, soccer I think he said it was. And one other thing, last I saw him, he was carrying an old shotgun. Spooked, I guess, by Fletcher's murder."

"Very interesting."

"Why's that, Stokey?"

"Can't say. But don't mention the Wade thing to anyone. You hear me?"

"I hear you, but why?"

"Could be dangerous. I mean it, Wiona. Not a word. Now take care."

"I will, Stokey. You too."

"So that was Stokey," she said to no one in particular. "He can't make it."

Wiona was sorry she couldn't tell Belen the news about her children. She didn't know enough Spanish to convey both hope and caution. She was concerned about Stokey's sudden interest in Wade. It was sobering to think he'd probably be tromping around the canyon while they were shooing cows. Belen was watching her as if reading her expression. Wiona smiled. "Muy buena comida."

Belen smiled faintly. "Gracias." She offered more coffee.

Beto held up his cup. "Solamente una mitad, por favor."

"Why can't you all speak English at the table?" Emma said through a mouthful of toast and jam.

"Belen doesn't speak English, Mother."

"Oh. Well, bless her heart." Emma looked up at the clock on the wall. "Where'd that thing come from?"

"I bought it to replace the old one."

"You can't just go out and by a new clock every time you turn around, Wiona. Money isn't toilet paper, you know."

"I know, Mother. But the old one didn't work."

"Worked good enough far as I could tell."

"Do you want more coffee?"

Emma got up from the table. "My program's about to start. I'll take it in the living room." She accepted more coffee and got up from the table.

"Why don't you brush your teeth first, Mother."

"Why don't you brush your teeth first, Mother," Emma mimicked in a singsong nasal, and walked out of the room, wagging her buttocks.

Montoya pulled the heavy glass door open and stood aside for his wife to enter. Since the kids were babies, he'd taken the family out to breakfast on Saturday mornings. It used to be a big deal. Now the older kids couldn't be dragged out of bed so it was just the little ones.

His granddaughter was jumping with excitement. "Pancakes, pancakes," she shouted. He took her hand. "Calmate, Camotita. Calmate," he said, and the little girl began the wedding walk she'd been practicing for the past two weeks. He took his wife's elbow, while she guided Junior with a firm hand on his shoulder.

As the hostess, a girl with pierces through one eyebrow and a nostril and a tattoo of barbed wire ringing her neck, led them to a table, Montoya rolled his eyes toward his wife. Kids today, he thought. He'd wring his daughter's neck himself if she ever defaced her body in such a manner.

Once they were all seated he studied the menu. He wanted the eggs Benedict but the guy at the tux rental who took his measurements had insisted his waist was 34. How could that be?

He'd always worn 32s. His uniform pants, the Charro pants he wore when he played with the mariachi band, all 32s. He stuck a thumb in his waistband. Not so tight, but his belt, also a 32, was on the last notch. He should have the oatmeal.

He looked up at his wife. "What are you having, mi amor?"

"Eggs Benedict."

He closed his menu. "Me too." Life was too short to deny oneself the pleasure of un plato de huevos Benedicto. Besides, he had a busy day ahead of him, he'd just skip lunch. In a few hours, certainly by midafternoon, he expected the search warrant to be ready. He planned to take every precaution. They would use the SWAT team for this one. Child Protection was at the ready to receive Dawn and whatever other children might be there. Stokelund would be on hand to deliver the children back to their mother. He could wait to get a deposition from them. If everything went as planned, it would be over in minutes.

Clear and cool, it was a perfect morning for the roundup. Wiona was mounted on Link, Beto on his roan mare, Niña. Gaby, who announced that she was expecting, due date sometime in November, got the ATV in deference to her condition. That left Lucy to straddle the little motorbike that had belonged to Frankie. With the exception of Lucy, they were all experienced wranglers, but they looked nothing like a person might see in the movies.

They had started gathering at the point farthest from the ranch up beyond the second tank where she'd seen some cows and their calves haremed up with a Brangus bull. When she'd blown her whistle, the group had ambled in for the treat they'd come to expect.

Now the cow with most seniority was at the head of a loose file of 40 or more cows, their calves and three bulls. Gaby and Lucy drove along their flanks, while Beto searched side draws where cattle were likely to hole up during the day. Out in front, Wiona blew her whistle again, and the swelling herd followed like children might the Pied Piper. At least that was the idea. Occasionally, a cow and her calf fell behind. It was Osa's job then to hurry them along, barking at their heels.

Altogether, there were some 80 cows and their calves to gather. Roundup was a leisurely labor – it was unproductive to hurry a cow. Still, the task took constant oversight. Just as well, Wiona did not want time to ponder the vision of Lucy, jittering along in a cloud of dust on that old bike. This was not the way to court friendship. Of greater concern was this morning's conversation with Stokey. What was the lead he was pursuing with the children and where did Wade Spalding fit in?

Alert, she studied each wash and draw as the group, cattle and ragged crew, lurched across the brittle landscape. She turned in the saddle. Lucy managed a wave. Heartened, Wiona waved back, then blew her whistle.

A calf was bawling, frantic, toward the rear of the herd. Wiona figured it had gotten separated from its mother. They were approaching the second tank, where they'd herd the cattle into the old mesquite corral, let them water and settle a bit while they waited for the errant ones to join the rest. Mama and baby would soon be reunited.

Dawn was slow to wake. She was still taking painkillers, but mostly now she took them to counter boredom rather than pain. If she woke up in the night, she would take another pill and fall back to sleep, the one thing that never bored her.

As she waited for her head to clear, she looked around the room. Adriana was gone, probably to the bathroom. What time was it? Carefully, Dawn rolled onto her side. The red numerals on the clock indicated nearly 11. Using the bedpost, she pulled herself into a sitting position. It was getting easier.

The carpet was strewn with scraps of paper. She and Adriana had stayed up late the night before going through her magazines, cutting out pictures, making lists of things they would buy on the shopping spree. It was something to do. She was sorry that Adriana wouldn't be able to go with her. Not wanting to disappoint her, Dawn never mentioned James' plans to her.

Where was Adriana? She was certainly taking her time and Dawn wanted to shower.

While she waited, she paged through her fashion album, then set it on the dresser alongside the scissors. Pancho Villa was carrying on in his cage. It took Dawn a moment to register the other wail twined with the parrot's enraged squawk. She looked on the dresser, then amid the sheets and blankets for her iPod, but couldn't find it. She put her fingers in her ears, but no matter how hard she pressed, Adriana's cries penetrated her brain like needles.

Why was he doing this now? Adriana was about to be adopted like the others, like her baby. Like her baby! Her baby! Fingers still in her ears, she rocked back and forth, back and forth until she was no longer aware of the cries or the pain in her belly. Soon she was in the bright place, his voice; she could hear the smile in it.

"*Hop, hop, hop, quick like a bunny*," he said.

Hardly aware of the scissors in her hand, Dawn hesitated at the door. She could hear whimpering on the other side. She nudged the door open with her knee. Naked and grunting, he was taking her from behind, his hand pressing down on her head, twisting her face toward the camcorder. She'd forgotten that, how he'd trained her to face the camera. She looked down and saw the scissors clutched tight in her fist. The first time she stabbed him, she used only one hand. Even so, the long, slender point sank easy and deep into his fleshy back.

Dawn had gone through his pants. She'd found his wallet, cell phone, keys and a notebook. She threw the notebook on the floor. The wallet was fat with bills. While Adriana was in the shower, she sorted them by denomination. There were seven hundreds, three twenties, a ten, two fives and seven ones. His pockets held a miscellany of change she didn't bother to count.

She took out her round, leopard print overnight case, which had never been used, and slipped the big bills in a zippered side pocket. From the dresser, she took out her best panties, newest Ts, shorts and a pair of jeans. These she folded carefully and put in the case along with a pair of red sandals with low, hourglass shaped heels. She regretted that she couldn't wear the heels and her jeans, but she could barely stand the pressure of her loose sweat pants as it was. She put the small bills and the change and one of James' credit cards, sunglasses and a makeup bag of essentials in a black patent leather clutch bag. After taking one, she tossed the bottle of Percocet into the purse and dropped it into a red plastic tote bag along with a fleece jacket and a bag of sunflower seeds.

What else do I need, she thought, looking around the room. The fashion album? She didn't need it anymore. She considered the various plush animals and dolls. Even the smallest one was too big to fit in her tote. In the living room, she watered and fed Pancho Villa, then flipped through the DVDs until she found *The Lion King*.

Montoya and Stokey walked out to the police parking lot. It had already been decided that Stokey was to follow Montoya in the Border Patrol vehicle and both would follow behind the SWAT team.

"So where are we going?" Stokey asked as he got into the truck.

"The house is out in Scottsdale." Montoya wrote down the address in his notebook, tore out the page and handed it to Stokey. "This time of day, it'll take us maybe 30, 40 minutes to get there."

Stokey nodded, then started the engine. As he turned on his flashers, his stomach did a little jig around the chicken Caesar salad he'd had for lunch. He'd been in on a dozen similar operations, but again, this one seemed personal, and that made him nervous. Stokey'd known good agents who'd made serious errors in judgment when things got personal. Some got fired for it, even went to prison, some got killed. Taking it personally, like impatience, was not a good thing when dealing with folks who are desperate.

Ahead, Montoya pulled onto the expressway. Stokey stayed right on his tail. He wished he had thought to bring some soda for the kids.

Both girls stood before the dresser mirror. Hands still shaking, Adriana combed out her wet hair. Dawn applied the last of her makeup, a pink blush, which she carefully brushed over her pale cheeks. She studied the effect for a moment then applied one last brush stroke to each cheek.

"What now?" Adriana asked her.

Wordlessly, Dawn pressed a button and handed her the cell phone. Before dialing, Adriana repeated her father's phone number. While she waited, her heart beat so hard, so fast, she felt like it might beat its way right out of her mouth. She didn't cry until she heard his voice. "Papá?"

As Montoya drove, lights flashing, he thought of the girl, Dawn. Given what she'd experienced in her short life, he wondered if there was anything to salvage there. What she needed was a good, stable home. He and his wife could become foster parents, they'd done that once. Maybe they could even adopt her and the baby. After their daughter's wedding, there'd be a big empty space at home. He let his mind entertain the fantasy for a few moments, Dawn and her baby filling the space in their home and hearts.

Traffic was predictably heavy, and they had to proceed with caution. "Vamanos!" he said. "Let's get this caravan moving."

The reality, he knew, was that kids like Dawn rarely were able to adjust to family life. He'd seen it before. She'd probably go into a group home. Yes, he could imagine her in a house full of other teenage girls, a sad, angry little sorority of wounded souls. Any other outcome would require a miracle. Some folks believed in miracles. He was certain that his wife was one of them, but he'd seen too much to know anything with certainty. Still …

He released a lungful of pent up air. It wouldn't be long now.

Dawn handed Adriana two plastic shopping bags. She opened the closet and dresser drawers. "Help yourself," she said, arms open wide.

Adriana shook her head. "No. I no need."

"You need. Here." She took the bags from Adriana and quickly filled them with clothing. "Now let's get your brother."

Adriana followed her, clutching the bags.

The three boys, dressed only in underpants, were watching cartoon figures race cars around a track. Only Edgar looked up.

"Ven," Adriana said to him. "Papá esta viniendo para nosotros."

"Papá!" Edgar began looking around the room for his clothing.

"Apurate! Papá ya esté viniendo!" she said, and the boy ran to her side.

"Let's go," Dawn said.

Though Honey continued to gaze at the television, Dante finally looked their way. "Where are you going?"

"Out."

"Can I come?"

"Maybe next time," Dawn said flatly.

"You always get to go," he said and turned his attention back to the television.

Dawn unlocked the front door, and the three stepped out into the glare.

Shading her eyes with her hand, Adriana looked up and down the empty street for her father. She took Edgar by the hand and started for the curb. "You no coming?" She asked when Adriana didn't follow.

Dawn shook her head.

"Come with us, with Papá. You can."

"I'm going to L.A."

"Where?"

"Los Angeles. I'll get my own ride."

Shortly Jacabo's truck pulled into the drive. Just then, the old lady who lived next door stepped onto her front porch. As if they were well-acquainted, Dawn smiled big and waved like this was normal, a little boy wearing only underpants and a girl carrying plastic shopping bags, a sleepover, maybe – that was a normal kid thing – and now their father was picking them up to take them home.

Adriana threw her arms around Dawn's neck. "Come."

She shook her head.

Adriana took Edgar by the hand and ran for the truck.

"Bye, bye," Dawn called after them. "See you later." She turned to the old lady and smiled once again. She allowed herself only a moment to watch the reunion, the father gathering Adriana and Edgar in his arms. With a final wave, she turned back toward the house, satisfied that her performance had been perfect.

Dawn stood with her forehead against the bolted door. She was crying. She didn't know why, but she must have been for some time because the neck of her hoodie was wet. She heard a moan, and allowed her body to slide down the wall until she was sitting. Her belly hurt, maybe that was it. For a moment she sat there trying to determine what was making her sad. She reached up and touched the bolt.

"*Hey, Bunny mine*," said the voice, warm and sweet. "*Let's sing. Hitch my old horse to the rack*," he began. "*Come on, Honey Bunny. You remember the words.*"

"Buckle my banjo on his back." She sang along with him until the tears stopped coming.

"Dawny?" James cried. "I know you're there. I'm bleeding awful."

Her iPod was hanging around her neck. Where had that come from? She put the earplugs in, turned up the volume then went into the bedroom to gather up her things. Standing before the mirror she corrected her makeup, erasing the dark mascara smudges with powder. Quickly, she swept all the makeup into the overnight case and snapped it shut. On her way out of the bedroom, she scooped up Romeo from his cage and tucked him into the pocket of her hoodie.

It was quiet when she passed by the set. She banged on the door. "James?"

"Unlock the door. Please, Dawny. We'll talk."

Once again, she put her hand on the bolt, hesitated, then let her hand fall to her side.

"Calm down, James."

"What? Are you just going to let me bleed to death?"

What would it mean if she did? She had to think about it for a moment. Did she care if he died?

"Dawny, honey, please. I'm begging."

"Everything is going to be OK, James. Just you wait and see."

"Dawny, baby."

"It's OK, James. This is just your period of adjustment. Everybody has one. You'll see; when it's over things will be fine." As if he could see through the door, she smiled her reassurance. "Trust me, padna. Everything's going to be just great."

Three cars pulled up next door, lights flashing in the most alarming manner. Initially, Frances Stillman was startled, but not really surprised. She'd been expecting something like this ever since her last conversation with Officer Montoya. He was standing out there now next to a gentleman from the Border Patrol. Border Patrol? What on earth was going on over there?

She watched from the window as three officers in complete

battle gear charged into the house. The girl had left the front door standing open, and Frances Stillman wondered why all the drama. Still, she waited for several moments. When she was satisfied that there'd be no gunfire, she stepped back out onto her porch.

"Officer Montoya?" She waved, arms frantic. "I need to speak with you right away."

He looked at her then, waved his arms, equally frantic. "Go back in the house Mrs. Stillman, now."

"But officer, I have important information about that girl, Dawn. And there were two other children, Mexican, I think." That got his attention! As he crossed the yard, she retreated into the doorway.

"Step inside, Mrs. Stillman."

Officer Montoya took her by the elbow then, Pogo barking furiously. Pogo never liked it when anyone touched her.

"Quiet, Pogo. Calm down, now. It's all right," she said softly. She stroked the dog's head, and he settled down.

"Now tell me quickly what you observed," Officer Montoya directed.

Frances Stillman bristled at his abrupt and officious manner. As a taxpayer, she was his employer, but she tried not to take offense. After all, he was merely doing his job, she supposed, and it was her civic duty to help him.

In the living room, a large, half-raw parrot raged from its cage. While they waited for an ambulance, the SWAT team administered first aid to a man, presumably James Trillig, who was bleeding from numerous stab wounds and was barely conscious. Stokey looked around the room, noted the bed with its canopy, curtained window. He pulled back the curtain, noted the plywood bolted over the window.

In the middle of the room was a camcorder on a tripod. Stokey pulled on a pair of latex gloves and pressed the rewind button, waited a moment, hit play. The bottom dropped out of his stomach.

He'd seen a lot of ugly, fucked-up things while deployed, a lot of fucked-up things along the border, but once again, this was personal. Stokey was certain the child in the video was Belen's daughter, though the face, distorted by fear and pain, bore little resemblance to the little girl with the shy smile he'd seen in the photo.

They could save a lot of time, effort and money if they just let the bastard bleed to death, was Stokey's thinking as he turned his back on the scene.

The bird continued its maniac screeching. He opened the door to a room that served as bedroom/office. In the closet was an assortment of men's clothing and more video equipment. He looked under the bed – nothing but dust balls.

The next bedroom was obviously outfitted for a girl, by the posters on the wall, a teen – the missing girl? He pulled back the curtain revealing the plywood bolted over the window. The dresser drawers were open, as was the door to the closet, evidence of a hasty departure.

There was a notebook splayed open on the floor. He thumbed through a few pages of names and numbers, then put it in his breast pocket. Montoya would be very happy to have a look at it, as would Rosy.

According to Montoya, the neighbor had seen two Mexican children, girl and boy, get into a truck, even heard them call the driver "papa." That answered one question.

He opened the door to the back bedroom. Blankets were in a tangle on the floor as if someone had been nesting there. Like the other rooms, plywood was bolted over the only window. Was this where Trillig had kept Edgar and Adriana?

As he looked around the mostly bare room, he noticed a musty odor. It seemed familiar, though he couldn't quite name it. He put his hand on the television. It was still warm, then he opened the closet door. Now he remembered. Unwashed children smelled a bit like mushrooms.

Stokey pulled back the blanket. "Hey, guys," he said to the two boys, huddled beneath. "It's OK. Nobody's going to hurt you." The younger of the two, a child of perhaps 4, climbed out of the lap of the older and held out his arms. Stokey picked him up, then held his hand out to other boy. "It's OK," he repeated. "Nobody's going to hurt you." After a moment, the boy shrugged and allowed himself to be pulled to his feet.

Montoya cruised down Camelback Road, figuring she'd head there to hitch a ride or catch a bus. Thought he'd go a mile or so in one direction. If he didn't find her, he'd turn around and go in the opposite direction. He imagined her walking down the road, thumb out. Mrs. Stillman said the girl wasn't pregnant. So what happened to the baby? If somebody's already picked her up, he might never know.

He was about to turn around when he spotted a small figure up ahead. He sped up, then pulled alongside her. He rolled down his window. "Dawn?"

The girl glanced at him, eyes unfocused, face pale except for the pink rouged patches on her cheeks, and kept on walking.

Montoya inched his car along. "Remember me? I came to your house last week."

She continued to walk.

"Why don't you get in the car. We could get something to eat. Do you like McDonald's or maybe Kentucky Fried Chicken?"

She paused as if considering.

He stopped the car and got out. "Come on, Dawn." He put his hand on her shoulder. "Get in the car."

Her eyes seemed to draw into focus then. "Is he dead?"

"No."

She didn't resist when he took the overnight case from her hand. "Is he going to die?"

"Probably not. What happened to your baby, Dawn?"

She passed a hand over her belly. "James sold him." She

rummaged through her purse a bit then carefully unfolded a slip of paper. "These are the people who bought my baby."

Montoya took the paper from her hand and looked at the names. He shook his head. "How did you get these names?"

"James. He made me promise I wouldn't try to find him until he was 18, but I've changed my mind."

Mr. James Trillig, he was thinking, was a real piece of work. He refolded the note and handed it back to the girl.

"So if I get in, will you help me find my baby?"

Montoya nodded. "I'll see what I can do."

"One more thing." She reached into her pocket and pulled out a small, brightly colored bird. "Romeo goes where I go."

"Sure." He opened the door then and guided her into the back seat of the car.

"Am I going to go to jail?"

"No, Dawn," he said. He buckled her in and shut the car door as gently as he could.

Cows liked to follow each other. Once they'd all been gathered up it had been pretty easy to keep them moving in a forward motion. Wiona had to hand it to Lucy. She'd hung in there.

Now the two women stood on a rail as the cows and calves milled around the corral. "So what do you think about the ranching life?" she asked.

"I think the price of beef should be a lot higher."

"I must say, I have to agree with you." Wiona studied the cows' haunches. "See how bony some of them are?"

Lucy nodded. "Not much to eat out there."

"Well there's that, but mostly it's because the lean ones are pregnant."

"But they're still nursing."

"That's why they're so skinny." She shook her head. "In a good year, about 95 percent of my cows would be pregnant. This year, with the drought? Well, it doesn't look so good."

"So now what?"

"We let them settle in for the night. Tomorrow's going to be a hard day for everybody, except for the bulls of course. They've already had their hard day." Lucy rewarded her with a laugh. Wiona leaned in a little until her shoulder brushed Lucy's. The light was already fading on the rhyolite cliffs.

"Supper's probably ready." Wiona hopped down from the fence. Held out her hand to steady Lucy's descent.

Flashers whirling, Stokey sped by Picacho Peak, just north of Tucson on I-10. At the moment, he figured Belen's husband was well on his way to Wiona's place. The man had less than an hour's head start; he would eventually catch up to him, might even beat him there. He could have radioed the station to have someone else apprehend him – the neighbor had provided a pretty good description of the vehicle, an older model, white Ford pickup with a dented right rear fender. That would probably be the most efficient way. Efficient, yes, but he wanted to see this to the end himself.

Increasing his speed to 90, his mind flashed back to the video. He shook his head to erase the image. Something else, he needed something else to focus on besides that twisted little brown face.

Well, there was Wiona. He'd long held the misperception that he had done her harm. He was relieved to know that he hadn't, though he supposed he hadn't done her any good either, and his thoughts turned to his old buddy, Frankie. What a bastard! Stokey never would have figured. But Wiona was strong, honest too. He liked her, admired the hell out of her, in fact. No doubt she'd be coming into some money. He had no idea what the reward was up to, but Wade Spalding, he was now sure, was the man who killed Fletcher Hart. According to Ochoa, Spalding was a middleman in the heroin supply line. Add that to the boot print at the scene and the shotgun Wiona said he'd been carrying, and bingo. Stokey could imagine how the geeky birder could wander along the dusty back ranch roads without raising the least concern. The old man stumbles upon Spalding in the midst of a transaction with a drug mule. Spalding shoots Fletcher in the back as he tries to get to the rifle in his ATV, and the mule takes off for the border.

As soon as Stokey was finished with this piece of business, he'd report directly to Garza. As long as Wiona got the money, it didn't matter who got the glory. Besides, he'd defied direct orders to stay out of it. Best to keep his head down.

And then there was Becka. What would it take to get her to … what? Snap out of her right to be pissed as hell. Well, if she didn't want to be his wife anymore, what obligation did he still have toward her? None that he could think of. Of course the baby complicated everything. He'd missed both Jack and Katie's births. He wanted to see this one born. How would Becka feel about that? Well, a lot can happen in six months. Hell, six months ago he and Becka were still together and working on making that baby.

Unwillingly, his mind circled back to the vision of Adriana, hardly more than a baby herself. Under the circumstances, he would certainly be able to arrange a humanitarian visa for Belen and her children, but a visa for the husband was much more problematic. If Jacabo had turned himself in with Belen it would be a different story. Now that window of opportunity was probably slammed shut and bolted over with plywood. The image made him wince. Clearly Adriana and Edgar, after what they'd been through, needed both mama and papa more than ever.

It wasn't long before Stokey spotted a white Ford truck ahead in the right-hand lane doing something below the speed limit – a common error made by folks wanting to be inconspicuous – and there was the dented rear fender. As he came alongside the truck, he could see three people in the front seat, a short, dark man and two kids, girl in the middle, boy riding shotgun. Willing invisibility, they all kept their eyes tightly focused on the road. Stokey didn't have to guess what was going on in Jacabo's head so clearly he felt it, felt the sick in his stomach, too.

Montoya still had three witnesses in custody who could testify against Trillig. And, of course, there were the notebook and the videotapes. Montoya didn't really need these children to make a case. Stokey considered the rules of engagement. His rules. Since his tours in the Middle East had failed to produce any positive results that he could see, maybe he could still provide somebody with a chance for a better life.

"What the hell," he sighed, then turned off his flashers. As he sped by, he could see them in his rearview mirror, Adriana's head now collapsed against her papa's shoulder.

Right or wrong it was done. As he continued south on I-10, the clouds gathered and teased as they had for the past three afternoons without yielding a drop of rain. Still, he was feeling lighter than he had in months. Stokey glanced at the clock on the dash. If he hurried, he could stop by the nursery in Tucson, pick up some bell pepper starts and a flat of marigolds. What the hell, he was feeling so optimistic he might pick up a red geranium for Becka's blue widow box, maybe slip a couple of arugula plants in there, too.

And maybe he'd get rid of the .48 after all. There's been so much hype lately about kids getting ahold of their dad's gun, not that he would allow that to happen. But with the new baby and all, it would make Becka more comfortable. What would she make of that?

He turned the flashers back on as he moved into the left-hand lane.

Rising from the table, Wiona began clearing the dinner dishes.

"Gracias, Belen," Lucy said. "La comida estaba muy sabrosa."

"Si, como siempre," Wiona added, assessing the leftovers. There wasn't much, just some green beans and a couple slices of bread. The rest was gone, chuck steak gone, refried beans gone, rice and the bowl of pico de gallo, that spicy mix of chopped tomatoes, onions, jalapeños and lime that Emma especially loved, all gone. Wiona put the green beans in the refrigerator and Lucy began to stack the plates.

Belen put out her hand to stay them and pointed to her chest. "Por favor, dejalo a mi."

Emma pounded the table with her fist. "If you all are going to speak Spanish, I'm going to go into the living room and watch my program." She sat there for a moment, waiting for a response. When there was none, she got up from the table and strode out of the room, mumbling about learning to speak goddamn English.

Lucy stacked the dishes by the sink.

"Dejalo a mi." Belen said again, this time a bit louder. She smiled and gave both Wiona and Lucy a little shove in the direction of the door.

Lucy stretched her back and sighed. "I guess I should be going."

"Stay for a cup of coffee. It's already made and it'll bolster you for the drive home." Wiona poured them each a cup. "Let's take it out on the porch."

The two women settled on the glider. Osa trotted out from beneath the porch. With a sigh, she collapsed at Wiona's feet.

"She worked hard today." Lucy said, reaching down to smooth her hand over the pup's head.

"We all worked hard today."

Covering a yawn with her fist, Lucy nodded. "So how's Punkin doing? I meant to pay her a visit, but it was so crazy at the clinic this past week."

"She's been clamoring to go outside so I guess she's on the mend."

"Cats are tough."

For a long moment they let themselves be lulled by the rhythmic protest of the glider, the jingle of crickets and katydids and the white-winged doves settling in for the night. Wiona had no idea what the life of a dove was like to a dove, but when they were roosting and cooing to each other, it sounded like it must be sweet.

Wiona patted Lucy on the knee. "For a city girl, you did pretty good today."

"Only you and the mayor would call Douglas a city."

"Well, it's not country, not the middle of nowhere."

"Not the middle of nowhere, but pretty close to it." Lucy inhaled deeply, smiled. "I think I could get used to living in the exact middle of nowhere."

Wiona wondered if Lucy considered her ranch the exact middle of nowhere. Lucy let her head fall against Wiona's shoulder, setting off series of small explosions inside her skull.

"Remember what fun we had that summer? I had such a crush on you, cowgirl."

A crush? The word slipped under her breastbone like a pry bar, but she was so conscious of the press of Lucy's head against her shoulder, the heat of her body, she could hardly think, let alone respond.

Lucy sat up, leaving the spot where her head had been to cool.

"Look," Wiona continued, determined to hurry on before she lost her resolve. "I realize you're not ready for another … ah … relationship, and I certainly don't want to run you off by saying this, but I figure … Ah, what the hell." She took a deep breath, let it out. "Everything I know about you today only proves … though of course I understand … "

"What?"

"Well, I mean I appreciate, you know, and all you've done for Belen and you doctored my cat, listened to me gripe about my mother and today, today you were such a help. Couldn't have managed without you and … well …"

"Well?"

"What can I say?" She was finding it hard to breathe. "I'm just grateful, is all. And I want you to know that, and I want you to know … I want you to know that even though … "

She looked at Lucy's face, her smooth, tea-gold skin. Lucy took her hand then. "Jesus, Wiona. Just say what you want to say."

Half-strangled by the heart that seemed to have climbed into her throat, she managed to whisper, "I've sort of gotten used to having Belen and the baby here. And well, it's going to be kind of lonely with just me and mother." She squeezed Lucy's hand. "I was hoping maybe we could be friends ... good friends like when we were young."

After Lucy left, Wiona fled to her office, Osa at her heals. She put a match to the fire, thinking of the kiss they had exchanged on the swing. It had been an awkward, sisterly kiss, their bodies barely touching, and now she was having an attack of the nervous shivers. Figuring this to be another emergency, she pulled out the bottle of tequila.

After a few minutes the fire and the tequila calmed her and she took stock. Maybe it hadn't been a total disaster. At least Lucy knew how she felt. It was a relief, really. Now there was nothing more Wiona needed to do. Either Lucy would call or she wouldn't. Either she would love her back, or she wouldn't. Life had just gotten simpler.

And pretty soon Belen and Jesús would be gone and her life would become simpler yet, just she and Emma on their own again. She looked at the fire. Eyes burning, she pushed the tears aside with the palms of her hands.

Osa started to bark just then. "Just a coyote girl," Wiona said, but the dog continued the alarm and ran out of the office.

She took a sip of tequila, and was about to put another log on the fire when she heard the truck pull into the yard. Lucy? Letting her heart get ahead of her brain, she raced outside. There was Jacabo's white truck glowing under the full moon. She watched him hop down from the cab and hurry toward the house. She hadn't heard from Stokey so she supposed the lead hadn't panned out. Well, at least Belen will have a little comfort tonight, she thought.

As she turned back to the barn, she heard Link nicker. She was too tired to go over and say goodnight, yet she didn't want to go back to the house. Didn't want to disturb Belen and her husband, one, didn't want to deal with her mother, two, didn't want to give up on feeling sorry for herself, three. She was allowed to once in a while.

She settled back in front on the stove, figuring the way her life was now was how it would always be, most likely.

"Better make the best of it, girl." She sipped the tequila, then closed her eyes. Tomorrow was another long day. Maybe Lucy would come by to help. Maybe not. Either way, she'd manage. She always had.

Belen had left her children sitting in the car, though it was hard to part from them even for a moment. Now, with only the moon illuminating the room, she quickly gathered up the baby things and the few clothes she owned and stuffed them into plastic bags.

She did not want to go to this Phoenix, did not want to stay in this frightening country where people steal children.

Jacabo had told her to hurry because la Migra could come at any moment. She almost wished that they would. Then there would be no choice but to go home. If it were up to her, they would return to their village and the coffee. At least there they would have peace of mind. She did not think there could be any peace of mind for her in this new land.

But it is God, not I, who decides, she countered. He would not have brought them all this way if he meant them to turn around and go home. She glanced around the room, sorry to leave without giving her thanks to Wiona. She owed her so much, perhaps her very life and the lives of her children, but there was nothing to be done. Her eyes fell on the blue rebozo hanging over the back of the chair. She picked it up, held it to her cheek for a moment, then carefully laid it across the bed. From the bedpost she took her jet and silver rosary, kissed it and placed it on the shawl. Wiona would see these and perhaps understand the depth of her gratitude.

She looked around the room one last time, patting the pocket of her housedress to reassure herself that Jesús' birth certificate was tucked safely inside. She picked up the plastic tub where her son lay sleeping and their few belongings then hurried down the hall.

When she passed the living room, she put her burdens down and crept up to la vieja where she lay sleeping in her big chair before the television. Belen tucked the afghan around her then made the sign of the cross over her forehead. Suddenly, the old lady opened her eyes wide and grabbed her tight by the wrist.

Belen placed her hand lightly over the old one's. "Adios y gracias," she whispered, and touched her cheek. There were tears there, and Belen wondered what she might be thinking. "Adios," she repeated.

"Adios y gracias," the old lady whispered, releasing her fierce grip.

Jacobo was waiting for Belen by the door. He kissed her forehead then took his son in his arms. "I bought him a crib."

Belen nodded, hand over her mouth.

The moon made long shadows over the dry, ragged grasses as they hurried to the truck where their children were waiting, safe for now, and anxious to be elsewhere, as children always are in the middle of a long journey.

About the Author

G. Davies Jandrey, whose friends call her Gayle, is a retired educa-tor, a writer of fiction and a poet. For five seasons she worked as a fire lookout in Saguaro National Park and Chiricahua National Monument. It was in these "sky islands" that she first learned to love the richness and diversity of southern Arizona. This double life, one spent teaching teens, the other focused on natural history, informs both her poetry and prose. She makes her home with her husband, Fritz, in the Tucson Mountains.

To read samples of Gayle's novels, both published and in progress, and her children's natural history in poetry and prose, visit her website: www.gaylejandrey.com.

A Garden of Aloes

G. Davies Jandrey

It's summer and hell in Tucson, Arizona. Leslie and her daughters, Sam and Audrey, land at the Oasis Motor Court along Miracle Mile, a street notorious for prostitution, drugs, and skin joints. They are at the tag end of everything from money to hope.

The story is told in four voices. The first is Sam's. A diminutive eleven-year old with angry blue eyes and a vampire phobia, she is the only one who acknowledges how far they've fallen. The second voice is Dee's, the 400-pound manager of the Oasis who befriends Sam. The one thing Dee is certain of is that God only requires her to put one foot in front of the other. Most days she's pretty sure she can do that. Chablee is next. The thirteen-year old biracial daughter of a topless dancer carries a chip on her shoulder the size of a small T-Rex. She and Audrey's forge a friendship based on their mutual interest in make-up and toenail polish.

The last voice is Leslie's. Fleeing her marriage was an act of courage, but now she's mired by guilt, doubt and poverty. Leslie had sought to protect her daughters and is devastated when she fails.

The Garden of Aloes is shocking, poignant, but also funny. When you least expect to, you will laugh out loud, yet the plight of the women at the Oasis is no laughing matter.

CPSIA information can be obtained at www.ICGtesting.com
Printed in the USA
BVOW08s0648270215

389454BV00006B/12/P